ALSO BY
CATHY PICKENS

Done Gone Wrong

Southern Fried

CATHY PICKENS

THOMAS DUNNE BOOKS

ST. MARTIN'S MINOTAUR ☙ NEW YORK

THOMAS DUNNE BOOKS.
An imprint of St. Martin's Press.

www.thomasdunnebooks.com
www.minotaurbooks.com

Library of Congress Cataloging-in-Publication Data is available
upon request.

ISBN-13: 978-0-312-35440-4
ISBN-10: 0-312-35440-1

First Edition: March 2007

10 9 8 7 6 5 4 3 2 1

DEDICATED TO MY NEPHEWS
John, Paul, Taylor, Hayden, and Jack:

DESPITE BEING RAISED AS "FLATLANDERS,"
MAY THEY LOOK TO AND LOVE THE HILLS AS MUCH AS I DO.

AND ALWAYS, TO MY PARENTS, *Paul and Kitty.*
AND TO *my husband Bob,* WITH MUCH LOVE.

Acknowledgments

Once again, many thanks to the readers and advisers who work to keep Avery out of trouble: Catherine P. Anderson, Barbara Anderson, Elizabeth Dickinson, M.D., Thomas Dickinson, M.D., Nancy McMahon, Terry Hoover, Paula Connolly, Ann Wicker, Tamara Burrell, and Robert Finley. They are my friends and family and they help me because . . . well, if they refused, (1) my mistakes would personally embarrass them and (2) their refusal might make holidays and get-togethers uncomfortable.

I've also called upon the good graces of others not bound to help me out of kinship or love, but who did anyway: S. Erin Presnell, M.D., of the Medical University of South Carolina; Emily Craig, Ph.D., state forensic anthropologist for the Commonwealth of Kentucky, for her gift of finding laugh-out-loud stories among the bones; Mark Kelso, Ph.D., political science department at Queens

University of Charlotte; Daniel "Chipp" Bailey, chief deputy of the Mecklenburg County (N.C.) Sheriff's Department and mystery author (who lovingly calls me "Unabomber Pickens"); Joyce Lavene, master gardener and with her husband, Jim, author of the Peggy Lee Garden Mysteries (among many others); and Donna Ashley, who read even though she had exams pending. Many thanks to each of them.

Thanks also to Meg Ruley, who knows a thing or two about small towns.

And with deep affection and admiration to Ruth Cavin, editor extraordinaire.

The remaining mistakes made and liberties taken are mine, all mine.

*The village idiot. . . kept sidling up, touching me softly
on the arm and bursting into fits of silent laughter.
I became quite used to him.*

—H.V. MORTON, *In the Steps of St. Paul* (1936)

Hog Wild

Friday Morning

"You haven't seen a pig, have you?" Melvin Bertram had strolled across the hallway from his office, ignoring the precarious stacks of boxes, packing paper, cleaning rags, and jumbles of unshelved books in what was supposed to be the offices of Avery Andrews, Attorney at Law.

"A pig?" I faced him, hands on my hips. Was that a smart-mouth indictment of my housekeeping?

"A pet pig," he said, not even looking at the mess that surrounded him. "Two-and-a-half feet tall, black, distinctive potbelly, waddles when she walks. Sheriff Peters put out an all points bulletin this morning."

"A pig." I stared at him. "Why's L.J. looking for a pig?"

He shrugged. "That's the most pressing threat to the citizenry's health and well-being, I suppose." ,

I couldn't tell whether his sarcasm was for L.J. or for the generally goofy backwater nature of Dacus and environs.

I shook my head and began unearthing a couple of chairs. "I'll let you know if I find a pig."

Melvin peered cautiously into the hardware-store bag sitting on my desk.

"Locks for the doors," I explained.

When Melvin's grandfather built the family's Main Street home near the turn of the century, the two spacious front rooms had flowed invitingly from the grand entrance hall. Now, with his investment office on the right and my law office on the left requiring separate entrances off the grand hall, I'd taken on the task of refitting the two sets of French doors with locks.

This batch of locks was my third attempt to get something that would fit the existing doors, provide enough security, and meet with Melvin's approval. I still wasn't convinced the glass-paneled doors were secure enough for our separate offices, but Melvin had argued we would simply lock the sturdy front door when both of us were gone.

If truth be told, I also wasn't convinced this whole office arrangement would work, but I'd agreed to give it a try.

"Can you help me slide these book boxes out of the way? I've got—believe it or not—a client. She's coming in a few minutes."

Melvin grabbed an open carton of books. "Don't want her suing you for personal injury."

We barely had time to shove the detritus of unpacking aside and create a conversation nook among the stacks of boxes before Magnolia Avinger arrived.

Melvin disappeared quietly across the hall into his office as soon as we heard footfalls on the porch.

The short woman with faded ginger hair and a tanned, lean face was my mother's age or older. She looked familiar—from church, I realized after a moment.

She stood taking in the entry hall, then she nodded to the sign beside Melvin's office door. "Bertram & Associates? That's Melvin Bertram?"

"Yes, ma'am."

"You're sharing office space with him?"

I nodded. She glanced through the glass doors into Melvin's parlor before joining me in my cluttered office.

"You really need to get a sign out front so people can find you."
Her tone was kind; she was simply stating the obvious, the way women
of a certain age do. Equally obvious, I wasn't set up for anybody to
find the law office of Avery Andrews just yet. But she'd called, and I
sure wasn't situated well enough to say no to a new client.

"I do appreciate you seeing me on such short notice. I really
needed to—talk to somebody."

She obviously wasn't one to waste time. "Come on back," I
said. "Please excuse the mess."

I led her through the front room, which would eventually house
a receptionist but now held boxes and mostly empty bookshelves.
My office proper wasn't in much better shape, though I did have a
desk—a massive one from my grandfather's old law office—and the
two chairs Melvin had helped me arrange. We took the seats facing
each other.

Magnolia Avinger skipped the preliminaries. "I couldn't take
this to any of the men lawyers in town; I'm too mortified. But I'm
desperate for help. I don't even know where to begin."

She handed me an envelope addressed to Innis Barker at Dacus
Monument Company, the top neatly slit open. I glanced at her, trying to read a hint in her expression before I pulled out a letter hand-
written on thick cream bond.

"My husband has accused me of poisoning him."

I'd never gotten a bombshell like that from a client. I held the
sheet of paper and waited for elaboration.

"Before he died, my husband, Harden, gave the executor of his
will instructions for his grave marker, to be forwarded after his
death. Mr. Barker at the monument company had the decency to
call me straightaway, as soon as he received this. Very concerned. He
wanted to do the right thing."

Her hand fluttered, then rested back in her lap.

"The monument itself is so ostentatious. It'll eclipse everything
else in the cemetery."

I tried not to register my surprise. He accused her of murder,
and she was worried about his taste in headstones?

"Then I learned Harden had written his own epitaph, which struck me as odd. Even after he got sick, he wouldn't talk about funeral plans or anything, except to say he refused to be cremated. He always made a rude joke about how he didn't want the evidence destroyed after I bumped him off. He'd laugh and laugh, but anyone used to his crude idea of fun paid no mind. I couldn't get any details out of him during his illness, about planning his funeral. Nothing except that sly grin of his, so I just didn't worry about it. Then he goes and orders his own grave marker, a giant stone angel to be shipped from Vietnam. Just like him to search out the cheapest source. As soon as he died, this letter was delivered."

She indicated the letter I held with another flutter of her hand.

Dear Mr. Innis Barker:

This letter is to be delivered to you by my executor after you have accepted delivery of the grave monument I ordered.

Inscribe the following on the marker in the space provided beneath the angel's feet:

Know all when this you see
My "faithful" wife, she poisoned me.
Harden F. Avinger
August 10, 1937–[add date]
From misery freed, my run complete,
May hers never be so.

I glanced up at Mrs. Avinger, then kept reading to avoid the embarrassed look on her face.

Within three weeks of receiving these instructions, you must complete the inscription and install the monument.

With this letter, you have received one-third the price agreed upon. Should you fail to complete the instructions TO THE LETTER, you shall FORFEIT the

4

remaining payment due you. Final payment will be made only after the monument with its completed inscription is installed.

My executor has a duplicate copy of these instructions and is charged with seeing them fully completed before authorizing payment.

Yours elsewhere,
Harden Avinger

I couldn't very well ask his widow, but what kind of nut would write such a letter? I tried to tamp down the small suspicion that reared up. Maybe she had killed him. True, I liked what I saw in Magnolia Avinger's face. No theatrics, despite her dramatic problem. But what did that really tell me?

"Mr. Barker wants to do the right thing," she said, "but he's in a bind. He's already paid for the gigantic stone angel and for shipping it from Vietnam. The thing is eight feet tall! If he doesn't comply with Harden's instructions, he doesn't get repaid for that expense. He can't afford to bear that loss. Frankly," she looked down at the handkerchief she had pulled from her sweater pocket, "neither can I. Harden didn't leave our finances in very good shape. I just don't have that kind of money." She shook her head, bewildered and frustrated.

"I simply can't have that monstrosity towering over our cemetery plot. I simply can't. I'm so grateful to Innis for warning me about this. I came to you and not to Carlton Barner. He's the executor, and I thought he was a family friend, but he never even breathed a word of this to me."

I scarcely knew where to start. Ordinarily, I might have explained why Carlton Barner couldn't warn her, but I didn't think Mrs. Avinger was in a mood to hear about attorney-client privilege. Maybe later I could defend Carlton, so she wouldn't harbor hard feelings for somebody she'd known as a friend. First, though, I had some uncomfortable questions to ask her.

"Miz Avinger, how did your husband . . . pass away?"

"Lung cancer. He'd had all the treatments; we battled it for three years. Wouldn't quit smoking, even with all that. Hospice helped him stay at home. His caseworker was even there with us the morning he died."

"Anything—unusual about how—" How the heck do you ask a widow about something like this? She would need to realize that, in light of what she'd face when her not-so-dearly-departed's angel made its proclamatory debut in the city cemetery, my questions would be tame.

She shrugged, her large brown eyes red-rimmed but dry. "I don't know. What's usual, really? He struggled for breath, for days. Each breath more racking than the next. I admit praying he would release himself, that he'd quit fighting. But that's all I did to hasten it. It was a horrible thing to watch. He was unconscious but struggling, fighting to stay, to breathe. A horrid, futile rattle, for hours and hours." Her voice tapered off, lost in bad memories.

"Someone was with you all through his final hours?"

She nodded. "From church or hospice or just friends. I couldn't have faced that alone." She blinked rapidly.

"Who was Mr. Avinger's doctor?"

"Oh, gosh. He had so many, here and in Greenville. Dr. Randel was his primary doctor in town. He saw an oncology group in Greenville, when he was taking treatments."

"So Dr. Randel signed the death certificate?"

She hesitated. "I think so. All that's still something of a blur."

I scribbled on my notepad, buying time to think.

"Miz Avinger—"

"Please, call me Maggy. Everybody does."

Her manner was direct and sensible. Maggy was slender, maybe a tennis player? Studying her face, I could see she was older than my mother. Too many years spent in the sun. Around here, that usually meant gardening.

"Thank you. Maggy. My questions may seem rude, but—"

"Ask away. I'm the one who came to you for help."

"Okay. Why would your husband accuse you of poisoning him?"

She raised both hands, beseeching. "I have no idea. It's the craziest thing I've ever heard. Harden was given to bad jokes. At least, he thought they were jokes, though few people ever laughed. No one will be laughing when that angel rises up over his plot. That's for certain."

I wanted to ask *Did your husband really hate you that much?* I'd been a lawyer long enough—and had observed the marriages of friends and relations for long enough—to know that more couples found themselves locked in mortal combat than bound in loving bliss.

"Maggy, getting the monument stopped is only one issue. The other is stopping the rumors."

At first, she looked puzzled, then she gave a dismissive shake of her head. "I'm not worried about that. This is a small town and Harden's stupid joke *is* bound to leak out, no matter what I do. I just figure if people know me and Harden, they know us both for what we were and are. Nobody else really matters. The truth will out, I always say. I just don't want that garish monstrosity perched on my head when I'm dead."

She paused, staring past my shoulder and into her own thoughts. "If I'm truthful with myself, the gaudiness of that ridiculous giant angel bothers me more than anything. I'm embarrassed to have it associated with the family, and I'm mortified at the thought of being planted underneath it. Why that should matter, it's only silly pride. But if I'm truthful with myself, it does matter."

"You also don't want the rumor and accusation following you around, either." Bad word picture—I imagined a rumor in the shape of a sepulchral angel, gliding along behind her. "Some people don't know you."

She sat a moment, thoughtful. "Guess it's not entirely rational, but rumors just don't bother me. I'm embarrassed more by the showiness, the poor taste—that's not who I am. The accusation doesn't bother me because it's so silly, no one could possibly believe it. Does that make any sense?"

Not really, but she was entitled to her inconsistencies.

"So what would you like me to do?"

"I don't really know, Avery. I want that angel stopped, but I can't afford to pay the rest of Mr. Barker's bill." She hesitated. "Do you think the police will—investigate me? How do these things work? I certainly would investigate, if I were the police."

"That's one reason why you need to confront your husband's accusation head-on. You don't want something like that haunting you." Another bad choice of words. Her mouth had a stubborn set to it.

"Did Mr. Avinger have life insurance?"

She nodded. "A small amount."

"You know a police investigation or even the accusation alone may prevent or delay your beneficiary payments. Even if the angel isn't erected, imagine the repercussions if you leave this unchallenged."

For the first time, she looked surprised. "The insurance they won't pay?"

"If they reasonably suspect you've been involved in your husband's death, they have every right to delay payment pending the investigation." I didn't want to add *and demanding payment won't make you look innocent.*

"Oh." Her voice was quiet. She balled her handkerchief in her hand and rubbed her fists up and down on the thighs of her khaki pants.

For the first time, she seemed subdued by what she faced.

I walked around my desk and fumbled in a drawer for a legal pad. "Jot a note to Dr. Randel, giving him permission to talk to me about your husband's case. Do you have a copy of the death certificate?"

She nodded as she took the pad and pen I offered her.

"Would you bring me a copy of that?"

I would talk to Sheriff L.J.—Lucinda Jane—Peters, but I wouldn't be trading on our old elementary school ties—more like seeking favor in spite of long-held animosities. Maybe she or Deputy

Rudy Mellin could clue me in on any domestic history Magnolia "Maggy" Avinger hadn't shared with me. I was glad Maggy had volunteered her innocence. I believed her, but clients don't always tell the truth and I can be gullible.

Friday Afternoon

Melvin must have heard Maggy Avinger leave my office. He returned to finish inspecting the sand-cast metal door locks and latches I'd chosen and pronounced them in keeping with the architectural integrity of the house and therefore acceptable. One hurdle crossed.

Rather than tackle the installation on an empty stomach, I decided to wander down Main Street for Maylene's lunch special. First, though, I called to get an appointment with Dr. Randel, a phone consultation at the end of his lunch break. His receptionist gave me the impression the quick appointment was a favor for Maggy Avinger rather than a professional courtesy to me. I'd need to eat fast so I wouldn't be late.

Maylene's was filling up early. With bright sunshine and a cool, clear March day hinting at spring, I wasn't the only one looking for an excuse to leave the office.

Deputy Sheriff Rudy Mellin waved from a back booth for me to join him.

"Figured you'd be out pig hunting," I said as I slid onto the patched vinyl seat across from him.

Rudy gave me a fish-eye stare. "How 'bout you just go back up to the door and wait on your own dang booth."

"You'd miss my company. Besides, anybody else who came to sit down would want an update, too."

Rudy snorted and stuffed a doughy white roll in his mouth.

I bowed over the menu too long, trying to decide what and how to ask Rudy about Harden Avinger without siccing him on my client. Rudy and I had known each other since kindergarten, had even been lab partners in high school chemistry class. I'd been surprised when I returned home to Dacus three months ago and found he was chief sheriff's deputy. Once upon a time, he'd talked of teaching high school history.

Now, I had to remember he was a cop.

I ordered the salt-and-pepper catfish with cole slaw and launched into my questions in what I hoped was a roundabout way.

"Rudy, hypothetically, what would you all do if somebody died following a long illness, with every indication it was a natural death? The doctor and everybody agreed on how he'd died. Then suppose a letter he wrote to somebody showed up, claiming he was poisoned. He didn't notify the cops. He just wrote . . . a friend. But you learned about it. What would you do?"

"Hypothetical, huh? This so-called friend have some kind of attorney-client privilege?"

I shook my head a bit too vehemently. "Just a hypothetical. Something I got to wondering about."

He held my gaze, looking for a telltale slip, then he shrugged, his belly tight against the table. "Reckon we'd start with the doctor, as well as background on the family. Any domestic disturbance calls in the past? Do friends or family suspect someone of wishing him ill? Someone stand to gain at his death? We'd handle it like any other investigation. Checking records, asking questions, digging around the edges to see what we unearth."

"What if you found nothing? No inheritance left to speak of, no signs of familial discord. The doctor was convinced it was death from a long painful disease. And what if the guy was known as a jokester and those who knew him thought it was just a bad prank?"

"This hypothetical of yours is awfully detailed." Rudy took a slow swig of his ice tea, watching me, waiting to see if I'd fill the silence with some explanation. I offered only a shrug.

He set his glass down. "If the doctor was convinced everything was on the up-and-up and we didn't have anything more than a letter to go on, we'd likely let it drop. If he was under a doctor's care, he might not have had an autopsy, though if he did, we would request a tox screen on the organ tissues, just to make sure."

"So if the doctor was satisfied and you trusted his judgment, you wouldn't try to exhume the body?"

"It would depend, but I doubt it. Too much red tape to exhume, and too expensive. The family could ask for one, but they'd have to pay." Of course," he snorted, "if his family offed him, they probably wouldn't be forking over big money for an exhumation, autopsy, and tox screen, now would they? Those are pricey items."

"You said if he'd had an autopsy, there'd still be tissue samples available? Who keeps those?"

"The hospital pathologist sometimes performs a limited autopsy. I don't know about your hypothetical case. With suspicious circumstances, the pathologist holds on to hunks of stuff, stored in jars, in case it's ever needed again for more tests. Mostly to protect the hospital in lawsuits, I'm sure. Quite a sight, I can tell you. These big glass jars with hunks of lung and heart and liver all jammed together with JOE BLOW writ large on the lid. That's what we come to, hunks of goo in a giant dill pickle jar."

The waitress plopped a plate of gelatinous beef stew, cabbage, and red beets down in front of him. He took a second to bow for grace, then dug in.

"Anything I need to know?" he asked around a mouthful of meat and potato.

"No. Just trying to think through a puzzle in my head." I'm not a good liar, so it's best for me to stick with manageable truth. Not too much false detail. That's where liars always mess up, too many false details.

He eyed me as he chewed. My plate arrived at that opportune moment, and I lowered my eyes in my own quick blessing.

Rudy had prepared me well for my quick conversation with Dr. Randel. Yes, Harden Avinger had terminal cancer. No, he had no signs of intestinal distress or other symptoms of poisoning of any kind. No, no full autopsy because he'd been under a doctor's care with no mystery about what had killed him. No, his wife couldn't have stockpiled pain medication and given it to him all at once; he'd had Dilaudid through a PCA pump.

"Miz Andrews, I'm usually loath to malign any patient of mine. Not because I have any compunction about showing disrespect for the dead but because I consider it unprofessional. However, many's the time I've wondered why Maggy Avinger didn't bash her sorry excuse for a husband over the head with a cast-iron frying pan and put them both out of their misery. He was insufferably cruel to her right up to the end, and she repaid him with gentleness and devotion. I don't know what's prompted your questions. If it has anything to do with something Harden Avinger stirred up, I don't want to know. That's blunt, but that's the way I see it."

He paused, then said, "If you want to know exactly what was going on with him at the end, call Rulill Evans. She was his hospice nurse. She can tell you better than I can."

Dr. Randel transferred me to his office nurse, who supplied Rulill Evans's phone number. Thanks to the wonder of cell phones, tracking her down didn't take but one phone call.

"Ms. Evans, Dr. Randel suggested I talk to you about Harden Avinger's last days. He said you'd know more about his condition."

"Well, I guess so. That's my job, isn't it? To keep doctors as far away as possible from patients who want to die in peace. Doctors prescribe whatever I tell them and trust I know my business. Just the way it should be."

I had to hold the phone away from my ear whenever she spoke. I pictured Rulill Evans as a battleship-sized woman cut along the same lines as my great-aunt Aletha. She didn't bother asking for a medical release form. Federal privacy laws have done little to change human nature.

"Some question has come up about Mr. Avinger's condition during his last days—"

"What kind of question?" She asked before I could finish, her tone defensive.

Might as well be as direct as she was. "Do you have any indication he'd been poisoned?"

"Poisoned? With what?"

"I'm not sure."

"Who throws around accusations like that without anything more than some general suspicion? Who'd you say you were?"

"Ms. Evans, confidentially, Ms. Avinger learned her husband accused somebody of poisoning him. She asked me to look into it."

Not exactly the way the story developed, but safer than volunteering what I was trying to squelch.

"Harrumph." Her snort forced me to move the phone farther from my ear.

"Harden Avinger was a jerk and an idiot. The only thing that poisoned him was his own black heart. Don't you think I'd have noticed if he had any signs of poison? He wasn't throwing up. He didn't even need anything for nausea from the narcotics. A lot of patients do, but he didn't. Didn't even require much in the way of pain meds. Poison."

She spit out the last word. "That man was poison, but he sure as hell wasn't being poisoned. Can I be any clearer than that?"

"No, ma'am. I appreciate your time." If I ever needed somebody to stand with me when I faced death, Rulill Evans was one I'd want. I sure wouldn't want to face off against her, though.

If Harden had been poisoned, it would be easier to suspect Dr.

Randel or Rulill Evans, with their passionate and professed dislike of Harden, than to suspect Maggy. Frankly, though, I couldn't see any of them playing angel of destruction. That left Maggy the widow of someone who gave meanness a bad name. Why had she stayed married to him? Silly question. A Southern woman of a certain age and a Baptist to boot. Divorce? Unthinkable.

I'd have to ask Mom and Dad what they knew about the Avingers.

"Knock, knock, anybody home?"

Maggy came through the front room into my office. I was momentarily flustered, interrupted by the very woman whose good sense I'd been mentally questioning. I needed to hang bells on the doors to give me some warning.

"You're here. I brought you that copy of the death certificate you wanted." She presented me with a manila envelope and stared at me a moment too long, as if trying to make up her mind about something.

To fill the silence, I said, "I talked to Dr. Randel this morning—"

"Avery, I'm—a bit embarrassed." She cut me off. "We didn't talk about money this morning. I don't know what I was thinking, but I can't—I just can't afford much of your time. I wanted to make that clear. I got carried away and didn't think—"

"Listen." I made gentle patting motions with my hands, what I hoped was a reassuring gesture. "Don't worry. It's not taking much time. Let me come up with a plan of attack first, then we can talk money. Okay?"

Attorneys are supposed to discuss fee arrangements with clients up front. Wasn't that somewhere in the Code of Professional Conduct? Or just common sense? In my previous life, I didn't set the fees for my services—and I didn't have clients who had trouble paying. What was I doing here? I had a familiar flicker of doubt about my decision to give up on a lucrative city law firm for a small-town general practice. Had I exhausted my options? Was coming home to Dacus really what I wanted?

Maggy let out the breath she'd been holding, but the worry wrinkles between her eyebrows didn't completely ease.

"I don't want charity. I like to pay my bills." Her chin jutted out, but her eyes gave a gentle pleading.

"I understand. But I haven't done anything to solve your problem yet. I'm still mulling over the best way to approach it. We'll talk on Monday, when I have a better idea, okay?"

She looked relieved. "Okay." Not that I'd dealt with many grieving widows, but Maggy hadn't said anything about missing her husband. Then again, given what I'd learned about her husband, what would she grieve?

She turned toward the front parlor, then spun around, a smile brightening her face. "I just happened to think. You're new back in town. Are you busy tomorrow? You might enjoy meeting some folks or renewing some acquaintances. And it's for a good cause. We've gathered a group for a plant rescue operation—to save some native plants ahead of the bulldozers. At a new development on the mountain."

"On the mountain?"

She nodded and fished in her shoulder bag for a paper. "Here's directions to the site. A beautiful cove forest. We need to save what we can, don't you think?"

I glanced at the map, which had a couple of pages attached explaining the what and the why of plant rescue. Too much to take in at a glance.

"We won't get started until mid- to late morning," she said. "Give the sun a chance to warm things up a bit. Just bring some gardening gloves and a trowel or shovel. We'll have everything else. I think your mother is coming, or you're welcome to ride with me."

"Thanks. I'll let you know," I said.

If someone was saving some part of the world, my mom was probably scheduled to be there.

I walked Maggy to the door. She started to say something but a sound on the porch caught her attention, and she turned to open the door for another visitor.

Mack MacGregor and his work boots thumped across the porch, a look of welcome surprise on his face.

"Maggy, how nice to see you." He smiled down at her from his lanky height, one heavy-knuckled hand clutching a large potted prayer plant to his chest. "Didn't know to expect you here or I'd have brought you one, too." He wiped his hand across his jaw as if checking whether he'd remembered to shave.

Maggy laughed. "Lord, Mack, I don't need another plant to take care of. Looks as though you have just the thing for Avery's office, though."

"I hope so." He indicated the leafy plant. "Can I set this somewhere for you?"

Suddenly I was six years old again and Mr. Mack was presenting me and my sister with red roses to wear at the Mother's Day church service. He'd made the presentation of our corsages such an event every year, I'd felt so special, so grown-up.

"That's beautiful! Thank you so much. Would it go right here?"

I indicated a spot beside the front door, where the plant could see the sunshine if it squinted across the deep-set porch and looked hard.

"That'll work." He ceremoniously set it down and centered it in front of the door's glass sidelight. "Just a little office-warming present."

"You'll need a small table, Avery," Maggy said. "If you don't have one, come by the house. I've got just the thing. Mack here would probably tote it over for you. He's my back-door neighbor, you know."

Mr. Mack nodded. "You'd think we'd see each other more often, wouldn't you?" He stared down at Maggy, searching her face for something.

"Isn't that always the way it is?" she agreed. "Folks are just too busy. And speaking of which, I'll see you two later." She was doing a good job not letting on about what had brought her to my office, Southern sidewalk casual.

Mr. Mack watched as she walked down the sidewalk to her car. "I've been so worried about her since Harden died."

"Did you know him well?"

"Sure. We shared a back fence for thirty years. Back when Lucy was alive, the four of us played bridge together."

Watching his face, I saw that look I'd first noticed when I was a little girl. He'd reminded me of a sad, long-faced puppy. Or Scarecrow from *The Wizard of Oz*. I'd first noticed that sad expression about the same time he'd begun delivering the roses from his garden, the year his wife had died.

"Here I am wasting your valuable lawyering time." He opened the door, then turned back to me. "You really need to get a sign out front, Avery. Some folks might not be able to find you."

"I know." I kept picturing a discreet wrought-iron post, white framed sign, black script lettering.

"That husband of hers."

He was looking down the sidewalk with a distant expression.

"Maggy's?"

He nodded, one fist jammed deep in his overall pocket. "Something Harden told me before he died, I just haven't been able to get it out of my mind. About how he had the chance to buy extra life insurance, at a really good rate, something from the navy, after he knew he was sick. He refused. Said he didn't want her being well off after he was gone, said somebody'd marry her for her money. Can you believe that?"

He shook his head. "It's made me sick at my stomach ever since. Because I know she struggles."

No wonder she worried about money.

"Figured Harden always knew she was too good for him." He gave a sad-puppy bob of his head, then roused himself from his ruminations. "I'd best get to work."

"Thanks again, Mr. Mack." I watched from the doorway and waved as he pulled his long legs into his pickup truck. A husband who wouldn't insure his life, who ordered his own outrageously expensive grave marker, and who used that marker to accuse his wife of murder. Dear Lord.

The afternoon's conversations tumbled around in my head while my hands tackled the door locks. I couldn't get my mind off Maggy Avinger and the glimpse Mr. Mack had given me into her life. My heart hurt for her.

The wood in the door frames was old, dry, and tough to drill. To get the latches and locks lined up in the French doors required shimming one of the hinges to correct for a slight warping in the door, then I filed the faceplate opening so the latch would catch. Buying new doors would have been much easier, but that would've forced me to endure another of Melvin's lectures on the value of architectural integrity.

By late afternoon, I was no closer to a solution for Maggy's problems but my office and Melvin's had lockable doors off the house's main hallway. Neither of the two former tenants—first the Bertram family, and later the Baldwin & Bates Funeral Home—had needed to lock the front parlors, but I now felt more secure.

I put Melvin's new keys on his desk with a note. Not that he could overlook them on the uncluttered leather blotter centered on the spotless expanse of desk.

As I'd wrestled with the locks, I'd argued with myself over how to deal with Maggy's problems. I was sure Mom and Dad could give me some much-needed background, though I'd have to be careful not to breach client confidentiality with a careless slip. I was realizing just how tricky that could be in a small town like Dacus. On the other hand, if everybody already knows something, is it really confidential?

My six-year-old niece, Emma, was supposed to stay with Mom and Dad tonight while my sister, Lydia, and her husband, Frank, rehearsed for an opera workshop production of *The Mikado*. Several professors and students were driving over from the university to lend their professional talents. Even with professional help, I suspected the Town of Titipu would still be populated with thick Southern accents. Light opera, sure, but shouldn't dramatic integrity demand verisimilitude?

If I hurried, I could invite myself to dinner and visit with Emma to see what sort of off-center observations she had on the world. As an afterthought, I grabbed up the papers Maggy had left about the plant rescue before I turned the key in my brand-new lock and went out the back door. Melvin hadn't said where he was going—not that he reported in with me—so I locked the back door, too.

"Plant rescue operation? What the heck is that?" My dad peered at Maggy's information through his reading glasses. Technically, he now owns the Dacus newspaper, but that doesn't mean he knows what's going on.

"Honey, I told you about that. Keena Brown and Maggy Avinger organized it. To rescue native plant species ahead of that new housing development going in, up above Walnut Grove campground. On Dot Downing's property. Apparently Dot's sold it to some developer."

"Mm-hmm," my dad said noncommittally studying the papers.

"You going, Mom?" I lifted a square of lasagna onto a plate, and Emma carried it to the table.

"I might join them later in the day. I work the First Fruits Food Bank in the morning. You ought to go up. Keena Brown has a business that salvages native plants and encourages people to use them in their landscaping. I never realized how many of the trees and shrubs we use originally came from Japan or China. Isn't that amazing?"

"Harrumph." Great-aunt Aletha—Letha for short—expressively summed up her feelings on the subject. She poured a glass of milk for Emma and put the carton back in the refrigerator. "Folks—and shrubs—ought to stay where they're planted. Nothing grows well away from its own home."

"Now, Aunt Letha. You know that's not entirely true." Mom said, tossing the salad. "Those gorgeous hollies you have outside your kitchen window aren't natives, but they sure seem to like it here."

Aunt Letha shot Mom one of her don't-prove-your-rules-with-my-exceptions looks and took a seat at the head of the table awaiting the start of the meal.

"Avery, you would enjoy getting to know Keena," Mom said. "She's led an interesting life, following her husband's career around the world."

"According to this"—Dad was still reading—"maybe twenty to twenty-five percent of the native plants around here are either rare or endangered? Never would've thought it'd be that many."

Aunt Letha snorted. "And exactly what are we in danger of losing that we really need? Precious little, I would imagine. What? Some subspecies of a chiggerweed? Big loss there. The English might like giant weeds and pollen breeders jumbling up their front yards, but I don't see that catching on around here. Folks here got sense enough to call a weed a weed and pull it up by its roots."

Nobody bothered responding. Mom, Emma, and I joined Aunt Letha and Dad at the table. Dad laid the paper aside and said grace over the food before reporting more information garnered from Keena's material that I hadn't bothered to read.

"I knew these plants were old-time remedies, but I didn't know some were now used commercially. Seems like those should be cultivated." Dad's engineering bias believes everything ought to have a rational solution or use.

"What's this development that's going in?" Mom asked. "The first I'd heard about it was when Maggy called about the plant rescue."

Everyone looked around, waiting for someone else to pipe up. Dad finally shrugged and said, "Heard something about a big golf community going in up there. That didn't make sense, though. Not enough flat ground up in there for a Putt-Putt miniature course or even a putting green."

"You can sell Yankees cockleburs and they'll sit around waiting for the baby porcupines to hatch out," Aunt Letha said.

Emma, sitting across from me, caught my eye. She took a sip of her milk to hide her smile.

"Speaking of Maggy," I said, changing the subject, "did you all know her husband?" I shoveled in a bite of whole-wheat lasagna and waited for my background research to come to me.

"We were in Rotary together for a while," Dad said. "He was right regular to come, when he had his accounting firm, but—"

"So's he could get you all as clients," Aunt Letha interjected.

"—he took sick soon after he sold his business and he quit coming."

"Been dead a long time ago if he'd died when he ought."

"Aunt Letha." Mom gently reproved her while glancing at Emma, hoping Letha would recall that a member of the tell-everything-I-hear club sat among us.

"You know it's true." Aunt Letha, undeterred, stated her case. "He treated his wife shamefully, his sales tactics were questionable at best, he squeezed nickels until they screamed in pain, and he coated it all with that shallow, saccharine hail-fellow-well-met act. Give me an out-and-out rounder anyday over one who dresses it up in sheep's wool."

"How long was he sick?" I asked, ignoring Mom's look.

"Morally? His whole life. Certainly from grade school on," Letha pronounced, a former American history teacher who also knew the personal history of most everyone in town. "Physically? He was sick two, maybe three years."

Emma and I both sat there chewing and taking it all in, each of us for our own reasons.

Mom just frowned. "Avery, could you come help me get the fruit cups?"

"Sure." I scooped the last bit of salad into my mouth and pushed back my chair.

When we got into the kitchen, Mom set her plate in the sink and turned to face me. "The conversation about Harden reminded me about a promise I'd made."

"Ma'am?" I'd expected a mild lecture.

Instead of going to the refrigerator for the fruit, she opened a drawer in the kitchen desk.

"Mr. Mack came to talk to me this afternoon, wondering if you could give him some advice."

From a file folder lying on top of the drawer's miscellany, she pulled a small newspaper clipping.

"Mack got this in the mail last week. Couldn't bring himself to throw it away but didn't know what to do about it and couldn't bear to keep it in the house."

Even though everyone called Henry MacGregor "Mack," Mom sometimes still calls him Mr. Mack around me and my sister, as she did when we were kids and she was trying to teach us the proper way to address adults. Thanks to her persistence, I still called him Mr. Mack.

I didn't mention his visit to the office.

The clipping was a banana pudding recipe. I had to turn the clipping around in circles to read the words as they turned the corners and filled the margins:

> *Stay away from Maggy Avinger's banana pudding. Her husband didn't survive his last meal, you know.*

I looked up at Mom, who stood propped against the sink.

"He got this last week?"

"I think so. It had to be sometime recently, after Harden Avinger passed. I told Mack to pay it no never mind, but I wanted to see if you could talk to him."

"About what?" About what, indeed. My brain flooded with oh-nos and what-ifs. Did she really do it? Had Harden somehow come back from the grave to scribble on a newspaper clipping? Could there be two people that mean? Or had somebody found out about Harden's sick joke and decided to fan the flame?

Mom shrugged. "Just reassure him. When he came by to talk to you today, he thought you were too busy. I tried to tell him you weren't, but he wasn't hearing any of that. You're a lawyer and he might listen when you tell him to just ignore this nonsense. Somebody who hasn't got gumption enough to sign a name hasn't said anything that deserves hearing."

"Did he bring the envelope it came in?"

Mom pulled it out of the drawer. I studied it. Postmarked Upstate South Carolina and dated last week. Harden couldn't have sent it; he was already dead. So who did?

The handwriting was shaky and cramped. Of course, the clipping's margins didn't allow much space to write in. No date on the clipping, but the typeface looked like the *Clarion*'s. Guess I could check to see if they'd run a banana pudding recipe and when, but I wasn't sure what that would accomplish.

"I'll talk to him. I'm just not sure what to say."

That satisfied Mom. She turned to the refrigerator and pulled out the bowl of diced fruit.

She could be satisfied, passing it along. She didn't know about Harden Avinger's eight-foot-tall accusation, coming soon to a neighborhood cemetery.

Mom pushed through the swinging door to the dining room carrying the large bowl. I followed with the dessert bowls, chewing my bottom lip.

"Aunt Letha, where did you say Aunt Vinnia and Aunt Hattie were going this evening?" Mom asked as she ladled up dessert. Emma and I exchanged glances, both of us disappointed that dessert turned out to be something healthy.

Letha wiped her mouth, the generous cloth napkin dainty in her large hand. "To see some picture show, with some other old farts. Can't stand the fare at the picture houses myself. Some tearjerker about a guy with dementia. Don't know what's entertaining about that. Besides, half that crowd won't remember what happened by the time they get home."

Aunt Letha is the oldest of my late grandfather's three baby sisters—and by far the oldest in the crowd of "old farts" her sisters had gone out on the town with. No one dared mention that. Mom didn't bother shushing her in front of Emma. Sometimes that just eggs Aunt Letha on. Besides, Emma had heard it all before.

Mom tried again to change the topic. "Are you going to the plant rescue tomorrow morning?"

"I might," I said.

Even though it was still March, it would be nice to be outdoors.

"You need to come by the house and pick up Bud, then. Take him with you," Aunt Letha said.

"Ma'am?" My eyebrows shot up.

"Take Bud with you, if you're going to be wandering around some desolate patch of woods."

"Bud hates hiking." Or just walking. Letha's Rottweiler likes his people settled and within his watchful eyeshot, preferably somewhere near his food bowl.

"He loves being outside. And you don't need to be wandering around up there without protection."

No point asking her who would protect the plant rescuers from Bud. He likes attention, doesn't like people moving quickly, talking loudly, or not paying attention to him, and is rather insistent on getting his way.

My dad bit his bottom lip and tried, not successfully, to hide his amusement. He didn't even attempt to rescue me, content to watch the inevitable unfold.

Saturday Morning

Saturday morning, I aimed the nose of my 1964½ Mustang up the mountain. Bud eyed me balefully as he scrunched into the blanket protecting the backseat upholstery from his toenails.

A mile or so outside town, Main Street becomes a two-lane state road and takes a sharp turn as it begins its ascent into the Blue Ridge, the southern end of the Appalachian chain. I love the abruptness of the climb and the sharp turns on the first stretch, where I know without a doubt I'm in the hills. I downshifted and pushed the accelerator. I heard Bud nestle down into the seat for the ride, happier than I was that we were sharing our journey.

I was concentrating on the series of sharp curves when a blue light popped in my rearview mirror.

A cop? On this road? I slowed and rode the right side of the lane so he could pass on the short straight stretch. In the mirror, I could see him making agitated pull-over hand gestures.

You gotta be kidding. Cops never clocked speed on this road. I had to drive another half mile before I could pull into a narrow gravel road, my stomach knotted in that irrational kindergartner-mad fit I get whenever a cop pulls me over.

The deputy took his time sauntering up to my window. His ears stuck out wide under his Smokey Bear hat, and he looked about sixteen years old.

"Ma'am, you have any idea how fast—*shee-ut!*"

With a roar, Bud rammed his gallon-bucket-sized head through the quart-sized window opening behind my seat. The deputy skittered in the gravel, backing away from the car, and almost fell. When he was safely out of Bud's reach, a slant-eyed anger replaced his wide-eyed fright.

"Get your dog under control. Now!" His hand rested on his pistol butt.

"Bud! Bud!" I couldn't get twisted around in the bucket seat to grab his collar, and his deep-throated barks drilled painfully into my head. Bud was enjoying this—he had something on the run, and he hadn't even broken a sweat.

I could no longer see the deputy in the side mirrors; he'd moved behind the car, squawking into his shoulder radio for backup, *Officer threatened.*

"He won't hurt you," I called out the window, struggling to reassure Officer Uptight and conk Bud on the nose at the same time. I didn't dare open the door so I could get hold of Bud. This guy was proving to be way more entertainment than Bud had enjoyed in a while. The car rocked menacingly as he barked and lunged.

"Get your dog under control! I'm warning you!"

"Officer—" I managed to twist around with my knees in the seat and reach between the bucket seats to grab Bud's collar. Bud rolled his eyes at me, as if to say *This is fun, isn't it?* He gave another throaty roar.

Through the back window, I saw the car carrying Officer Scaredy's backup whip off the main road behind us. That was quick.

Oh, no. Deputy Rudy Mellin's familiar shape emerged from behind the driver's door, a smirk on his face and his hand on his gun belt.

The junior deputy danced around on first one foot, then the

other, regaling Rudy with a roster of my offenses. I bent over the seat and wrestled with Bud's collar, trying unsuccessfully to pull his massive head back in the window and wishing I could evaporate.

Rudy stepped up to my window and leaned over so he could look me in the eye—and study my rear end. He cupped Bud's head, scratching his ears with one hand and smoothing his throat with the other. Rudy's cooing sounds hushed Bud's barking and set his giant Tater Tot tail wagging.

"Exceeding the speed limit in excess of fifteen miles an hour. Threatening an officer with grievous bodily harm. Failing to comply with an officer's request to stand down. Tsk-tsk-tsk."

"Stand down? Nobody said stand down. What the heck does that mean, stand down?"

Rudy studied my jean-clad rump to further irk me, and smiled. "Busy this morning, aren't we, counselor?" He kept rubbing Bud's ears.

I glared at him. This was all Aunt Letha's fault.

Rudy turned to the deputy, who had taken a brave step closer to the back of the car. Bud eyed him, but was too happy with the ear-scratching to take up a now-old game.

"Officer Caudle, I think this situation's under control. You may resume patrol."

"But I witnessed her speeding. And—"

"Deputy. I have this matter in hand now."

Bud hassled happily.

Junior stared at Rudy a couple of beats too long, mentally searching for some way to legitimately defy him. I was his big catch for the day—heck, for his whole career so far—and he knew Rudy was declaring a catch-and-release day.

Rudy's rank meant Junior couldn't even sputter with indignation, so he huffed back to his car. After maneuvering forward and back a few times to get unsandwiched from between Rudy's cruiser and my car, he couldn't resist spraying a little gravel as his tires barked back onto the paved two-lane heading for town.

I turned loose of Bud's collar and slid back down in the driver's seat. Bud was too enamored to eat Rudy and save me from a lecture.

"A'vry, you gotta slow this crate down."

"I wasn't going that fast. How would he even know how fast I was going? The Sheriff's Department doesn't have——"

"Yes, we do have radar and we use it on this road to keep hot dogs from toasting themselves."

"I'm not going to wreck." Being chastised made me sullen.

"I'll take care of it this time. You don't want to know what happens to your insurance when you get a ticket like the one he was about to write."

Rudy obviously hadn't checked my driving record.

"Thanks, Rudy." I gritted my teeth in frustration, but I didn't want to sound petulant. Junior had been mad enough to haul me to jail, if he could've found a way to get me out of the car.

"Where you headed?"

The plant rescue sounded lame as I explained it to hulking, bemused Rudy.

He cooed at Bud and gave him one last pat on the head, like he was palming a basketball. "Keep 'er in the road, A'vry."

Bud craned out the window to watch his new friend return to his patrol car.

Steep roads and sparsely populated hills don't present many turnoffs, so I found the plant dig without getting lost. Bud stayed in the car happily dreaming of his morning spent meeting new enemies and old friends.

I carried the gardening gloves Mom had encouraged me to bring. I doubted their marks of wear would camouflage my inexperience, but I joined the other plant rescuers. Thanks to Bud's antics and that baby-faced deputy, I was late for whatever speeches everyone had gathered around to hear. The group—mostly older women—were bundled in L.L. Bean jackets and wool scarves, their cheeks pink and their eyes bright with gardening zeal.

At the center of a loose half circle stood two women: Maggy Avinger, in her practical corduroy pants and faded plaid shirt coat, and a young woman dressed in a wool pantsuit who clearly had no intention of digging anything. As I joined the edge of the group, Maggy gave me a small wave and kept talking.

"—Lisa Livson, the sales agent for the development, has graciously helped us get permission for our efforts."

Lisa, the woman in the pantsuit, nodded to the group and flashed a quick smile, her teeth peroxide-bright against her dark lipstick.

"You all know our sense of urgency," Maggy continued. "Lots of native plants to be relocated and not much time to do it."

Even by late morning, the weak winter sun hadn't done much to warm this hollow. I glanced around at the group. Nobody else had donned their gardening gloves, so I folded mine and jammed my hands in my pockets to keep my fingers warm. Despite the cold, maybe because of it, the assembled looked eager to start digging.

"Dot Downing has marked each plant or cluster with one of these flags." Maggy held up a tiny caution-orange flag on a coathanger-wire stake. Easy to spot, the flags dotted the winter-brown hillside all around us. "Dot certainly knows whereof she speaks. These have been her woods for—how long?"

A stocky woman wearing a tatty oversized sweater, gray frizz sticking out around her wool toboggan, stood next to Maggy and looked a bit embarrassed at the attention. Or sad. "Longer than we'll mention," Dot said, her voice soft.

Maggy slipped her arm around Dot's shoulders. "Dot and Keena Brown also wrote down for us some information on the plants and their degree of rarity. None of us really appreciated how special these cove forest habitats were until Dot and Keena began doing some research."

I studied Magnolia Avinger with a new appreciation, amazed at her good humor and calm when I knew what hung over her like a malevolent threat. Her abusive husband's long illness, the embarrassment and expense of his garish gift to himself, and his dangerous accusation would have swamped most anyone. She could try to ignore the threat his accusation posed, but it had already leaked out—Mr. Mack's anonymous letter proved that. As I watched her pull everyone together to save some plants, I realized I'd have to pull her along to save herself. She'd have to deal with the problem her husband had bequeathed whether she wanted to or not.

"Typical, isn't it?" An unusually husky voice murmured close to my ear. I turned, startled by how close he stood. A pair of thick-lashed brown eyes and a face that hadn't said good morning to a razor were capped by an unruly mass of too-long brown curls. His outdoor gear looked more gonzo snowboarder than master gardener. "We value what we have only after we destroy it," he said, still standing too close, but turning back to face Maggy.

I didn't respond to the cynic philosopher.

"Did I see you on the road, on the way up?" he said, his voice just above a whisper. "Pulled by a couple of cops?"

"What makes you think it was me?" I whispered, feeling guilty talking during Maggy's instructions, like naughty kids whispering in the back of math class.

"Not many burgundy 1960s-vintage Mustang convertibles around here—or anywhere, for that matter." A wry grin lifted the corner of his mouth.

"You aren't from around here, are you?" I said.

"Ah, the classic hold-'em-at-arm's-length-but-feign-interest question. Gosh, how did you know?"

"Because you stand too close."

He grinned broadly, flashing perfectly straight teeth, but he didn't step back.

The group was breaking up, shuffling off in clusters. Thanks to Chatty Boy, I'd missed my assignment.

"Glad to see you two know someone here." Maggy approached, offering us copies of Dot Downing's plant research.

"No," he said, taking a paper. "We haven't met."

"I thought surely—well, Noah works at your dad's newspaper. Avery Andrews, Noah Lakefield."

We studied each other, reprocessing previous misconceptions.

"You're the lawyer."

I nodded, at a disadvantage. My dad, an unreconstructed engineer, had bought the Dacus newspaper more to have old machines to work on than from any affinity for disseminating information. He hadn't said anything about hiring a new reporter. Then again, I'd been in Charleston for several weeks working on a case. I had to wonder what this guy was doing in Dacus, besides scraping the bottom of the journalistic barrel. A really bad journalist? A checkered past? The witness protection program? To be fair, he might be thinking the same thing about me. At least I belonged here, I told myself.

"Your patch is right over here. We'll put you two together. Noah, let me get you a shovel. We need some brawn to get those saplings up. We're not sure we'll be able to salvage any of the dogwoods. I won't think about that. It'll make me cry."

She led us across a clearing to a shaded slope. "Here's the wrapping material. Cut out well around the roots, lay the plant on the fabric, and wrap it up, like so. Don't shake the dirt loose from the roots." She deftly dug around and lifted out something that looked like a dull, shriveled weed and rolled it into a square of some kind of space-age material.

"We're lucky it's been a mild winter. The dormant plants will have an easier time of it. Just stack them loosely here, and the trailer crew will come by for them."

Noah and I stood awkwardly on either side of her. He looked even more intimidated than I felt. Somehow, knowing these were endangered plants made me nervous. They were too valuable to be trusted to my inexperience.

"What are these?" Noah asked, surveying the brown weeds marked by orange flags.

"These are nodding onion," Maggy said. "That's faded trillium. For poultices and to stop bleeding. You'll have to look carefully, because they've browned back a bit for winter. Those are monkshood, for making aconite."

Maggy must have noticed Noah's discomfiture. "Here's a trowel. Why don't you work here on these smaller plants for a while.

Avery can help you if you have questions. I'll get you later, for some heavy lifting with the shrubs."

I started to admit my inexperience but then bit my lip. Judging from the way he held his trowel, like a chopstick, he knew even less about gardening than I did, sad to say.

Maggy headed toward another group but froze, staring up into a tree so large I could have disappeared behind it. "I had no idea Dot had black walnut in here," she said, more to herself than to me or Noah. She blinked, her eyes damp. "There's more here than we can possibly save. Why, oh, why did she sell?"

She cut herself off with a shake of her head and moved on to join the next group, focused on what she could fix and walking past what she couldn't. Noah and I both stared up at the wide-arching branches of the winter-bare tree.

"Black walnut?" he asked.

"A dark, very hard wood, for furniture. Very expensive, I guess because it's rare. My dad likes to work with it, and so did my granddad."

Noah craned his neck back to see the tree canopy, the leafless branches spread far above us in a delicate filigree. "It's beautiful just as it is, isn't it?"

It was beautiful. What would happen to it? Surely, if it had to be cut down, they'd sell the timber so someone could make something beautiful with it. They couldn't just lay waste to it all.

To keep from thinking about the tree and the look of loss on Maggy's face, I turned my attention to the huddled little weeds at our feet. I was, after all, the closest thing to an expert in our group. I had to set a good example.

After our first hesitant efforts, we fell into a reasonably productive rhythm and didn't have to concentrate on every move.

"So," I asked, "who talked you into spending Saturday morning up here playing in the dirt?"

"A couple I met at a university lecture last week—local Sierra Club members—mentioned it, said they were coming. Seemed like a worthwhile project, and a good story for the paper at the same time."

"Sierra Club, huh?" Up here, that name elicited visions of granola crunchers and leftover hippies with canoes. Natives who have lived here for generations distrust outsiders who preach about how to be stewards of the land, but as better roads and too much discretionary income brought more outsiders in, I was beginning to see that stewardship was easier when developers weren't waving huge wads of cash in somebody's face.

As if he read my thoughts, he asked, "Do you know Dot Downing, the lady who sold this land?"

"No, not really."

"I just wondered why she'd sell to somebody like Lionel Shoal."

"Who's he?"

"Thought you were from around here," he teased.

I didn't grace him with a response.

"He's moved in touting his new conservancy development. Golden Cove, he calls it. He's got a story for every listener. Pure bullshit. Allegedly, an abandoned gold mine sits somewhere on the property, so he's talking to some people about the investment potential in mineral rights that'll help pay for their vacation home up here. To others, he's talking about the conservation easement on common areas that'll preserve a huge chunk of pristine cove forest. It's all gold-plated bullshit. Somebody's not reading the fine print. Including, I'm afraid, Dot Downing."

"What do you mean?" I stopped digging.

"I mean she's the first one he sold—how do you say it here?—a pig in a poke? She swallowed his snake-oil spiel. Now that reality is dawning, she's got serious seller's remorse. With good reason. Didn't you notice her crying this morning?"

I did remember Maggy's consoling arm around Dot's shoulders, but I hadn't seen the tears. I pulled a square wrapper off the stack to sit on. The time-honored mountain tradition of hunkering—sitting on the heels of your work boots—is a male-only tradition. Most women aren't aerodynamically built for that. Noah, with his long legs and nonexistent backside, had hunkering mastered, though.

"Why don't you talk to her?" he said. "Can't you lawyers find some clever way to out-con a con artist?"

Before I could explain that lawyers in South Carolina can't solicit clients and that land sales aren't easy to set aside, the sound of scuffled leaves interrupted us. Maggy was coming down the slope with a girl in tow.

"Good job, there. Good job. Noah, make sure you're getting all the root you possibly can. That one there was once used in rheumatiz ointment. I've brought you some help."

A long, wispy girl with flyaway waist-length hair and doe eyes peeking through her bangs let herself be drawn forward, tucked under Maggy's arm. She was older than I'd first thought—maybe fifteen or sixteen.

"This is Jesse Ruffin. Avery. Noah. It'll be good to have you here with these delicate plants, Jesse. They need your gentle touch. Do you have any gloves? Good. Keep your fingers out of your mouth and away from your eyes and nose. Some of these"—she pointed to where Noah was digging—"are poisonous."

Noah jerked his hands back as if he'd been burned.

"No, no. Didn't mean to alarm you. Just be aware they can be irritants."

Noah didn't look reassured.

"I'll round up some gardening gloves," she offered.

He nodded, grateful.

Jesse settled down to work without a word, her hair over her face and her grasp of the trowel clumsy but determined.

"Avery," Maggy said, "could you come with me a minute?"

I stood and started after her, then thought to toss Noah my gloves. He was surreptitiously contemplating his fingers as if wondering what poisoning himself would feel like.

Maggy marched off some distance before she stopped to talk to me. The small groups had been strategically scattered to get the best coverage of the area, so no other groups were in view. Military generals could take notes from this woman's tactical planning.

"Avery, I wasn't expecting Jesse up here today. She grew up down the street from me, so I feel more than a little protective of her. I'd like her to work here with you."

"Sure."

She must have noticed my puzzled expression. "Jesse needs some friends right now. Her dad took off a week or so ago for parts unknown. Good riddance, if you ask me, but her mother isn't taking it well. Lots of people around town know the story, so I'll just be blunt. Len Ruffin abused his wife, and I fear he turned his attentions to Jesse before he left town."

"Dear Lord." I kept myself from glancing back at the willowy twig-girl and tried to stop imagining too much.

"Her mother hasn't been able to give Jesse enough support. She's wrestling with her own guilt and her money troubles. Planning to go back to college, finish the schooling she interrupted to marry that sorry excuse of a man, but it'll be a while before she can get a better job. She's a mess right now."

"So he ran off with another woman, or what?"

She shrugged. "Who knows. Probably. They can always find a new victim."

"Maybe Ms. Ruffin is afraid the—" I cut myself off before I spit out an expletive. "Afraid he'll come back," I said.

Maggy blinked, as if she hadn't considered that possibility. "That may be."

"Sounds like a candidate for the better-off-dead club." I regretted it as soon as I said it, remembering too late her own not-much-lamented husband had been dead less than two weeks. Here she was, so fiercely protective of little Jesse Ruffin. I wondered again why she wasn't able to defend herself.

She looked startled. I shouldn't have been so blunt. After all, I didn't know Len Ruffin or his wife. I'd only seen their daughter, her eyes downcast, looking as rare and fragile as the wildflowers she was tending.

"Has her mom got somebody tracking him down, trying to get some child support?"

Maggy shook her head. "Absolutely not. I discouraged that. No need drawing him back into their lives."

That made sense. But only if Jesse's mom could find a way to keep the family afloat.

"Thanks for telling me," I said. Likely nothing I could do but be nice to her, but at least I could avoid treading carelessly on a sensitive subject with Jesse.

Maggy wasn't listening. She was staring so intently over my shoulder that I turned to follow her gaze.

"What in the world . . . ," she muttered.

Across a ravine, hidden behind a slight rise and a hedge of undergrowth, I glimpsed faint outlines of caution yellow.

"Is that what I think it is?" Her voice was raspy, angry. "They aren't supposed to be working with equipment anywhere near that area. They aren't supposed to be there at all."

She looked around, as if for backup or guidance. Then she strode down the hill to get a better look, leaving me wondering whether I should go back to saving shriveled weeds or follow her. I glanced back where Noah and Jesse sat hunched over their digging, then turned to see Maggy disappear alone down the sharp slope.

I didn't take long to decide. I began my own shambling descent down the hill.

Midday Saturday

We hopped and slid down the hill into the ravine, then I followed Maggy as she pulled herself from tree to tree up another, steeper slope, then down into a broad, sheltered draw.

In the clearing sat a large bulldozer, eclipsing the toy-sized Bob-cat beside it. The equipment sat silent, with no one in sight, but the size of the dozer implied power and noise and destruction.

The clearing where we stood was deserted. I looked across the ravine, but couldn't see Noah and Jesse. In these steep, heavily forested hills, things are quickly lost from view, even in winter.

"They weren't supposed to be anywhere near this area with equipment." Maggy's voice was raw with emotion. "Look at the damage they've already done, cutting in here with that dozer. This is a wetlands area. They aren't supposed to be here."

She paced, unable to catch her breath. "They can't do this! He said—Avery." She spun to face me. "You can figure out a way to stop him. Can't you? This isn't right. They weren't supposed to do this."

She stopped, struggling for breath, angry that words or actions couldn't convey her fear and frustration. She'd feel a lot better if she let fly with a string of cuss words. That's what I would have been tempted to do.

We stood in a thick forest lush with undergrowth even in the winter's-end March chill. But I didn't see any water anywhere.

"Wetlands?" I asked.

She nodded, her eyes red-rimmed, angry. "The water table is high here. In summer, it supports plants between summer rain showers. He agreed to leave this area as a conservancy easement, not to disturb it. That was what finally convinced Dot to sell her land, that he would maintain this and other natural areas. Guess he couldn't resist selling the view. And selling his soul at the same time."

She turned, surveying the thick-trunked trees all around us, including at least three black walnuts easily identified by their tough, riveleted bark. Past the trees, the views off the mountain to the east toward Dacus were breathtaking.

"This was no accident. He lied." Her voice was a broken whisper. "Why?"

"Lionel Shoal?"

"The brains behind Golden Cove." She spit the words out. She really would feel better if she let herself cuss.

"This section has the richest variety of plant life and animal habitat on the property. He promised Dot it would be set aside as a preserve. That was the only reason she agreed to sell." She sighed. "Dot's getting to the age where it isn't smart to live off up here by herself. She figured this deal would make provision for herself and protect the land at the same time."

She gestured around her, impotent, frustration choking off her words.

Maggy turned away from the two dozers. In cutting the jagged, muddy swath through the undergrowth, they had shredded several giant laurels. She took a few slow steps and stopped. At her feet lay a large dogwood, the bark scraped off one side exposing splintered white wood. Without a word, she turned and purposefully started back down the ravine.

I struggled after her on the lumpy hillside, concerned she was overexerting herself. She certainly kept in good shape, but she wasn't a young woman. Even so, she was whipping the daylights out of me.

When we got to the top of the rise on the other side, I was out-huffing her. Her ire must have given her an extra push.

"I'm going to find Dot. And that Lisa Livson with her sales brochures. I intend to find out what's going on here."

She started to march off, then hesitated. "Would you stay and keep a watch over Jesse?" She didn't wait for an answer. She headed down the almost-reclaimed logging road, one probably left over from the turn of the last century, the last time progress had skinned these hills bare.

Back at our digging spot, I found Noah's and Jesse's collecting had taken them several paces apart. The small mound of uprooted plants, carefully wrapped and stacked on their sides, had grown. The hillside where we'd been working was now dotted with little holes and disturbed mulch. It smelled wet and earthy and primitive.

I didn't like the holes. The plants belonged where they'd grown, not wrapped in space-agey cloth waiting to be carted off to some less hospitable and certainly less serene environment.

We had no choice, though. We had to move them or wait for them to be plowed under.

"Oh, decided to get back to work, I see." Noah called over to me. He didn't really expect a reply.

I'd forgotten to ask Maggy about the extra gloves. I picked up my trowel and moved closer to Jesse. She gave me a shy sheepdog glance and a faint smile before she bent again to her careful digging.

I couldn't think of a good conversational gambit. What do you talk about with an uncomfortable fifteen-year-old? How 'bout them Tigers? Read any good books lately? That dad of yours sounds like a real sumbitch, bet you're glad he's gone? I chose something safe.

"You go to Dacus High School?"

Her head jerked up. "Mm-hmm." She nodded.

"What grade are you in?"

"Tenth."

I nodded.

"What's your favorite subject?" *Arrgh.* I was asking the same lame questions I hated to be asked when I was her age.

She shrugged. "I dunno. English, I guess."

Five words strung together there. Okay. "Is Miz Patterson still teaching English?"

She shrugged. "I dunno."

"I had her in tenth grade. She could make even the good stuff boring. 'Bout made me swear off poetry."

That didn't even get a shrug or a *dunno.* Best let it rest.

Bound in our own thoughts, our digging moved us farther apart.

After a long while, Noah stood and stretched. "Thought I might get some lunch," he said. "You guys want something?"

I pulled back my sleeve to check my watch. "Gosh, I didn't realize how late it was." Or how hungry I was. I dusted off my knees and shook the kinks out. Jesse stood, too, and carried more wrapped plants over to add to our collection.

The three of us wandered down the logging track to where most of the cars were parked. Other diggers were also drifting back down the road from other sites, as if some primitive, unheard dinner bell had summoned the workers in from the field.

Someone—probably directed by the well-organized Maggy Avinger—had set up a makeshift serving table on collapsible sawhorses, with sandwich fixings, fruit, Oreos, chips, trail mix, an industrial-size water can, and a stack of paper cups and plates. A black plastic garbage bag hung from a stob on a nearby tree trunk. All the comforts of home. Except a potty. I'd head for home before I needed to take to the woods—too chilly out here for that and too many people milling about.

I settled down with a peanut butter and jelly sandwich, an apple, a handful of nuts, and three Oreos. Some sweet ice tea would've topped it off, but the fresh air made up for that one lack. I munched and enjoyed the woods, blocking out the voices of the others gathering around the midday repast.

After my morning hike with Maggy, I saw our reason for being here in a different light. It had started as a little gardening project, a small do-good for the environment, akin to recycling newspapers and drink cans. Now, after the mud-red dozer tracks, the broken dogwood, the frustrated tears in Maggy's eyes, and the little holes in the rich black topsoil, it was more urgent. And more futile. This was too beautiful, too quiet and rich and older than we could imagine. Soon it would be gone.

The Cherokee who'd roamed these hills knew the truth. None of us can own it. It's not ours. Why didn't we all go home, with our chattery voices and paper plates, and leave it to the jays and salamanders and hawks and deer? Just being here messed it up. Trying to enjoy it, make some part of it ours, we ruined it.

I didn't want to dig any more disturbing little holes. I wanted to get in my car and—Bud. *Damn.*

I scrambled up, filled my paper cup and two more with water, and carried them back to the car, trying to hurry without sloshing out all the water.

Bud filled the entire backseat, lying on his back with his feet in the air, sleeping the sleep of the satisfied. I called softly through the crack in the window, not wanting to startle him. He blinked, yawned, and struggled to right himself.

He daintily lapped the water from two of the cups and most of the third before he looked up at me, satisfied. I clipped a leash on his collar and he lumbered out, arched forward, then stretched each of his hind legs.

A one-hundred-forty-pound bear of a dog, Bud appreciates his own majesty and demands the appreciation of others. When no one joined us to admire him, he did his business, sniffed the air, took a ho-hum look around at the woods, and sauntered back to the car.

Bud didn't look pleased when the car door closed with me on

the wrong side of it. But better him inside, his yawn seemed to say, even if I refused to make a sensible choice.

I didn't see Mom's minivan. The logging road cut an eroded and healing swath for a winding distance into the forest, so she could have parked farther down toward the main road or farther up, past where we'd eaten lunch. Maybe she had been distracted with some other project and hadn't come at all. No telling.

When I returned to our assigned hillside, Noah had Jesse talking up a storm. Sometimes eight or ten words to a sentence. He kept firing questions, about music and bands and movies and stuff I'd never heard about. She smiled and even laughed soft bird twitters. At least she wasn't ducking her head and shrugging.

They left me to dig in peace. I tried not to look around at the woods, at the big picture, just focus on each plant as I came to it.

We worked only an hour more before rain came unexpectedly. March clouds had rolled in, and I heard gentle rustlings in the branches before I felt the drops hitting my bare head.

In silent agreement, we walked back to the staging area, hunkered into our jackets. No point in hurrying. The branches overhead shielded us from the light rain, but we were going to get wet, no matter what we did. I didn't see Maggy or Dot Downing or the sales lady or anybody else in charge. Maybe they were down at the sales office having a powwow. As mad as Maggy had been, I felt a flash of sympathy for Lisa Livson.

Two men were gathering tarpaulins laden with plant bundles and gently laying them in a truck bed. A sign on the truck read DO-MESTICATED GODDESS NATIVE PLANTS, with an address in Cashiers, North Carolina.

An uncharitable thought crossed my mind as I blinked a raindrop off my eyelashes: Was I slave labor for the Domesticated Goddess's profit center? Mom would say my cynicism canceled out any martyr points I'd earned by good works. I'd see how cynical I felt tomorrow, according to how sore and angry my muscles were after digging all morning.

"Avery!" Noah jogged over to join me. "Your gloves. Thanks. I know it's short notice, but would you like to grab an early dinner?"

"Uh, sure. I guess so."

He grinned and looked relieved. "Figured you'd know the best places, being a hometown girl. I haven't found a good pizza yet."

"There isn't one, unless you rate grocery store frozen pizza as good."

Judging from his clipped city accent, I could've predicted the sad shake of his head, but he'd picked the right Dacus local for his restaurant dining guide since I never cook. I eat out whenever I can't find a free meal with my family.

"Your choices are simple," I said. "Barbecue. Fried chicken. Hamburgers. No vegetables until Sunday dinner tomorrow."

"Barbecue sounds good. Five o'clock too early?"

Not too early in a former cotton textile mill town like Dacus. And never too early for me. I eat anywhere, anytime. I gave him directions to Runion's, and he strode off down the road, which was quickly becoming slippery with rain-slick red clay. I figured he, like the rest of the volunteers driving low-slung cars, hadn't wanted to risk his car's suspension or oil pan driving far on the abandoned logging road. My Mustang, on the other hand, could climb trees. I should have offered him a ride. Always too late with the polite gestures.

When I pulled past him a few minutes later, he was climbing into some tiny beat-up foreign box. With a canoe strapped to the top. What had I gotten myself into?

Saturday Evening

I dropped Bud off at Aunt Letha's house, assuring her that he'd behaved himself and that he'd provided admirable personal security for me and everyone on the mountain. Bud hassled and grinned in his sappy Rottweiler way, dropped to the floor with a thump beside Aunt Letha's armchair, and closed his eyes.

Rather than drive the distance to my grandfather's old lake cabin, I decided to shower and dress at my parents' house before dinner at Runion's. That would give me some extra time to make a couple of detours.

I'd left a big law firm in Columbia and had been back home in Dacus since November. Except for the few February weeks I'd spent in Charleston helping plaintiffs' attorney Jake Baker try a sad case, I'd called my grandfather's lake cabin home. Theoretically, I'd been staying there to fix it up. That's what I told everyone. In reality, as much as I love my parents, I didn't figure any of us wanted this chick back in the nest. My living arrangements and cabin fixer-upper jobs provided family peace, a face-saving explanation, and property value enhancement all around.

Luna Lake was isolated and the cabin rustic, with only a rudimentary kitchen and wall pegs instead of closets. Most of my business suits hung in the closet in my old bedroom at my parents' and, even though racing my grandfather's vintage Mustang up and down the mountain made the commute fun, it still took twenty minutes each way—if I didn't get stuck behind a poky tourist or in front of a sheriff's deputy testing out his new radar unit.

In November, shortly after we met, Melvin Bertram had started talking about refurbishing his old family home place—the grand Victorian that had served for a time as the Baldwin & Bates Funeral Home—and turning it into offices. He suggested that would be a good place for me to open an office, well before I'd seriously thought about moving back to Dacus. He had also graciously—and persistently—offered to let me live in the other half of the upstairs. Melvin knew how hard it was to find rental property in Dacus. Beyond that, I don't think he wanted to be alone in feeling the uncertainty of a return to Dacus.

Making two offices out of the downstairs parlors and dining room had been easy. However, I wasn't sure we'd have enough privacy, splitting the upstairs into separate living quarters. More important, though, did I really want only a few steps between my office and my bedroom? Particularly since some of my clients could copy my number from a scribble on the holding cell wall. Not people I wanted visiting me at home.

In the last few weeks, I'd traded anxiety over my job limbo for housing limbo. Opening a single practice in Dacus might not be the best career move, but this living quarters thing was another whole fret.

The Dacus real estate offerings were haphazard, everything from million-dollar lake homes to double-wide trailers, with the occasional badly located brick ranch or badly built subdivision trilevel thrown in. I wasn't sure what I wanted, and mentally trying on houses and locations tired me. Still, a FOR SALE sign could make me cut a sharp right or left, just to see what was available.

In the extra few minutes I had before meeting Noah, I drove by a white clapboard house completely overgrown by kudzu, then a sad 1970s-vintage Colonial sitting on a weed-choked pond with a sign in front advertising it as "waterfront property." When I finally got home, I took a few minutes to catch Mom and Dad up on Golden Cove, Maggy Avinger, and Dot Downing. Thanks to my detours, I arrived at Runion's fifteen minutes late.

Noah's dented, canoe-laden car sat near the entrance. Only an early arrival could capture such a prime spot at Runion's on a Saturday night.

He stood to wave me over and pulled the rickety ladder-back chair out for me, which made this feel more like a date than I was ready for.

"Sorry I'm late."

"No problem. Can I get you a beer?"

The waitress walked up, ready to take our orders. Runion's isn't a dine-at-your-leisure place, especially on weekends. Before long, they'd have a line waiting for seats. To allow us a little extra time to order, she got my ice tea while I explained to Noah the merits of chopped versus sliced barbecue.

"What kind of meat is it?"

Poor boy. "Pork. Nothing but pork barbecue around here."

"No beef brisket?"

"Nope. No mustard-based sauce; that's Columbia and Charleston. Or vinegar-based sauce; that's Low Country and eastern North Carolina. Tomato-based red sauce, slightly sweet, not as smoky as Texas. Cooked into the meat, not poured on afterward."

The waitress slid my drink in front of me on the red-checkered plastic tablecloth and wrote down our orders, not wasting a motion.

"Hushpuppies or loaf bread?"

Noah glanced at me, confused.

"Hushpuppies," I said, and she sailed off, her jeans tight on her well-padded hips, her movements quick.

I was really too tired to play cultural attaché tonight, but he asked, so I explained. "Hushpuppies are deep-fried balls or squirts of corn bread. Some are oniony. These are sweet and really crusty. The honey butter there is to dip them in, but even I think that's a bit too much."

"And loaf bread?"

Gee whiz, kid. "From a loaf of bread? The square white stuff?"

He'd obviously never eaten Carolina barbecue or sat down to supper with a working family who didn't have time to make up corn pone or biscuits or money to waste buying brown-and-serve rolls.

"I gotta ask, Noah. Where're you from?" It hadn't taken long back in Dacus to slide into old habits. Here it seemed more important to get background on anybody who'd found his way to Dacus—not *into* Dacus, just *to* it—than it had been in Columbia or Charleston. Getting *into* Dacus could take at least a generation.

He took a swallow from his beer bottle. "Everybody always asks that."

I shrugged. "Don't take it personally. People just tend to know one another and they know when someone's new.

"Colorado. What's that tell you?"

"What part?"

"Vail. Actually, a little town near there."

"Mm-hmm." That might explain a bit of the California quality he had about him. "What brings you here?"

"A job." His voice carried a mild challenge.

"You strike me as bright, capable. You're inquisitive, not afraid to work, if today is any indication. Pardon me, but there are better jobs than the Dacus *Clarion* for guys with those credentials."

"That's your dad's paper you're talking about." More challenge.

"Don't let the title 'publisher' fool you. My dad's a recovering engineer. But that's another story. So you left Vail and came here."

"Not directly. Stops in graduate school, the University of Washington, San Francisco. Bouncing around."

Granted, I didn't know him well, but he didn't strike me as a drifter. True, he had a scruffy quality, his hair too long, his jeans a bit raggedy. But that could be attributed to his age—early thirties, I'd say—and his maleness.

I have a working hypothesis: Most people don't move idly about. If someone leaves home voluntarily, it's to follow a job or a girlfriend or boyfriend or to try something new in school. A few bounce around looking for something they're unlikely to find with a change of scenery, but most—not all, but most—settle near people they know or places that look like home. I personally prefer my time-worn, blue-tinged Blue Ridge Mountains.

Nothing about this guy supported my hypothesis. These hills look nothing like his home near Vail, the Dacus *Clarion* wasn't much of a job, and if he had a friend here, he wasn't volunteering the information.

I changed tack. "What got you interested in the plant rescue?" I'd asked earlier, but maybe he had another answer.

He shrugged. "It'll make a good story."

"Doesn't mean you have to get gardener's knees to get the story."

"No." He chuckled. "That's true. Just seemed like a good deed. And"—he offered his beer bottle in a mock salute—"seemed like a good way to meet people."

Strange fellow if he hoped to pick up chicks at a plant rescue. Me and fifteen-year-old Jesse Ruffin had been the youngest females there, by at least a decade or two.

He took a long swallow of beer. "Probably sounds corny, but I watched my hometown disappear. The trails where I hiked, my cross-country skiing routes, the wildlife. Even the people became an endangered species, once the moneyed people rolled over the pass with their fume-belching urban assault vehicles. They priced the land out of reach of the people who had lived on that land, had cared for it. The newcomers had to grab their piece of it, so now there's none left for those who'd called it home."

The anger and pain in his voice and in his eyes stung me. His thoughts traveled lines too close to mine, almost as though he'd read my mind earlier in the afternoon. What do you do when you don't have a home anymore?

"What was Vail like when you were growing up?"

"Mostly ski bums, guys looking for fresh powder and a free-wheeling lifestyle. Two guys started a sort of door-to-door traveling salesman bit, selling interests in the resort to wealthy guys around the country. We all grew up knowing the story—or the myth, more likely. The first President Bush even put up money. That was all good—people who liked to ski using money from people who weren't around much.

"Then corporate big business arrived and perfected the law of unintended consequences. They had to calculate a return on investment, and that meant growth. No matter that the water resources wouldn't support golf courses and snow machines and insatiable expansion. Never mind that lynx, grizzly, and wolf habitats were sliced to ribbons. Never mind that the magnificent vistas people traveled to enjoy were now filled with glistening glass castles—which, incidentally, require obscene amounts of energy to heat because of the lack of solar conservancy design. So much destruction and waste, just so somebody can fly in for a few weeks a year, then shutter it up and jet on to the next site of conquest."

His diatribe ended almost as unexpectedly as it had begun, with one hand around his bottle and him gazing off across Runion's rustic dining room.

His passion stunned me. Was this more than a history of his home? Was it a prophecy for mine?

The waitress plopped two plates of steaming barbecue, baked beans, and fries in front of us, and Noah ordered another beer. I introduced him to the sauce selection—mildly sweet or spicy sweet—and he set to experimenting with both and neither.

"It's got to be hard to watch a place you know as yours disappear," I said, picking the conversation up where it had dropped.

He looked at me, maybe surprised because somebody was inviting him to stay on top of his soapbox.

"Yeah. The ironic thing is, they drove property prices out of reach for the ski bums who made it so colorful, the shop and restaurant owners who fed them and repaired their gear for cheap, even the people who cleaned their megamansions. Eventually somebody figured out rich people need worker bees—after it was too late for the natives. They've got crowded enclaves for their immigrant labor now."

He shoveled in a forkful of pork and took a few thoughtful chews. "That's why Golden Cove grabbed my attention. You people don't understand zoning laws, as is evident driving down any road in this county. Unless the state or federal government owns it, the land around here is pretty much open to whatever somebody wants to do with it."

I bristled. "This is South Carolina, you know. States' rights? Self-determination? Staunch individualism?"

"Okay, I'll give you the states' rights thing." His expression was almost a sneer.

"People around here hate being told what to do. They're mostly live-and-let-live kind of folks."

"So if I move a ratty house trailer next door to your family's home, that's okay?"

"I should have bought more land, if I find that objectionable. I let you alone, and you won't be complaining about target practice in my backyard or howling hunting dogs."

"You got hunting dogs?" He crinkled his nose, incredulous.

He'd missed the point of my colorful illustration. "You got a house trailer?" I didn't point out that we'd let him ride around with a canoe lashed to the top of his car, poking dangerously out front and back, and I bet no one had said a mean word to him about it. We'd let him do it, even if we found it a bit *quair*, as folks would say.

"You need mechanisms to protect what you have." He continued the argument. "Have you seen Tryon? North Greenville County? Golf courses galore. Extravagant uses of land. Huge houses perched all along the ridge line, destroying the very views everyone comes to enjoy. Who's managing that? Who's trying to contain it?"

He'd mistaken my corny attack on zoning for disagreeing with him. His words had grown shrill. No point explaining that South Carolina did have a ridge law preventing new construction over forty-two feet high on the ridges. Unfortunately, it had come too little, too late, and didn't restrict the houses dotting the sides of the mountains.

"Do you have any idea what all that development in Cashiers and Highlands is doing to your own little corner of the world?" he said. "The water runoff from their paved parking pads and dishwashers and 3.5 toilets per house all runs downhill, right into the Chattooga River."

The Chattooga was one of only a handful of rivers in the United States designated Wild and Scenic by the federal government. Locals tend to curse the memory of poet James Dickey and his novel *Deliverance*. However, had it not been for the twenty-plus drowning deaths in the months after the Burt Reynolds film hit theaters, when wannabe he-men flocked to the river like lemmings to replay the man-against-nature-against-man battle, the river might not have been federally protected. Another reminder that we don't do anything until it's too late.

"That's an exaggeration," I said, taking up the argument. "Wastewater has to be treated. They wouldn't let—"

"They don't treat water running off pesticide-treated golf courses or off asphalt parking lots. You think water coming out of some enclave's privately owned wastewater treatment plant is water that mountain trout thrive in? The trout don't think so."

He leaned across the table. "Ever hear of the edge effect?"

I shook my head. Might as well let him talk himself out, even though I wasn't liking anything he had to say.

"Just the act of cutting a break through a forest endangers the wildlife there. Predators roam the edges. Just like in an urban area, there's a fringe element."

He sliced along the tabletop with the edge of his hand. "Hawks swoop in on small birds or ground squirrels when they break cover, out into the open. Birds find lizards or insects that wander into an open spot. Deer, rabbits, all are more vulnerable to whatever hunts them as soon as they hit an edge. That old logging road we were on today, how long's that been there?"

I shrugged. "Don't know. They've been logging these hills since the early nineteen hundreds."

"A hundred years, fifty, five. It doesn't matter. It can't heal. It creates two edges, either side of the road. It separates the populations on either side, walling them off from habitat, from mating choices. How many cuts, how many edges before they're walled into extinction? The cask of amontillado, in the wilds of Southern Appalachia. Walled off and dying."

He pushed the cole slaw around on his plate. He hadn't eaten much.

"Did you know this area boasts richer biodiversity than just about any other place on the planet? And you people aren't protecting it. You're letting the Lionel Shoals of the world fly in and crap in your nest and you stand idly by, full of sweet Southern charm, and don't fight to protect what you were given."

He was about to tick me off, coming in making pronouncements. *If things are so good back home, go back home.*

But I kept my mouth shut because a part of me knew he was right. That cove forest, with more rare trees and plants than I even knew existed, was going to be bulldozed down behind a sign announcing GOLDEN COVE. Gold, all right—in somebody's pocket.

"According to you, folks in Colorado didn't do such a hot job protecting themselves and their land, either."

He'd started eating again. My plate was almost clean, and what was left, I mopped up with a hushpuppy.

"They fought, at least. Hard. About ten years ago, someone set fires, burned several lift shacks and a huge lodge, trying to discourage construction of a new ski slope on what was probably the last breeding ground for lynx in Colorado—probably the last outside Montana. Huge blaze. Perfectly orchestrated and timed. Quite a commando operation."

"That's smart. Who sets a fire to save animals?"

He crinkled his nose, puzzled for a moment at my sarcasm. "No, no. They didn't endanger any animals. The shacks at the two lifts were isolated, with deep snow all around. Not much chance of it spreading or burning anything except what they wanted to get rid of."

"So who burned it?"

"They never found out, though I know they had their suspects."

"But it kept anyone from building the new slope?"

He was quiet a moment. "No. You can't fight that kind of money and power. All they understand is more money and more power. Or force. The company opened more new slopes anyway. The new lodge was even more monstrous than the old one. No one's ever seen another lynx." He sounded sad. "But it did draw attention to environmental issues, helped attract more money and members, more energy behind both traditional lobbying efforts and more—unconventional warriors."

The fires set in Vail. "Eco-terrorists, you mean."

"Radical disruptors. Yeah," he fired back.

Who was this guy? "Does Lionel Shoal have that kind of money and power?"

"He's nothing but a pissant. He's stupid and greedy—the kind that *can* be fought. That's why stepping back and letting him roll on through is so unforgivable."

"How do you know people aren't fighting back?"

He gave me a pitying gaze. "Where were those dozers parked today?"

Maggy Avinger hadn't been the only one who'd spotted them. For the first time, I realized I hadn't seen her after it started raining. What had happened to her?

"So what would you propose?"

"Somebody needs to get hold of that land-sale contract. Some smart lawyer." He cocked a bushy eyebrow at me. "Get hold of the lady who sold it to Shoal, see what loopholes there might be. Digging up plants to transplant them where they won't survive is a painful exercise in futility."

"You think I'm that lawyer."

"I think you could get started on it, maybe bring in some of the environmental defense folks for help."

My only environmental law experience, my first case in Dacus, had been representing Garnet Mills—right before the inspectors showed up and found a dead body in the torched plant. Not an auspicious opening to an environmental law career.

"I can't solicit clients, Noah. That's not allowed in South Carolina. But I do have a friend . . ." I began mentally exploring options, even though most weren't realistic.

That he'd captured my interest seemed to satisfy him. He polished off his barbecue and refused the waitress's offer of another beer. I had a flashback to my last visit to Runion's, one of my first meetings in November with Melvin, who got drunk because he'd just found out his long-missing wife was dead. Next time I wanted barbecue, I'd come during the week, and I'd come by myself. Best way to avoid both crowds and drama.

Sunday

By spending Saturday night with Mom and Dad, I saved a drive up the mountain, making time to walk on their treadmill to work out the kinks from yesterday's digging. I also got to visit with my niece, Emma, while her parents rehearsed again for *The Mikado*. Rather than sit around the drafty community theater auditorium, Emma opted to stay with my parents, make popcorn, and giggle uncontrollably while watching Three Stooges videos with Dad.

Sunday morning in church, I sat between Mom and Aunt Vinnia in our usual pew and studied the crowd. Mr. Mack came in the door beside the choir loft—the door in front of the congregation that, for some reason, everyone called the back door.

He nodded and exchanged greetings with people as he came up the aisle and gave me a quick nod as he took his seat a couple of rows in front of us, at the end of a pew. I could see his face in profile but couldn't draw his attention again. I'd have to catch him after the service.

As the congregation settled in for the sermon, the bodies in front of me arranged themselves so I had a clear view of both the watchers and the watched. That's one of the benefits of being a back-row Baptist—a broader perspective.

In her usual spot toward the front, a few rows from the pulpit, I saw Maggy Avinger's short ginger-gray hair and the petite shoulders of her tweed suit. I couldn't help noticing that Mr. Mack's attention alternated between the hymn book in his hand and Maggy. He could have been looking at Pastor Richards, but what I could see of his expression said otherwise.

Great-aunt Letha, sitting to my left, fished the stubby pencil out of the pew holder to scribble something for her sister to read—probably a comment on the inappropriateness of the scripture choice. Good thing she couldn't tell I hadn't been paying attention to the sermon.

After the service, I stood in the pew, sandwiched between Mom and Aunt Vinnia while they visited with those strolling past. Maggy waved at me and mouthed, "See you later?"

I nodded, and she moved in the slow tide toward the front of the sanctuary. She didn't even notice Mr. Mack in the aisle behind her, part of the rear half of the congregation headed for the main door. His gaze settled for a moment on the back of her finger-combed hair as she moved away from him.

When he turned and caught my eye, he motioned Vinnia and me out ahead of him in the aisle.

"Have you got a minute? Outside?" I asked him as we shuffled out with the crowd.

"Certainly." He gave a solemn nod.

The pastor and I exchanged perfunctory greetings as he stood in the doorway shaking hands. At the bottom of the steps, most people turned left toward the parking lots behind and beside the church. I turned in the opposite direction and waited on the sidewalk.

When Mr. Mack joined me, I didn't waste words. "Mom gave me that clipping you received. Kind of nasty." I had to tilt my head back to talk to him. Even though he tended to slouch, he towered over me.

Without fanfare, he said, "If I didn't know better, I'd say Harden

Avinger sent that. Just his idea of a joke. Truth be told, Harden wasn't the easiest man to get along with."

"According to the postmark, it was mailed after Harden died." I couldn't let on about Harden's beyond-the-grave "gift" to his wife, but that had been sent by his lawyer.

"I noticed that. I know it's crazy to suspect him. He's been gone for two weeks now." He sighed. "I didn't want to bother you. I just didn't know what else to do."

"No bother, Mr. Mack. Please don't say that." I patted him on the arm. One of my mother's gestures that I now felt compelled to offer Mr. Mack. I didn't know if it felt as reassuring to receive as it did to give.

He sank his teeth into his bottom lip as he considered something. "You in a hurry? Can you come to the car a minute?"

"Sure." The touch of urgency in his voice hinted that whatever he wanted to talk to me about was more important than lunch at Maylene's. Besides, Mom hadn't come out of the sanctuary yet, so no need to rush to meet her and Dad at the restaurant.

Mr. Mack had parked his sedan half a block down the street. He unlocked the passenger door and retrieved a large white envelope from the front seat.

He turned back to me, holding the envelope to his chest. "I got another letter. So I'm doubly at a loss what to do."

He glanced behind me to make sure no one was nearby and offered me the envelope.

Mr. Mack's address was typed on the nine-by-eleven-inch envelope, and the printed return address read *Carlton Barner Attorney at Law.* Inside the large envelope, I found a cheap letter-sized envelope; its flap was sealed, but the end of the envelope had been neatly torn off. Hand-lettering on the front read FORWARD TO HENRY "MACK" MACGREGOR. I glanced at Mr. Mack, slid out the thin, slightly yellowed piece of paper, and unfolded it.

The letter had been typed on a manual typewriter, the keys jumpy and several of the letters blocked solid.

Dear Mack,

When you get this, I'll be pushing up dandelions in that poor excuse for perpetual care at the edge of town. Or paying for past sins, if all those emotional, intellectually stunted preachers have it right—which I doubt.

I wanted to do you one last favor, old friend, perhaps to earn myself some penance.

I will be dearly departed some weeks before you receive this. If you receive it, that means my dear wife Magnolia is still among the living. That, of course, depends on my lawyer doing exactly what I ask him to do—and he's being paid enough not to screw up.

I felt compelled to tell you—our longtime friend and neighbor—why Maggy is still among the living and I'm not.

It's simple: She killed me.

Now, don't act so startled. She and I have been married 26 years, so you must admit I know her pretty well. She's been planning this for some time. Not that I necessarily mind dying. I just hope it is—was?—relatively painless. She's not a cruel woman, so I think I can count on that. Life's not been exactly roses with this cancer—too constrained, too many rules.

So I suppose she did me a favor, and I've decided not to send a letter to the police. However, I wanted someone to know.

Don't hold it against her. Just do be careful of her cooking. Remember, by now, she's an accomplished poisoner.

Farewell to you, Mack.

Harden Avinger

I looked up from the letter to find Mr. Mack studying me intently, watching for something in my expression. Shock? Confirmation? Something.

I struggled to keep my face straight. I couldn't let slip that Harden Avinger had opted to proclaim his murder with an eight-foot angel rather than a letter to the police. Had he been crazy? Prophetic? Or just mean?

"You can see why that banana pudding recipe I left with your mother set me back on my heels," Mr. Mack said. "Harden used to make rude cracks about her cooking, about everything she did. Always put-downs. Maggy Avinger wouldn't hurt a fly, but forgive me for saying it, Harden Avinger could kill a nest of angry hornets with a sideways glance."

"When did Harden's lawyer send this?"

"I got it a couple of days ago—Thursday? No, Friday."

Harden had kept Carlton Barner busy last week mailing letters, to Innis Barker and Mr. Mack. Were there others?

"You mind if I take this with me?"

"Take it. Nasty thing makes me sick. It's like something slimy slithered through the mail slot."

I paused, choosing words. "I'm sure you know this already, but Maggy Avinger could use a friend right now." I couldn't say more than that. But Harden's darkness seemed to circle her. To say I feared for her sounded melodramatic, but I didn't know how else to explain the nagging sense of dread.

"We-ell." A sweet, light voice trilled behind me, startling us both. "If it isn't little Avery Andrews, back to practice law, I hear. My, my."

I recognized the woman from church but couldn't put a name to her. She minced toward us clutching a foil-wrapped dish. I didn't risk a look at Mr. Mack, but he too probably hoped it wasn't banana pudding.

Her navy wool skirt had the tautness achieved only by an industrial-strength girdle, and her feet spilled over the tops of her low-heeled pumps.

"Henry." She purred. "I was fixing apple cinnamon bread for the women's club tomorrow and just made up some extra while I was at it. This is still warm, so you'll want to have some with your lunch." Her voice supplied all the butter needed.

63

"Why, thank you, Estelle. Still warm, you say." Hypnotized by the scent of cinnamon, his eyes were only for the foil-wrapped package.

I backed down the sidewalk a couple of steps. "I'll see you all later."

Estelle stepped closer to Mack with a beaming smile and a decidedly proprietary air.

After church, Mom and Dad sometimes try to beat the crowd to Maylene's for lunch. Futile, since the Presbyterians always get out that little tick before the Baptists—more responsive readings but shorter sermons.

This Sunday, some unchurched people must have eaten early and left Mom and Dad a table because they were already seated by the time I got there. They exchanged nodded greetings with a few others in the restaurant. Dacus isn't small enough that you know everybody, but you do recognize lots of familiar faces—and you expect to run into somebody you know just about anywhere you go.

The last ten years has brought in a lot of retirees, some to the lakeside resorts, some spilling down from Highlands, where average home prices rival San Francisco's. A few couples looked like retiree imports. Of those, one group was dressed for church, two others for golf or an afternoon of antique shopping. But most of the folks, even those I didn't recognize, looked like natives. Conservative dress, conventional haircuts, no overly bleached teeth or surprise-eye facelifts. The women who spent time with their makeup and hair stood out from those with some lipstick and wash-and-wear hair, but those with dye jobs and eye makeup were still much more subdued and natural-looking than a similar gathering in Atlanta or Charlotte or even Greenville would offer.

For the couple who pushed around the crowd at the door, that lack of subtlety was one of the things that made them stand out. Her hair was too platinum, her boobs too large to occur naturally with those boyish hips, her lipstick and eye shadow too dark and overdone. He looked more conservative in his blue blazer and open-collar shirt—and more pushy, rocking up on his toes as if he were trying to spot the maitre d' so he could slip him a twenty for a good table. Clearly a newcomer who didn't understand the wait-patiently-in-line protocol of Maylene's.

Staring is an accepted form of public entertainment in Dacus, much as street musicians and artists entertain spontaneous crowds in large cities. When I first came back to Dacus, having a whole restaurant full of people turn to watch me when I walked in the door unnerved me. It took a while for primitive memory to return, to recall the motivation: Check to see if you know them; if not, where are they from and what might they be doing here?

"Who's that?" I asked Mom and Dad, nodding toward the crowd at the door.

Neither had to ask who I was talking about. Dad just shrugged, out of the rumor loop, as usual.

Mom said, "Lionel Shoal and his wife. Valerie, I think."

"The Golden Cove guy?" I leaned closer so I could keep my voice low.

Mom nodded.

Lionel Shoal looked like he'd be more at home in Las Vegas than negotiating a land conservancy or running a Sierra Club meeting. He picked his way through the tables to accost a waitress when his attempts to catch her eye from the door failed. She pointed him back to the doorway, and he rejoined the crowd, none too happy, judging from his frown.

I changed the subject. "So, Dad, why didn't you tell me you'd hired a new reporter?"

Mom cut her eyes at him, but didn't say anything.

He looked puzzled for a moment. "Oh, him. Boy with the wild hair. Walter hired him."

Walter Vann was the *Clarion*'s editor, the guy who really put out the paper three times a week and, at the same time, managed the piece-rate print jobs for restaurant menus and sale flyers that paid the bills for the whole operation.

"Seems to be pretty good. Knows how to roll up his sleeves and get busy. You met him?" Dad asked with only casual curiosity as he focused his attention on his fried okra.

"Yeah, I did. He was telling me all about Vail."

"Vail, huh? That where he's from? Could've sworn Walter said he was from Phoenix. Tucson. Somewhere dry. Out west."

"How'd Walter lure him to Dacus?"

Dad shrugged. "Reckon he wanted a job."

"Noah seems very experienced, um—" I stumbled, not putting into words that Dacus's paper wasn't exactly an incubator for Pulitzer Prize winners.

"Guess he wanted to get out of the city, to something simpler."

That would make sense to Dad. He had, after all, moved to Dacus himself. I wasn't quite convinced that it made sense for Noah. Noah Lakefield would bear more study.

"You coming to the plant rescue today?" I asked Mom. At the last minute, she'd had to fill both the morning and afternoon shifts at the First Fruits Food Bank yesterday, so she hadn't made it up the mountain.

She nodded. "You want to ride together?"

Most of the same faces returned to the dig, but I didn't spot Noah or his amphibimobile. I hadn't talked to Maggy Avinger since she'd marched off the day before looking for Lisa Livson and some explanation of Shoal's bulldozers. Taking Maggy's place, a no-nonsense woman with a clipboard deployed Mom to work with me and Jesse Ruffin. This endeavor was a bigger operation than I'd realized, with lots of worker bees.

We carried our plant wrap and tools to a new area and a new set of little orange marker flags. Yesterday's rain made the digging both easier and messier. Even before we'd bent to our task, Mom had Jesse talking, about school, her mom, where her mom worked, how glad she was her dad ran off but how scared her mom was that she might not be able to support the two of them and at the same time how scared she was that her dad might come back. A torrent of words. Even—shyly—about her boyfriend.

"Aren't you young to be settling on a boyfriend?" My mom fights the local tendency to marry too young by nipping the first tender buds of romance before they spread like kudzu. "There's a wide wonderful world out there you need to explore first. A boyfriend will just slow you down."

I know Mom wanted to say *hold you back* or *strangle your dreams completely,* but the day was young. She'd just met Jesse. She still had time to work around to that message.

Jesse looked startled but said nothing. A new concept for her. No boyfriend? Probably from a family where adults started asking five-year-olds, *Who's your boyfriend?*

"Sorry I'm late." Noah loped up the hillside, his unruly curls jammed under a knit toboggan, his borrowed trowel and a brand-new pair of gloves in hand.

My mother's eyes lit up when I introduced the two of them. She studied the newspaper's employee, intrigued with the new reporter. So I wasn't the only one who didn't know about the new hire.

"Breaking story?" I asked.

His withering gaze surprised me. I was just trying to make small talk.

"You don't want to know," he said.

"Sure we do," Mom said, her voice chipper. She was bent over the black cohosh plants in front of her, so she didn't see Noah's expression.

He was too polite not to respond to her. "A pig sighting."

"Pig?" Mom said, not even looking up from her digging.

"Yes, ma'am." The look he shot me said, *I'm dying of embarrassment here.* "A runaway potbellied pig. The Sheriff's Department and the city police are both on alert. Somebody spotted the pig in the field beside the elementary school this morning, but it disappeared into the woods." He finished his news recap with an attitude of finality.

"I heard about that. One of those cute little pet pigs?" Mom said. "I'm sure the owners are frantic."

"It's no cute little pet pig." The frustration was obvious in his voice. "It stands thigh-high and weighs a hundred and fifty pounds. Apparently some family got tired of their cute little pig when it started weighing more than all the children combined, and they threw it out." He acted as though he ought to be covering bigger stories. Didn't he realize this was the big story?

"Oh, dear," Mom said. "I had no idea they got that size. Surely it can't live on its own."

"It's pretty well suited to outrunning sheriff's deputies." I didn't add *and newspaper reporters*. Noah was new in town, and Mom would fuss at me for being mean.

"Pigs are such smart animals. I can't believe somebody would do that," Mom said. "Of course, people with children throw them away after they tire of the novelty. Folks just don't think—got to have what they want, whether they're ready to take care of it or not."

Mom didn't finish her sermonette on the mount. She was distracted by a young man sauntering toward our small group, looking as out of place as a plate of spaghetti on a communion table.

"Hello there," Mom stood to greet him, brushing dirt off her knees. "Did they send you to work with us?"

He slouched inside a scuffed brown leather jacket, and his gaze darted toward my mother, then me. He didn't smile or take his hands out of his pockets.

"Naw," he said, finally. Even with heeled boots, he wasn't much taller than my mother in her scuffed walking shoes.

He ignored us and walked over to Jesse. Her face was a confused mix of girlish delight and—was it fear? Something unpleasant.

"Jesse," he said. "We need to talk."

He grabbed her elbow and led her away without a glance or a word in our direction.

We couldn't hear the conversation, though he appeared to do most of the talking. Jesse kept shaking her head, leaning away from him, even taking some tiny backward steps. He looked like he'd be more at home in a bad teen-gang movie than in these woods. His dark, unkempt looks contrasted sharply with Jesse's fair skin and frail build. Where do girls like Jesse find guys like him? More likely, how do guys like him always spot girls like her?

Noah went back to digging, oblivious to the tension. Mom made no pretense of digging. She stayed on her feet like a sentry on alert, her trowel held at her side like a weapon at the ready.

About the time I noticed how intently Mom was watching them, he grabbed Jesse's arm and shoved his face close to hers. That was Mom's cue. She flew at him like a banty hen on a stray dog.

"That's enough." Her voice cut sharp with authority. The boy spun around, his arms bowed up at his sides, his fists clenched, his face red.

"That's enough. You leave. Now." Mom barked the words like a drill sergeant and took another step toward him.

His jaw muscles worked. For an instant, I feared he would hit Mom. But her forcefulness seemed to take the air out of him, his eyes darting around as if he expected attacks from behind the trees.

He didn't say a word. He didn't even glare at my mother. Instead, he spun on his high heel, with a sharp glance back at Jesse, and strode down the road, stumbling once on a tree root.

Despite her middle-aged ordinariness and her all-weather gardening jacket, my mom can be one scary lady. What she would've done had the little jerk come at her, I don't know. She was probably relying on me for backup. Noah sat on his heels watching it unfold like a TV show, unaware that things had almost gotten ugly.

"You okay, honey?" Mom tucked Jesse under one arm, trying to calm her uncontrollable shaking. Big tears spilled down Jesse's cheeks.

"Let's go over and get some water. Walk off what's bottled up inside you."

Mom led the slender girl, wobbly on her long fawn legs, away from the direction the punk had taken.

Boom!

"What the heck was all that—" *Bo-om!* Noah's question was cut off by a loud echo of what sounded like gun blasts.

I instinctively hunched close to the ground before looking around, all too familiar with the dangers of out-of-season hunting and stray shots. Noah jerked upright, turning first one direction, then another.

"What the—"

Only one other group of diggers was in sight. They, too, stood frozen, looking around in the silence.

We looked up the road, away from the direction our bad-tempered visitor had gone. An angry voice, the words indistinct, carried from the direction of the gun blasts.

Self-preservation and curiosity warred inside me for a moment, then I took off toward the noise, moving as quickly as I could in a slight crouch, trying to see over the rise toward the logging road without making myself too big a target. A rustling in the dry leaves behind me drew my attention. Noah, outdoor guy that he was, knew to keep his head down as he inched up the slope.

Below us, five or six people stood in the leaf-strewn roadbed, their backs to me. In a lopsided Wild West parody, they faced two men. The larger of the two wore a hunting jacket and held a shotgun, the barrel broken over his right forearm. He provided backup for a shorter man who was red in the face from yelling.

Lionel Shoal, the giant with the shotgun, looked like a dog on point, ready to snap the barrels up and take aim at any provocation. I assumed he'd broken it open to reload after firing both barrels, the source of the two shots we'd heard. The smell of spent gunpowder hung in the air.

The shorter man was doing all the yelling, pointing his finger threateningly at the group facing him. Everyone stood frozen and showed no sign of challenging him.

"—don't care what you were told. I want you off my property now."

Members of the group shuffled their feet, uneasily eyeing each other and hanging back from Shoal. I got the sense that, with one exception, they would be happy to leave Shoal's property—if they dared turn their backs on him.

The one exception took a brazen step toward Shoal: Magnolia Avinger.

"Surely, Mr. Shoal, you don't want to go back on your word. Lisa Livson said—"

"I don't give a good goddamn what Lisa Livson said. I'm saying get the hell off my property. Now!"

The group behind her took a collective step backward. Maggy didn't budge. If anything, she leaned into the fight. This was getting out of hand.

"You—" Maggy started.

"You violated your end of the bargain," Shoal shouted her down. "Straying into areas off limits. That's the final str—"

A *whoop* sounded over the hill behind Shoal. Startled, Shoal spun around. Down the rough logging track jogged a pudgy man with a fringe of hair around his glistening bald head. Between huffs, he waved his arms and bellowed.

Paying no attention to the awkward standoff he'd interrupted, he stumbled to a stop. His manicness created even more of a stir than Shoal's cussing and screaming had, maybe because he looked so wild-eyed and scared.

"Does anybody have a cell phone?" He faced first Shoal, then Maggy and the group at large, struggling for breath. "One that works up here? We got to get the cops. There's a body. In a hole. We found it."

The energy that had propelled him pell-mell down the hill now spilled out in his words. He kept glancing over his shoulder, as if what he'd seen might have followed him.

"What the hell you talking about?" Shoal said. "A body. Get hold of yourself. Lew, go see what the hell he's blithering about."

"We gotta get the cops up here." The unchecked raw emotion on his fleshy face was almost embarrassing.

Everyone stood frozen, trying to process what to do. I checked the signal on my cell phone. No service on this side of the hill. I constantly alternate between hating the things and wondering what we did without them.

I broke the silence. "I'll climb the hill and call the sheriff."

To reach the easiest route up the hill and a better signal, I passed close by Shoal without a glance in his direction. He grabbed my elbow, turning me to face him. "I said get off my property." He was so close, I could smell cinnamon on his breath.

He'd passed the point of gentle reason. I jerked out of his grasp. "Mr. Shoal, someone may need help. I'm going where I can call the sheriff's office. You can discuss your property rights with Sheriff Peters when she gets here."

"Don't nobody need any help," the message bearer muttered, bent over with his hands on his knees, catching his breath. "Trust me on that."

I gave Shoal a final stare before continuing up the logging road, picking the shortest route through the trees to higher ground.

After some wrangling, I got the dispatcher to put me directly through to Rudy Mellin. He could call in Sheriff L. J. Peters if he wanted to; I preferred to avoid dealing with her.

Rudy wasn't enthusiastic about driving up the mountain based on nothing more than, to quote him, what some guy said.

"So you didn't personally see the body."

"No, Rudy, I didn't. But the guy looked green around the gills and blithered like an idiot. He didn't make it up."

"He said it was in a hole."

"Yep."

"Like a grave or something?"

"I don't know."

"For love and money, A'vry. It's probably a deer carcass. I had a rough night last night and I'm scheduled to clock out in another hour. It'll take longer than that to drive—Why don't you go look at the so-called body yerself and call me back."

"Rudy—"

"Come on, A'vry. As a favor to me. Least you got sense enough to know if it's a dead deer. That, or get yerself a new best friend in the Sheriff's Department. L.J. would love to come up there if only you'd call her."

True, the trip to check it out was much shorter for me than for him. It might be nothing, after all. I gave Rudy a dramatic sigh. "I'll call you back in a few minutes."

He gave me his direct number. I continued over the hill, then down the other side to rejoin the logging road as it circled the hill. When I rounded a curve, I saw a small group gathered in the lee of an abrupt outcropping of rock.

Lionel Shoal had beaten me to the scene, taking the shorter route along the logging road to check things for himself. He was walking away from the small clump of people, fumbling for his cell phone. His bluster had evaporated, and he looked gray and shaken.

I didn't have to ask where to look for the body. Everyone faced, at a respectful distance, the rock embankment. Some still clutched their garden trowels. Nobody was talking. When I joined the group, I could see what looked like a dark slash in the bank and could smell what had sobered Lionel Shoal and the others.

As soon as I saw the lace-up work boot sticking out from an opening in the rocks, I knew it was no deer. Judging from the swollen, mottled skin peeking out of the dark blue pants leg, the guy who'd run downhill to report the body was right. Whoever it was didn't need any help.

I searched among those who'd gathered. Noah was nowhere to be seen. Chasing the story elsewhere? Looking for somebody to take charge, I spotted the two most sensible people I knew: Mom and Maggy Avinger. I made my way over to them and quietly asked if they'd herd everybody away from the shaft. I climbed back up the hill to call Rudy, huffing to get the sticky sweet smell of decay out of my nostrils.

Late Sunday Afternoon

"Whew! Wisht somebody'd found him sooner. Gawd, what a smell!" Rudy Mellin sauntered over to join me on my perch in the sun, upwind from any stray odor but with a good view of the logging road, the surrounding forest, and any movement by curiosity seekers or four-legged scavengers around the narrow opening in the rocks below.

In the short time since I'd returned to Dacus, I'd increased the amount of time I'd spent in criminal matters several hundredfold, from near zero to too much. Before November, I'd spent my time in civilized lawsuits, defending doctors and large corporations, making only occasional forays into the criminal courts as a guardian ad litem, usually for children who had a parent heading off to jail and who needed somebody representing them in a custody hearing. I'd also done some pro bono plea agreements and had been intrigued enough to study up on investigation procedures, hoping to find something to aid my admittedly guilty clients or their kids. That had not prepared me for Dacus.

First, I'd had to deal with Donlee Griggs—a gigantic goofball who'd fancied himself my suitor in high school—along with his buddy Pee Vee Probert and their frequent drunk-and-disorderly charges. Then the Garnet Mills fire I'd witnessed in November while helping Melvin when he'd been suspected of his wife's murder. And now a dead body in an abandoned mine. Nothing had fully prepared me for this.

I had hoped Rudy would handle the investigation but, forty minutes after I called him back with the bad news about the body, Sheriff L.J. Peters herself led the procession. Three patrol cars and an ambulance crept up the logging road, dragging oil pans over the rocks and tree roots. L.J. brought the coroner—who was a life insurance agent when he wasn't pronouncing decomposing bodies dead. Rudy and another deputy drove the other two patrol cars.

L.J. carefully covered her bowl-cut black hair with her Smokey Bear hat as soon as she unfolded her six-foot self from behind the cruiser's steering wheel. She fingered the butt of her gun and the baton handle with that hint of official malice that drives me mad.

I'd known L.J. since grade school, when she'd periodically slammed me against the wall in the restroom just to prove she could. Now she could wield power without violence—unless, I'm sure, someone presented a situation where violence might be both entertaining and within the definition of "reasonable force."

It didn't take long for L.J. and Lionel Shoal to square off. Predictably, Shoal made the mistake of trying to out-officious Lucinda Jane Peters. Distracted by watching the coroner try not to get too close to the ripe corpse, I didn't notice how the meeting between L.J. and Shoal began. I only saw how it ended. This was the third time I'd seen Lionel Shoal in action, and not once had he impressed me as a man of tact or diplomacy—or good sense. He preferred bullheading his way through the middle. Maybe that's how developers got things done where he came from. I could've told him it would not be a good way to handle L.J., but he never bothered to ask. Not too smart for a guy in his line of work.

By the time I noticed their encounter, Shoal stood toe-to-toe with L.J. In high school, L.J. had been a basketball standout. She was beefier now, which only added to her intimidation factor.

"Mr. Shoal," she said, her voice calm and dangerous, "we need to continue this conversation down at the Law Enforcement Center."

She stood so close that Shoal had to crook his neck back to stare at her. He belatedly began to realize his disadvantage. On many levels. He let her lead him to her patrol car. She gave him the courtesy of not handcuffing him since he wasn't under arrest, but with a slam of the door, she cut off his pleas to let him sit up front. He probably thought she'd let him play with the siren.

L.J. removed her hat, tossed it in the front seat, folded herself behind the wheel, and drove slowly away, with Shoal's head bouncing from side to side in the rear window as the car wallowed over the deep ruts.

Rudy and the other deputy L.J. had left at the scene took down information from the plant rescuers before letting them go home. Camden County doesn't have enough crime to justify a full-fledged crime scene crew, so we had to wait on a team from SLED, the South Carolina Law Enforcement Division. Lester Watts and a kid with a crew cut arrived after L.J. left. While the kid shot some videotape, Lester halfheartedly took a few photos, but nobody could count on Lester's results. Everybody stayed back from the body itself, awaiting the experts.

"Any guess how long he's been there?" I asked as Rudy joined me, propping his rump against the boulder where I sat cross-legged.

Rudy shrugged. "He's bloated and his skin's so black you can't even tell what color he started out being. We've had some pretty nice days, up in the fifties, but the nights have been near or below freezing. Who knows what being stuffed in that hole has done. He's been there more'n a couple of days, but I wouldn't say he's been there for a couple of months. Nothing more than a wild-ass guess, though."

Rudy wouldn't have seen a lot of dead bodies in Camden County, but his wild-ass guess would still be better than mine.

"What's that hole he's stuck in?" I asked. Rudy had been closer to the body than anyone else, and even he'd kept a good distance, not wanting to contaminate the scene but wanting to get an idea of what they were dealing with.

"If I'uz to guess, I'd say it was an abandoned mine shaft."

"That's what somebody else said. That crack in the rock is a mine?"

Rudy nodded. "There's quite a few up in here, most of 'em just places cut back into a hillside, like that one. Some go back far enough to need timber supports. Most of those larger mines are all rotted and tumbled in by now, though. Nothing like the mines you see on those old TV westerns. These are small, hard-scratch holes."

"What'd they mine here?"

"Gold, mostly."

"You gotta be kidding. That's really a gold mine?" Rudy had to be pulling my leg.

"Sure. Lots of people dug or panned for gold up around here, from before the Civil War, some up into the thirties. The Depression, I guess, had people looking for any way they could to get some money."

"Gold mining in Camden County. Imagine that."

"Where do you think they got the name Golden Cove?"

"Thought it was just some cutesy stupid name. Was there much gold up here?"

"Naw. Guess they got the fever because of the richer veins just to the east and west of here. But around here, it was mostly just something folks did to tide 'em over after the crops were in. Or to keep from having to find honest work."

"How'd you know so much?"

"My grandmother had an abandoned dig on her place. She allowed as how it just gave my granddad somewhere to hide out from chores. Said the little bits he found never amounted to a knot on a gnat. Said he could've made more working a week's shift in a cotton mill."

"You ever dig for gold?"

"Naw. Granny would'a tanned my hind end good if I'd gotten

near that tumbled-in hole. My uncle did show my brother and me how to work an old sluice he had. We got some little flecks of gold we kept in a glass aspirin bottle filled with baby oil. But that'uz a potload of work for a teaspoon, let me tell you."

I'd read about gold veins farther east in North and South Carolina. Charlotte had even boasted a U.S. mint at one time to process the gold discovered nearby. Then gold fever struck in Dahlonega, Georgia, to the south and west of these mountains, before San Francisco and Alaska lured the dreamers even farther from home. That had been a hundred-plus years ago. Three hundred years before that, the local Indians had suckered de Soto into leaving them alone, each tribe passing him along by telling him of other tribes with golden riches—always over the next hill.

I could imagine some dirt farmer up here scratching away, hoping to hit it rich or just to afford some little extra for his family—or to sucker his wife into leaving him be. As good a way to waste time as any, I guess.

"Reckon he was digging for gold and something fell on him?" I asked.

"Hard to say." Rudy shifted his weight, trying to find a comfortable spot on the boulder. "Hard to say."

"How long before these crime scene folks get here?"

"Also hard to say. I promise you, we're not high on their priorities. I can also promise you, I'm not going to be the schmuck who spends the night up here guarding the scene."

"I hadn't thought about that. Guess somebody has to keep an eye on things until they've finished. Can they work after dark processing it?" I pictured huge klieg lights and generator trucks. The sun was already angling low through the trees. It would slip behind the ridge before long, bringing early dark.

Rudy just shrugged.

We sat companionably studying the crevice in the hillside and the leafless trees and the glint of sun on the mica-flecked soil. Rudy resettled his backside on the sloping outcrop and chewed on a piece of broomstraw. L.J. hadn't reappeared, not that I'd expected her back. A couple of other deputies sat in a patrol car they'd managed to maneuver down the rock-strewn road to within thirty yards of the no-longer-abandoned mine.

"I'm going to head back into town," I said after a while. "Unless you need me for something."

Rudy spit out a stray piece of straw and looked a little disappointed. "Sure you don't want to volunteer to keep an eye on things here tonight? That'd be enough to interest some deputies in the assignment."

"Fill me in later, okay?" I had to admit to more than a little idle curiosity, but I had some work to do, like reading case law and puzzling over what to do about Maggy Avinger and her husband's little elegiac.

Rudy startled me by reading my mind. "You gonna fill me in on that hypothetical you were chewing over the other morning?"

I know I must have looked guilty. "Um—no. I mean, there's nothing to tell. If there was, you'd be the first to know."

His eyes narrowed into slits and one corner of his mouth crooked up. "You sure." It wasn't a question.

"Sure." I meant to be sincere. "See you later."

He hooked a thumb in his belt loop, up under his overhanging belly, and gave me a knowing nod.

Sunday Evening

By the time I got back to Dacus on Sunday night, it was dusk, the time of day when I either have to be distracted or depressed.

All weekend, I'd mulled over what to do about Harden Avinger's poisonous tombstone. After watching Maggy, I was even more convinced that she and my mother had been cut from the same world-beating, earth-saving bolt of cloth.

Though Maggy didn't agree, I knew the accusation, not the angel, was her biggest problem. Even if I found a way to stop Innis Barker from installing the angel, everybody in town would eventually be whispering about what was hidden, buried. Short of exhuming Harden—which would create almost as much stir as the tombstone itself—what else was there?

After much thought, I decided I would call the hospital pathologist tomorrow morning. If she had kept tissue samples, I'd find out what was involved in getting them tested and how much it would cost. That could settle the first part of Maggy's problem, the accusation.

Then I could focus on what to do about the angel. I needed to reread the copy of Harden's letter Maggy had left with me. Tomorrow morning, I'd go by and see Innis Barker at the monument company, talk to him about options for keeping Harden's hateful words from achieving the immortality of granite.

I also needed to puzzle my way through what Dot Downing could do about Lionel Shoal's double-dealing. Of course, without seeing the deed, I couldn't know what legal covenants had been made as part of the sale. I also needed to learn more about wetlands protection. Only four states in the nation have a greater percentage of land mass in wetlands than South Carolina. As a result, the state legislature has seen fit to supplement federal environmental protection with some stiff laws of its own. Frankly, though, I hadn't known we had wetlands in the hills.

Maggy had spoken so convincingly about protecting the cove forest, and after seeing the vulnerable trees and delicate orchids and habitats that no rescue efforts could save from the bulldozers, I wanted to know what the options were.

So I did what lawyers with legal questions do: I logged onto my office computer and searched the specialized legal databases and some environmental Web sites. Too much fringe-element nut stuff in some of the environmental sites, and too little explanation of the reach of statutes onto private property.

Despite masses of environmental protection legislation at both the state and federal levels, the law governing whether a property owner can plow under wetlands on his own property was confused and mired in controversy. The U.S. Supreme Court had ruled recently that the Army Corps of Engineers was reaching too far onto private property to prevent development; the court interpreted the Clean Water Act more narrowly than the Army Corps of Engineers had wanted, so the Corps had continued to find new ways to push against the restrictions.

For a moment—just a blink—I felt sorry for the guy in one of the cases who'd purchased a lot and couldn't build on it because of the wetlands. In another blink, the sympathy was gone. Buyer beware. Was there ever a way to know ahead of time what the Corps or any other regulatory body was going to allow or condemn?

Congress has the power to regulate activities in interstate commerce. As a result cases had held that any river regulated by federal law had to be navigable and thus able to be used in interstate commerce. Wetlands had to drain into a navigable river in order to be federally protected. Otherwise, the wetlands were governed by the state.

If the wetlands were protected, an Army Corps of Engineers permit was required before any building could commence. The Corps and the federal courts were in a tug-of-war: The Corps wanted to regulate every damp patch of ground in the nation, and the courts kept limiting the reach of regulations. In short, the law wouldn't be clear until the Supreme Court settled the issue—if then.

Did the wetlands on Dot Downing's property drain into a navigable river? Did it drain into the Chattooga? In that case, would the federal Wild and Scenic designation protect the river's watershed, even though the river wouldn't be termed "navigable" for interstate commerce? No, according to the documents I pulled up, the Wild and Scenic protection extended only to development along the river, not to its wetlands and feeder streams. Still, if he didn't have a required state or federal permit, siccing the regulators on him could mean fines, a possible jail term, and an order to stop work.

The staunchly independent personal rights part of me hated government telling somebody what to do with his property, but it warred with the part of me that had spent the last two days wandering under a thick canopy of poplar and black walnut trees. The plundering of those woods disturbed and saddened me.

A floorboard creaked. I jumped, startled.

"Don't you need some lights on in here?" Melvin came into my office from the hall.

I'd been so engrossed, I hadn't realized it had already grown dark outside. The laptop screen gave the only light in the room.

"Don't hit the switch. You'll blind me." I fumbled for the chain on the walnut floor lamp beside my desk, a lamp hand-turned by my granddad.

Melvin walked over and joined me in the pool of light, taking a seat in the armchair beside my desk.

"Where's your cell phone? I've been calling you most of the afternoon."

"Hmm. Plugged into the charger? In the cabin?"

"And your office answering machine?"

I turned to the mahogany buffet that served as a credenza behind me. Only after I shifted some of the stacked books and files could I see the message light blinking.

"From you, I presume?"

"Several," he said.

"Do I need to listen to the messages, or are you going to break the suspense?"

"I had a client who needed some legal advice this afternoon." He sounded irritated. "Just trying to steer some business your way."

"So, who needed help on Sunday afternoon?" A gentle reminder that I'm not required to be on the clock on Sunday, even if he insisted on working all the time. "Or did you get it taken care of?"

"I tracked down Lincoln Graham on the golf course. Your buddy, the sheriff, had Lionel Shoal in for questioning. Things got pretty tense. Shoal called me for advice."

The lamp apparently didn't highlight my surprise at Shoal's name. "Long story, but it's probably best you couldn't find me."

Given our brief encounter on the mountain, Shoal likely wouldn't have been excited about having me come to his rescue.

"Just trying to help get you on your feet."

I didn't respond to the pique in his voice. "Why did he call you? I mean—" I didn't want to sound rude, but who calls his financial adviser from the sheriff's office?

"I was on the board of directors for his company and the only board member in Dacus. He didn't know who else to call."

The light from the floor lamp encircled my desk with a warm glow. Melvin studied my desktop. Only a few papers, a notebook, and my almost empty calendar in view. With the rest of the room in shadow, I couldn't see the jumble of boxes and disarray in the rest of the room, just the little sanctuary of my desk.

"You hungry?" His tone said he was offering me an olive branch.

"Ravenous," I realized as soon as he asked. "Let's go exchange our long stories." He'd been trying to do me a good turn. I'd wait to ask how he got hooked up with Shoal.

Sunday nights offer sparse pickings in Dacus, unless you want moderately edible pizza. Which lots of people who'd been to Sunday night prayer meetings obviously did. While we waited for a table at The Pizza Wheel, we watched a bunch of ten-year-olds playing video games and spilling energy and gum balls all over the place.

Once we were seated, I gave Melvin the thumbnail version of the plant rescue efforts and the afternoon's drama. The description of the mottled, swollen leg wasn't appetizing, but sharing it with Melvin helped me process just how horrible it was, that I hadn't exaggerated it in my mind.

He took a sip of his sweet tea. "No wonder Shoal was rampaging. He didn't give me the details. Now I'm especially glad he fired me from his board."

"Fired you? Melvin. How scandalous."

"I'm not the scandal." He didn't elaborate.

"Okay, you can't leave it there."

He toyed with his red plastic tea glass for a moment, deciding what he could say without violating any confidences. "Lionel Shoal came here from Phoenix with the idea of setting up a development company to sell limited partnerships in his projects. The initial landowners would finance the development of the property, as an investment interest."

What little I knew about limited partnerships came from a textbook and a single law school course on business organizations. The use of limited partnerships had fallen out of favor thanks to some tax shelter abuses in the seventies, but it could still be a useful investment vehicle for the right project.

"Sounded like an interesting plan," he said. "I agreed to join his board—an advisory board, really, as he did the setup and got things rolling. He proposed a housing development bordering the national forest land. Rather than a golf course—ridiculous on land that steep—the drawing card was a tax-sheltered investment in lands reserved in conservancy. I'm sure you're familiar with that. Tax benefits would accrue to the limited partners, the initial investors. They and the later homeowners would enjoy access to the conserved lands and to the national forest for picnicking and hiking."

I gave a half nod, half shrug to keep him talking. No lawyer can know everything about the law, and Melvin, the financial whiz, often filled in gaps in my business law knowledge.

He must have read my puzzled look because he continued. "South Carolina has favorable conservancy laws that shelter against property taxes if land is maintained in its natural state. I'd never seen that employed on a real estate development project, and I was intrigued."

"Interesting." I'd made small gifts to the Chattooga Land Trust, which buys land in the river's watershed, but I'd never heard of a for-profit conservancy. I didn't share my ignorance.

"He also had another draw, though I was skeptical of that one. The land includes an abandoned gold mine. He thought people would enjoy telling their friends they owned part of a gold mine. I thought it sounded dopey and too much of a hazard. Somebody goes poking around in that thing and it collapses, guess who gets sued."

"You've been hanging around me too long, seeing lawsuits lurking in every hole. So what got you kicked off the board?"

"I didn't really get kicked off. I quit." He paused, weighing his words. "Let's just say I didn't agree with some of Shoal's tactics, and I'm picky about my business associates."

"That's where they found the body today, in the gold mine. Reckon that's what happened? It collapsed on him?"

"I'm sure I don't know." Melvin looked surprised. Lionel obviously hadn't explained what prompted his visit with L.J.

Except for the swollen leg, the body had been out of sight in the dark slash in the hillside, so I hadn't been able to see much except the jumble of rocks surrounding the opening. Maybe a rock had fallen and hit him on the head.

"If it was an accident," I said, "why did L.J. haul Shoal into town to grill him?"

"Don't ask me. She's your buddy."

L.J. and I have that loaded relationship that can only exist under the weight of childhood rivalries and playground battles—the kind of memory-bound relationship you don't develop unless you know people over the changing of decades. In other words, L.J. and I had baggage. We certainly weren't buddies and never had been.

"Speaking of our erstwhile men in khaki . . ." Melvin nodded toward the door. I turned to see Rudy Mellin saunter into The Pizza Wheel.

"They let you come in out of the cold tonight, huh?" I said as he caught sight of us.

Rudy gave Melvin an abrupt nod, then ignored him. Once a suspect, always a suspect in Rudy's book. "That's what rookies are for, spending the night out in the cold."

I thought about some kid propped up on a rock outcropping all night, keeping watch in the dark, alone.

"Hope you had two rookies. That'd be a spooky place to spend the night."

"Just one." Rudy looked down at me with a grin. "Little chicken-'ll likely huddle in his patrol car, where he can't see the scene he's supposed to protect, and run out of gas trying to keep warm. I can tell you, if I have to haul a can of gasoline up there tomorrow morning, we're going to be short one rookie."

He cocked his head. His tone loaded with implication, he said, "I'll let you two get back to your dinner. I'm gonna go over here and bite into half a hog. I missed—"

The cell phone on his belt buzzed. With the ease of much practice, he pulled it out and turned away, muttering into the phone hidden in his beefy hand. I like somebody who doesn't include me in his phone calls.

87

After a quick conversation, he snapped his phone shut and turned back to us, his mouth slightly agape. "You won't believe this. Both the real estate office and the model home up near that gahdam mine just blew sky-high."

"What?" Melvin and I reacted in unison.

"Neil said it sounded like an atom bomb. Just lit up the sky. Gotta get up there. Shit. I'm starvin'."

"Get them to fix you a sandwich, Rudy. You know you'll be out there all night." I sounded like my mother.

Nobody has to twice urge Rudy to eat. He flagged down a waitress and headed to the register to pay. I really did feel sorry for him. I get horrible headaches when I don't eat.

"I can't believe it," I said, as much to myself as to Melvin.

The two of us sat for a moment lost in our own imaginings. I'd planned to go up to the cabin to spend the night. The real estate office could be on my way home—if I added a twenty-minute detour to my twenty-minute drive home.

"You're going up there, aren't you?" Melvin said.

His gray-blue eyes studied me, and he allowed me a bemused grin. Melvin and I hadn't known each other but a few months, but I've learned he has an uncanny mind-reading ability.

"Want to come with me?" I asked.

Sunday Night

At my invitation to drive up the mountain to the explosion site, Melvin hesitated only a moment, wrestling between dignity, maturity, and the nine-year-old's sense of adventure that lurks in every adult male.

"Long way for you to bring me back," he said.

"That's okay. You're there to provide a grown-up explanation for our presence."

"We were in the neighborhood and just decided to stop by?"

"That'll work."

We paid—separate checks after a short battle—but Melvin won the battle over who would drive. He thinks I drive too fast. He proceeded to poke around the curves in his Jeep Cherokee like Aunt Letha's Rottweiler on a stroll around the neighborhood.

When we got to the turnoff marked by the Golden Cove model home sign, we had no choice but to keep driving. Trucks and cars were parked thick along the side of the narrow two-lane highway, some with official markings, most of them the nondescript vehicles of looky-loos like us. Melvin passed twenty or so cars before he could park on the narrow grassy strip along the roadside. We walked back to the Golden Cove road.

A few feet down the gravel road, the police had established a perimeter with yellow crime scene tape more than a football field's distance from what had been the office. The cute little cottage with its shutters and flower boxes was splintered rubble, as though some little girl's brother had stepped on her dollhouse.

Spotlights from the two fire trucks and the police cars lit up the area like a shadowy black-and-white photo blurred by distance. On the hill, the model home was still standing, but it had sharper, more awkward edges than when I'd seen it yesterday morning. The roof canted over the porch. The side windows were ragged black holes.

The air carried faint whiffs, but not the smell from a fire. This was a dusty smell. The firefighters stood inside the perimeter tape. With their coats hanging open and their helmets off, they were nothing more than casual spectators, like the rest of us.

On our side of the yellow tape, mostly guys crowded along the gravel road, all staring, talking, shuffling aimlessly.

The scene was surreal, hard to grasp. As my eyes adjusted to the sharp light and deep shadows, I noticed a second line of crime scene tape had corralled the idle firefighters and some paramedics and sheriff's deputies away from the active scene investigation. No need to have the idly curious messing up evidence, even if they were wearing official uniforms.

The tape lines disappeared into the trees past the huge glass and shingle house on the hill. In the woods far up the hill, I saw movement. An officer was stationed on the back side of what remained of the model home. Guess they wanted to make sure nobody snuck up the far side of the mountain to contaminate the scene. Like somebody was going to climb miles straight up through dense forest.

Though this looked like the aftermath of a tornado, this was no act of nature. I'd seen an old furniture plant immediately after a gas explosion, one caused by arson. A huge fire had raged afterward.

This was different, unusual enough to merit standing around contemplating it on a chill March night.

"Avery." Noah Lakefield appeared at my elbow, a bit out of breath. "What happened? Any idea?"

He wore a toboggan hat pulled almost to his eyebrows and a much-worn down jacket. Melvin, standing on the other side of him, turned to study the newcomer in that unnerving way he has. I introduced them. Noah's nod was polite, but he turned quickly back to me, the fount of no knowledge.

"You been here long? What do you know? The cops said anything?"

I shook my head. "We just got here. What you see is all we know." I didn't tell him about the call Rudy Mellin had received at The Pizza Wheel, labeling this an explosion. It wasn't much news and it wasn't mine to tell.

Melvin stood with his hands deep in his cashmere overcoat pockets and watched the scene, leaving Noah and his questions to me.

"Avery, which of those guys over the line there would most likely talk to me?" Noah nodded across the crime scene tape.

Two young deputies stood inside the first tape, facing the crowd, keeping gruesomely curious civilians at bay with stern, unamused stares. They also served as gatekeepers into the limited sanctum between the two tapes, the area reserved for officials who had no official reason for being on the scene. A Dacus city cop came up and chatted with one of the deputies, who held the tape up and let him join the crowd of officers and other semiofficial attendees who needed to feel important inside the first yellow tape.

"I don't know, Noah." In scanning the official-looking folks, I spotted Rudy. For some reason, I didn't sic Noah on him. Rudy certainly knew how to handle reporters, but he'd already had quite a day. Even Rudy hadn't made it inside the second tape, so he probably didn't know much more than we did.

"Ask those guys guarding the line if there's a spokesman." There probably wasn't one, but they might have some tidbits to offer, if he asked nice. The cops were kids. They'd love the attention.

Noah hesitated. He'd hoped I could offer a better inside track. When I didn't, he stepped over to the nearest protector of the peace and was back almost immediately.

"They've called in the ATF. No official—or unofficial—comments until after the feds arrive."

"ATF, huh." I looked first at Noah, then at Melvin, who seemed intent on not joining in our conversation.

Even Melvin's concentration was broken by a sharp, loud voice.

"Melvin Bertram! Finally, somebody who can tell me what the hell is going on here."

Lionel Shoal, unfazed by his afternoon with L. J. Peters.

"My gahdam business is destroyed, and I can't get one of these stupid hicks to talk to me. They act like mouth-breathing morons."

I felt spines all around us stiffen, and eyes cut toward Shoal. Not heads, just eyes. Shoal seemed unaware that he was surrounded by hick morons. Did this guy really not have a clue?

Melvin murmured quietly to him about the ATF, probably wanting to send a subtle message that he needed to quiet down.

"This is a royal effin' joke." Shoal jabbed his fist at nothing, paced a half step and spun in frustration, anger on a short leash. "I got to find one of these morons that can tell me something, gahdammit."

He stomped off toward the nearest fresh-faced deputy, who'd heard most of the exchange.

Good luck, Lionel.

"That guy's got some anger-control issues," I said.

Melvin agreed with a curt nod. "Ready to go?"

"Yep. Least we can say we attended this event."

"No postcards to show for it, though."

Noah had picked the wrong time to disappear into the crowd. Shoal's lack of control could be a reporter's dream. My feet were numb and tired. I'd forgotten to bring my earmuffs, so I was glad to climb into the heated seat in Melvin's Jeep.

"So, this Noah works for your dad?"

I snorted. I'd have to start calling him Clark Kent—there when things started, then gone in a blink. "I'm not sure he even knows what Noah was hired to do."

"Having a go-get-'em reporter in Dacus, that'll be news."

"Yeah. I can't quite figure him out. He seems a bit too . . . I don't know."

"Out of place?"

"Overqualified. This can't be his dream job. But he apparently loves the outdoors. Drives around with a canoe on top of his car all the time, like he might need to use it at a moment's notice."

"Waiting for God to break his promise and flood us out again?"

"Who knows." I couldn't read Melvin's face, but something in his tone hinted that he'd taken a dislike to the Dacus *Clarion*'s new ace reporter. I'd leave that topic alone for the time being.

When we got back to the office, I climbed into my car. It was well after midnight and too late to wake up Mom and Dad, so I took the direct route to Luna Lake, not the least tempted to take the long way around by Golden Cove.

Monday Morning

Despite my late night and black-and-white dreams filled with a sense of anxious waiting, I woke early Monday thinking about Maggy Avinger and her angel. My subconscious had hatched a plan, or at least a likely path.

I sailed down from the mountain cabin, trusting all the junior deputies were sleeping in after their late night at Golden Cove.

I caught the hospital pathologist in her office and got answers to my three questions: No, they hadn't done even a limited autopsy on Harden Avinger; yes, they could do a tox or heavy metals screen on an exhumed body; and yes, it would cost a lot of money.

Okay, I had answers. No solutions yet, but some answers. The more I mused on it, the more convinced I was that Maggy needed hard evidence to dispel even a hint of wrongdoing. Then she could worry how to keep the monument from being erected. The epitaph would loom larger than the angel, even though she refused to see it.

I drove over to Innis Barker's monument company. Both "monument" and "company," singularly or together, implied a concern of more substance than the reality. The Dacus Monument Company was a portable metal shed, dented and surrounded by a scattering of sample headstones on the little patch of grass that fronted Cane Street.

As I drove up, Innis Barker peered out the door. He looked like he'd been planted on this spot about the same time as the rust-flecked shed. Wiping his hands on a cloth, he had to stoop to step out the door. His overalls were covered in dust, and instead of offering to shake hands, he nodded a curt hello.

"How do, ma'am." His greeting was somber. Guess in his business it was bad form to appear too happy to see customers.

"Mr. Barker, I represent Maggy Avinger. Do you have a minute to talk about her husband's memorial?"

He shook his head and wiped more dust onto his face from the rag in his hand. "A bad business, that is. Don't know how I can help. A bad business. Come around back."

He led the way around the shed to a wooden barn that stood in back, under a sheltering oak. Through an opening in a sliding door, I could see blank stones and what I took to be carving tools and equipment. So this was where letters appeared on a headstone, in an orderly, though dusty barn.

He motioned to a sunny spot and a weathered picnic table under the leafless oak. Even on a March day, it was certainly more inviting here in the sun than in that rusted, cramped office shed.

He settled across from me at the table, his sun-deep wrinkles arranged in a morose expression.

I didn't want to waste his time. As soon as I'd mentioned Maggy Avinger, he knew why I was here. "Mr. Barker, I believe I can prove Mr. Avinger's accusation is false. From all I've been able to find, Harden Avinger was a prankster, and Maggy Avinger doesn't deserve a cloud of suspicion hanging over her head because of a joke." I was choosing my words carefully, in case Innis Barker had considered Harden a friend.

As I talked, I pulled out my copy of Harden Avinger's letter. He knew what it was as soon as he saw it. He sat slumped on the picnic bench, his head bowed.

"Once I prove this accusation is false, then the second problem is how to stop the monument from being erected."

He shook his head emphatically. "I can't do that. I got to be paid. That thing cost almost what I make in a whole year. That lawyer fella who sent the letter said I wouldn't get the rest of the money—two-thirds what I'm owed—if I don't do what Avinger said. The lawyer said put that poem on there. 'It's mean,' the lawyer said. 'And it's not even a good poem, but do it.' Them bills come here, not to nobody else. I gotta get this settled."

Barker kept shaking his head, both hands clutching the rag as his voice grew sharp with urgency. A terrible burden, either being a party to wrongly accusing someone of murder or to wrongly covering one up.

"How about this: What if Mrs. Avinger paid you for the monument? That way, you could pay off the bill and Mrs. Avinger could decide what she wanted to do with the angel."

He looked skeptical, trying to figure out what I was trying to pull on him. "I—don't know."

"From my reading of the letter, that's the only control Mr. Avinger had from the grave, withholding the final payment. If Mrs. Avinger bought the monument, then she could have it say whatever she wanted. He might not be happy, but the Avingers can argue over that later."

He didn't smile.

"I don't know about that. She went a bit crazy when she heard about it."

"Could I see it?" I'd heard so much about this angel, I was intrigued.

He bent forward, braced his hands on his knees, and stood. "She's back there."

He slid the barn door open a notch more and led the way inside. She stood in the center of the workshop, with crating boards stacked against the lesser monuments at her feet.

She filled the shed, glowing with the pearly light of polished marble. Her wings flared from her shoulders, then folded reverently down her back, the tips dusting the hem of her robe. She wasn't the sword-bearing, vengeful angel I'd pictured. With her head bowed, she raised one hand prayerfully against the fluted stone obelisk. On her stone pedestal, she stood at least eight feet tall—almost three feet taller than I am.

The blank rectangle of stone where Innis Barker was to add the epitaph covered the base of the obelisk. Harden Avinger was one of the few people who could've found a way to desecrate such a beautiful work of art.

"She's gorgeous," I breathed.

Innis Barker turned to stare at me, one eyebrow raised in disbelief. I could see her through his eyes. After all, he was in a solemn business. Traditional rectangular headstones lined his workshop, none sporting anything fancier than a demure vase or a heart-shaped silhouette.

"Probably wouldn't fit in the Dacus city cemetery," I said. But she was breathtaking.

We stood staring up at her face.

"Don't know what Mrs. Avinger would do with it if she bought it," I said more to myself than to Innis Barker. "She was mortified that he'd put something like this on their plot."

"Sure ain't much of a garden adornment," he said.

Maggy Avinger would have to spend eternity resting under an accusation of murder by poison, borne on the wings of an eight-foot angel. Harden Avinger hadn't left her any financial resources, yet he could buy this for himself. Studying the blank rectangle, I didn't see that he'd left any room to include her name and dates, to commemorate her life. Nice guy, Harden Avinger.

"Maybe she could sell it back to the manufacturer."

Innis shook his head. "Nope. Harden had this special made. They ain't takin' it back. I done asked."

"There's always eBay, I guess."

Innis didn't respond, his face solemn as a death-penalty judge.

"How much did she cost?"

"The price of a new pickup truck."

"That much?" My mouth gaped open, more in shock than in awe. I could understand Barker's melancholy panic over being paid. A charge like that would rack up some credit card interest.

Maggy Avinger had hesitated over paying my bill. She surely didn't have that kind of money lying around. So much for my smart solution. On the good news side, that made the cost of an exhumation and tox screen look like pocket change.

"Wow. Mr. Barker, I've got to think this over some more." I hesitated, knowing he wouldn't like my next question. "Can you hold off just a bit longer on the carving?"

He looked pained. More head shaking. "I got to have that money by the end of the month. I got to. That lawyer said he couldn't pay me until it was carved and installed." He resumed wringing his dusty rag.

"I certainly understand. Can you just give me until Wednesday? That's day after tomorrow. Then, if I don't come up with a solution, you'll still have time before the end of the month, won't you?"

He relaxed a bit, but only a bit. "Not past Thursday."

"Great." I stuck out my hand and, after a hesitation, he shook on it. His hands felt dry and dusty and hard.

I walked back around front to my car, a granite lump in my stomach. *Some solution, Avery. Now what?*

I'd skipped breakfast, so I headed for Maylene's and an early lunch. Can't think on an empty stomach.

Rudy Mellin was finishing a late breakfast as I slid into the booth.

"People gonna start talking, we keep hangin' out like this." He sopped up the last of his fried egg yolk with his white toast.

"Probably. What's new?"

"Other than I hadn't gotten enough sleep? Let's see. ATF guys are fixing to descend on us to investigate the explosion. A DHEC guy has already come up from Columbia, something about somebody destroying a wetlands site up there. How can you have a swamp in the mountains? Can't say I've ever run across that before. But if you work for the government, I reckon you can find a swamp any blessed where you want one."

I didn't admit it had been news to me. Had Maggy sicced the state's Department of Health and Environmental Control on Lionel Shoal? She hadn't wasted any time, if she had. Not that Shoal didn't have plenty to tangle with already, between a dead body and an explosion. Would the Army Corps of Engineers be far behind? I was beginning to feel a tinge sorry for him. Just a tinge.

"Any word on what happened to that guy in the mine?"

Rudy sat his empty coffee cup down. "Len Ruffin, according to his wallet. Never seen anybody look even worse than his driver's license photo. Funny thing, he'd been gone a couple a weeks, but his wife hadn't reported him missing."

"Ruffin?" *Missing. Jesse Ruffin's father?* "Does he have a daughter, about fifteen?"

Rudy's eyes narrowed with a suspicious frown.

"Just a coincidence. I met her this weekend, at the plant rescue. Somebody mentioned her dad had run off. Said it was a good thing."

Rudy studied me, trying to put pieces together, figure out if I was holding anything back.

"What about the explosion?" I asked.

He shrugged. "With two separate buildings at once, not a chance it was an accident. Other than a quick check to make sure nobody was inside, we left it for the big dogs."

"Any connection with Ruffin?"

"Who knows, at this point. Did get an interesting lead on the explosion. Guy works for the highway department told his buddy this woman needed some dynamite and she was willing to, shall we say, entertain him in exchange for a couple a sticks."

"Huh?" Surely I'd misunderstood him.

"Yep. Just when you think you've seen it all. Sex for dynamite. Nookie for nitro. Said she didn't have any money to pay for it and her boyfriend needed it bad."

"Dynamite."

"Yep. Guys at the office are having a hoo-ha over that. Everybody wants to be the one to question her. Trying to pick her up this afternoon. I won't repeat any of the jokes going around." From his expression, I could tell he was tempted to share one or two with me, then he'd thought about how embarrassed he'd be. He even blushed.

"No need." I could imagine. Guys get awfully free with the wordplay among themselves when just the right thing sparks their creativity.

Rudy's phone buzzed. He listened and rolled his eyes. "Be right there." He flipped his phone shut.

"Great. Somebody croaked at home over on Liberty Street. Probably some geezer, but gotta check it out."

"You're a wonderful public servant, Deputy Mellin." I saluted him. He thanked me with a withering roll of his eyes. He slid his belly out from under the table and rearranged the implements on his belt.

The waitress cleared Rudy's dishes and handed me a lunch menu I didn't need to read. "I'll have the fried chicken, fried okra, and squash casserole." All Maylene specialties. The waitress, a young woman I hadn't seen before, scribbled it all down on her pad as Cissie Prentice slid into the bench opposite me.

"Gawd, I'm so glad to see you."

Cissie and I have known each other since kindergarten, but she's rarely exuberant about running into women friends. Men, that's another matter. The deep V of her sea-foam green cashmere sweater showcased her gently tanned breasts. Push-up bra or implants? I was no expert. I just knew from high school gym class that Cissie had been only modestly endowed then, which matched her slender hips and long legs.

"I need to talk to you." She plopped the papers and envelopes she'd been clutching onto the table. "I just got the most disturbing thing. At the post office. It's nasty and creepy and—I don't know."

She pulled out an envelope buried in her stack of mail and handed it to me. Printed in a neat spidery script was Cissie's name and address: Priscilla Prentice, 19 Lake's Edge Drive, Dacus.

"Read it." She held a deep wrinkle between her brows as she chewed the lipstick off her bottom lip.

The creamy paper felt oiled and elegant. Glued to the bottom corner of the stationery sheet was a small, carefully clipped three-inch square of newspaper. Cut from an advice column and glued so firmly it became a part of the stationery, the headline read, "Hubbie's New Friend Means Trouble."

Written in the same cobalt blue ink and graceful school script as the envelope, the words themselves were anything but graceful.

Dear Mrs. Prentice,

I have watched your licentious behavior for many years, as has the rest of the town. I can keep silent no longer.

Your constant attentions to the new minister at the Presbyterian Church can come to no good. He certainly shares the blame, but he was not the instigator. Men are foolish, particularly men with little experience of women like you.

Leave him be. There are plenty of men versed in base behavior who do not have wives, small children, and vulnerable parishioners relying on their good example.

Stick with your own kind, Mrs. Prentice.

"Women like me?" Cissie whispered. Tears threatened to spill over the thick mascara coating her lashes. "Avery, do you think I'm—licentious?"

"Cissie, don't be silly." I turned the envelope over. Of course it had no return address; the postmark was yesterday, Upstate South Carolina.

"Who do you think sent this?"

"I have no idea." She hugged herself, making her breasts pop farther out of her V-necked sweater. "The more I think about it, the more it creeps me out."

"It is pretty creepy," I had to admit. Surprisingly creepy. "Is this—true? About—?"

Cissie drew herself up. "Reverend Stanton and I have played tennis together a couple of times. That's it. He's new in town and is just now meeting folks."

I didn't answer her indignation by pointing out he had a whole church full of new folks to meet—and some of them probably played tennis, though few would dress the part as well as Cissie did.

"Besides," she said, "he's not my type. What use would I have for a preacher man?"

Seeking repentance obviously wasn't on her self-improvement list this year.

"Anyway, I'm seeing a man in Highlands. He retired there, owned a big company."

"That's your type, all right. Well-to-do. Widowed?"

She nodded, but didn't fire the return volley I'd expected in our well-worn banter. As the waitress approached with my steaming plate of food, Cissie laid her hand on the letter and wadded it up in one fierce motion.

"Just some hot tea for me," Cissie said, "and some cottage cheese and pears."

I reached for the letter. "This may sound strange, but you need to hold on to that for a while."

"Why?" She kept the paper wadded in her fist.

"I don't know. Just the lawyer in me. You never know." The more I thought about it, the more disquieting it became. Who could feel strongly enough about Cissie to take time to write a letter? The writer had to be a "she." The handwriting, the formality, the sense of moral outrage. Women I knew in Dacus had no problem delivering subtle but unmistakable guidance to other women, without ever once damaging the bonds of sociability. Why write an anonymous letter? First Mr. Mack and now Cissie. Was there a club for this in Dacus now? Instead of knitting, did women get together to sip tea and write nasty letters?

Cissie smoothed the crumpled paper, refolded it into its envelope, and slipped it deep into her coat pocket rather than into her stack of mail. Best to tuck something like that away, out of sight.

Cissie, whose resilience had moved her through widowhood and three divorces in a little over a decade, dipped her spoon into the cottage cheese and canned pears the waitress plopped in front of her and changed the subject.

"Did you hear about them finding that woman dead? In her home? Just over on Liberty?"

"How did you hear about that?"

"Well, you obviously know. What, I can't have sources, too, Miz Lawyer Lady?"

Sources that beat the chief deputy to the scene? I didn't reply, not wanting to give away my source.

"Heard it at the post office. They say she was murdered. A horrid scene, mess everywhere." She swallowed a dainty spoonful of cottage cheese. "What is this town coming to, I ask you."

What indeed.

Monday Afternoon and Evening

About the time everyone else in Dacus would start heading to lunch, I made it back to the office, ready to work. I thumbed through my old hornbook on contracts, hoping to find something that would help Maggy Avinger with her eight-foot angel, but nothing joggled loose a good idea.

Frustrated, I soon turned to putting books on the shelves, trying to decide on some sensible order and how much room the sets of state statutes and case reports would take, a challenge since boxes were scattered here and there, all poorly labeled.

Lots of lawyers were opting not to maintain expensive libraries, relying instead on computer searches, but I liked being surrounded by these hefty, well-thumbed tomes, as though surrounded by history and memory, part of my grandfather's legacy. I vacuumed the closed pages of each one as I unboxed it, lovingly stroking the baby-smooth beige leather. Search as I might, not one of these books was going to yield the lawyer's holy grail—a "case on point," the answer to Maggy Avinger's problem. Sometimes lawyers solve problems with law and cases, sometimes they solve them by being wise. I needed to get hold of some wisdom.

I was lost in thought, and the rapping at the front door had to be repeated several times before I was certain I'd heard something. When I didn't hear Melvin heading to answer it, I climbed down off my ladder.

I swung open the front door, delighted to see my Luna Lake neighbor. "Sadie Waynes! How nice to see you! And Ms. Downing." Sadie lives on the other side of the hill behind the cabin, which is a long drive around by car, but up there, that counts as a neighbor. From a long affection for my grandfather begun in her childhood, she keeps an eye on me.

She looked out of place in my Victorian entry hall in her baggy work jeans and plaid flannel shirt, her gray hair hanging in a thick braid.

"Hope you don't mind us stopping in. You know Dot."

"Sure." The lady who'd once owned Golden Cove.

"We're very sorry to barge in unannounced," said Dot, "but we just left the courthouse and we didn't want to wait."

"Come in, come in. Things are still a jumble. I'm sorry. We can clear off a couple of chairs."

I pulled the French doors closed—the ones I'd dressed up with locks and new latches on Friday. Not that visitors would notice the new hardware as quickly as they noticed I was sitting on a stack of book boxes while they sat in the only two uncluttered chairs. I needed to get this office finished and get down to business.

"A'vry, I made Dot come," Sadie said, taking the lead. "What's been done needs to be put right."

Dot, dainty in her slacks and windbreaker, was almost a foot shorter than Sadie. Both had the same tough, nut-brown gardener's tan and both spoke with the same hill-country twang, though Dot had a bit more polish and didn't tend to parcel out her words as sparingly as Sadie.

"That Lionel Shoal pulled a fast one, and I fell for it," Dot said.

"Sadie here and Maggy Avinger had a talk with me, made me see the light. With Shoal, what got said and what got done aren't atall the same. But what can I do now?"

"Horsewhippin' would be a start," Sadie offered.

Dot barely paused, doubtless having heard Sadie's extreme views repeated often. "Maggy took us to the courthouse, showed us how to look up deeds and such. She had to learn things, probating her parents' estate—and for her husband. Sadie's seen it, too. Right there. What's on those papers don't read like what he told me."

"Give her the copies." Sadie waved her hand at Dot as if shooing a cat.

Maggy pulled a folded sheaf of papers from her coat pocket.

"We copied these at the courthouse."

She handed me a registered deed of trust for a parcel of land, transferred from one Dorothy Brandt Downing to Lionel Shoal, d/b/a The Shoal Company Properties.

"This is the deed for what Shoal's calling Golden Cove?"

"And it's one fat lie." The anger built in Dot the longer she sat, as though walking from the courthouse to my office had dissipated it some and inaction allowed it to build strength.

"What do you mean?" I skimmed over the deed. The only real estate closings I'd been in were when I bought my condo in Columbia and when I sold it. Based on my book learning and limited experience, the deed looked standard.

"For one, he promised it would keep a sizable section in what he called a conservancy, so nobody could ever build on it. He said he'd have to pay me less because of that, because he couldn't build on it and he'd make less money on his development. Said he thought it was the right thing to do. Said it would attract the right kind of people to live there. People who would care about the land and preserving it. It's all lies." Her voice spit with disgust.

"How do—"

"Maggy said it should be in that deed, in something called a covenant. Like God's covenant. God keeps his covenants. Lionel Shoal ought to roast over his broken ones for eternity."

Remind me not to make little Dot Downing mad.

I turned through the pages, scanning the traditional boilerplate language.

"There is something about a conservancy," I said.

They both stirred, surprised.

"It also mentions mineral rights. What was your understanding about that?" I asked as I read, trying to make sense of this unusual provision.

"Mineral rights? We never talked atall about that."

"Shoal as the grantee retains all mineral rights, in both the conserved property and fee simple—the nonreserved property."

I looked up from the handful of papers.

Sadie's eyes narrowed.

"What's that mean?" asked Dot, her fingers twining and untwining.

"I don't really know." I didn't want to tell them what was on the tip of my tongue—that I wasn't sure what good a covenant to protect land was if somebody had the right to tear up parts of it looking for minerals. I also doubted the tax shelter offered by the conservancy would hold up if the grant didn't effectively protect the land. I wasn't fluent in the language of South Carolina land conservancy, but from a practical point of view, this didn't seem to offer much protection.

"Can you leave this with me? Let me study it some more? I'd like to check a few things."

The two friends looked at each other for confirmation, then Dot nodded.

She leaned forward. I thought she was about to impart an important bit of information, but she whispered, "Do you mind if I use your restroom before we go?"

"Not at all. It's down the hall, tucked behind the stairs."

Yet another thing I needed to be more businesslike about. Was the bathroom clean? Did it have paper and towels? For Pete's sake. I'd never had to worry about such things in a big law firm with a downtown city office.

After Dot left the room, I said to Sadie, "I didn't realize you and Ms. Downing were friends."

She nodded. "We go a long ways back. She's older, but we kinda grew up together."

I had no way of knowing how old Sadie was, with her weathered face and her sturdy, hard build.

"Hate I missed you at the plant rescue," I said.

"Wadn't there."

I must have looked surprised.

"Didn't really see any point. Plants don't much live except where they choose for theirselves. No need to go moving 'em around."

"The nursery lady in charge of it all, she helped flag particular plants and told us how to handle them." I'm sure my voice carried my hopefulness.

Sadie shrugged. "Just haven't seen it myself. Guess if you make money moving plants into people's yards, you must know." She sounded skeptical.

Sadie stood with her hands in her pockets, looking around the two large rooms and through the French doors into the entry hall. In the front room where we were, a bay window opened onto the generous front porch. I planned on using this as the reception area, though I had no plan about who would be here to do the receiving. On the opposite side from the bay window, wide pocket doors led into the bookcase-lined study that was becoming my office.

Melvin's offices were a mirror image of mine, also with a bay-windowed parlor in front. His back office occupied the old dining room and boasted a breathtaking crystal chandelier heavily iced with prisms. His rooms lacked the massive bookcases that his grandfather had built into what was now my office. Fortunately for me, investment gurus don't need as many books as lawyers do—and maybe the crystal prisms could serve as multiple little crystal balls for Melvin's financial forecasts. So we were both happy.

"Nice place," Sadie pronounced over my two rooms.

"Thanks. I really like it here. Moving in is taking longer than I'd planned. Lots of work to do in a place like this."

"I remember the funeral parlor," she said, surveying the rich wainscoting and the trimwork on the bookcases.

I'd never stood here imagining these rooms as a funeral parlor. They had probably held viewings in these rooms. I shivered a bit.

Sadie walked over to examine the molding around the floor-to-ceiling windows, then craned her neck to take in the plaster medallion around the ceiling fixture.

"This has a good feel," she said with finality. "A good place." She turned to face me, her black eyes piercing. "Your grandfather would be pleased. Very happy. This is a good place. You belong here."

I was surprised—and oddly comforted.

"Thank you." It was as if she had pronounced a benediction, blessed me on my way.

Dot bustled in from the hallway. "A'vry, I don't know how to thank you. I hate to burden you with my problems, but Sadie insisted, and I know how very wise she is about such."

I walked them to the front door, making what I hoped were reassuring sounds. From the porch, I watched as they strode down the short walk to Main Street, Sadie towering protectively over her friend.

Here it was, late on Monday afternoon, the start of another week, and I didn't have a paying case in sight. True, living could be done with remarkable frugality in Dacus—no house payment, no car payment. I had my savings, the proceeds from the sale of my condo in Columbia, and the generous sum Jake Baker had paid me for helping him with a case in February.

Also true, I'd only been back for a while, didn't even have my office set up. But the cases wandering in my door thus far weren't going to buy many meals at Maylene's or whatever rent Melvin decided to charge me for this office. I had left behind my courtroom life. Now I needed to master the bread-and-butter work of lawyers: title searches, real estate closings, and wills. Things people expected to pay for when they walked in a lawyer's office. The boring stuff.

I looked back at the top of the box where I'd laid Dot's sheaf of papers. Too many puzzles. And too many things taxing the limits of my knowledge. Give me a courtroom with a complicated lawsuit involving a drug company or a knotty business fraud. Let me immerse myself in that, learning unimaginably arcane bits about processes and problems I never knew existed. Oh—and include the resources for sophisticated computer searches, for flying around doing research, for hiring experts, and for support staff. Don't leave me here with clients who couldn't pay, problems that didn't have solutions, and me worrying about soap and toilet paper in the bathroom. What had I gotten myself into?

This is a good place. You belong here. My benediction.

I picked up the pages of the deed. No mention of an attached trust. What did Lionel Shoal want with the mineral rights? Had he been fooled into thinking an abandoned gold mine might have potential? I faintly remembered something about an old mine reopening in South Carolina, but nowhere near here.

I couldn't afford the time, but I needed to walk. I went out back to my car and, from the rear floorboard, dug out some sweats and tennis shoes. I'd taken to carrying my worldly possessions with me—or at least comfortable clothes and shoes and a book to read—since I never know where I'll end up for the night.

The five-mile trek I'd measured out took in parts of Dacus twice, as well as some country roads. The whole hour I walked, gold mines and mineral rights kept tumbling around in my head. I decided to make a detour to the library.

I always think of it as the "new" library, though it had celebrated its fifteenth anniversary in its quietly carpeted building with vaulted ceiling and tinted-window walls. I still fondly remembered the creaky, bright library I'd grown up in, housed in a former community-center basketball court, outfitted with peeling floor tiles and scarred maple tables. This one was nice, but the old one would remain "the" library in my mind.

The librarian unlocked the Carolina Collection room and showed me more on gold mining than I could read at one sitting. Large-scale strip mines on reopened veins in Lancaster and Kershaw counties and a new operation in Fairfield County had been operating in South Carolina for at least two decades. Other than a few roadside operations farther into the North Carolina mountains where tourists panned for gold or gemstones, no commercial gold-mining activity had existed in these mountains since the Civil War.

Gemstone deposits were more common in North Carolina. Even day-trippers had unearthed rubies, sapphires, quartz, and emeralds of news-reportable size. A magazine article detailed one man's zealous search, farther east around the North Carolina Piedmont town of Hiddenite, a particularly rich mineral region. His persistence had paid off when he discovered an eighty-carat emerald, the first of many lush finds on his property. But again, no articles mentioned any major gemstone veins or finds in the mountains around Dacus.

After the 1799 discovery of a seventeen-pound gold nugget on the Reed farm near Charlotte, the whole region went crazy. A United States mint had to be built in Charlotte to handle the gold that was carried out of North and South Carolina, but the mint didn't last long after the California strike proved richer. Historically, gemstone and gold mining here had been small stuff, from small veins—as Rudy had said, mostly farmers supplementing their crops and filling in time with a pickax along a quartz vein or, more often, a pan in a stream.

When the librarian—a young woman with rich, waist-length brown hair—politely shoved me out the door at closing time, I still didn't know why Lionel Shoal was so bent on obtaining those mineral rights. He either knew something several hundred years' worth of hill folks hadn't found, or he was an idiot who thought that shallow crack in the rock hid the Lost Treasury of the Confederacy and the locals had been too stupid to find it.

I strolled the few blocks back to the office. The lights were on upstairs in Melvin's apartment. I had no reason to go back in my office, so I headed up the mountain to my little cabin.

The winding road was fun, though I didn't push it too fast—hitting a deer, or a whole herd of them, was a real risk this time of year. Cars and people don't always survive those meetings. Not too good for the deer, either.

As I drove along the two ruts that lead through the woods, I realize that, somewhere in the last few months, I'd stopped constantly referring to the cabin as "my grandfather's cabin." He'd built it both as a retreat and as a gathering place. He'd come here to write and think, but also for picnics and barbecues when he called together his family: my parents, his younger sisters Aletha, Hattie, and Vinnia, various friends. He'd built it close enough to town that everyone could drive home after the festivities, and he'd built it small, so few people presumed they could stay. I'd often spent the night, after those picnics, tucked up in the loft under the eaves, listening through the soffit to the wind blow whispers through the evergreens and oaks outside.

Now, with Emma the only child and most of the family too busy to spend time canoeing or fishing or playing horseshoes, we usually gathered at my parents' or great-aunts' houses in town rather than here. So it had returned to my grandfather's original purpose, a retreat. Part of me would be content to stay here forever.

As I unlocked the door, I glanced up at the loft, the ladder still propped in place. I needed to bring Emma here. I doubted she'd ever stayed in the loft, but she was the kind of kid who would appreciate it.

To feed my nostalgia, I popped some popcorn in the unnostalgic but convenient microwave, settled on the cracked leather sofa, and started flipping through one of my grandfather's thick bound journals. He'd kept several, and I kept finding them in odd places— tucked in his old desk or behind some dusty *Reader's Digest* magazines in the cabin or in a dresser.

At first, reading what he'd written had been guilt-tinged. But then I realized, Granddad was a deliberate man. He could have gathered his journals all in one place, or he could have destroyed them. Everyone could've found them, or no one. Instead, he'd scattered them about, not buried, just not displayed. Somehow it felt as though he'd left a trail of bread crumbs. For one particular bird?

On occasion, in a ruminating mood, I would randomly pull one out. The faint odor of his pipe tobacco lingered in this volume, perhaps because some flecks had sifted into the seams. In this sofa, with dusk closed in, his words felt as though he'd come back for a visit.

Had to get up in front of Judge Mabry today and argue with a straight face that the Grubie boys should be let out on bail and that they'd pledged to quit cooking liquor. The bail request wasn't funny, but their pledge was, and the judge knew it.

They still refuse to tell where their still is. Their story—to me and everybody else—is that they bought that truckload of corn liquor off "some ol' boys" up in Bear Wallow Cove. Can't tell us who those ol' boys are. Even the bailiff was grinning like a mule eating briars at the thought of a Grubie buying liquor off somebody when they got one of the proudest shine traditions in these hills. I don't know what made Judge Mabry maddest, them refusing to tell about the still or the high-speed chase. As high speed as you can get in a Model A Ford truck rattling full of quart jars. Come to think of it, it was probably the part when they took off from the traffic light with the deputy riding the running board and clinging on for dear life that got to Judge Mabry. Wouldn't have been as funny if somebody'd gotten hurt, but nobody did and what a picture that must have been. In the hallway later, the judge laughed until he had tears on his cheeks. Too little opportunity for such mirth in his job, I'm sure.

Have been reading about a fellow—a lawyer—who came from Tennessee to log this part of the country around the turn of the century. He got tired of starving doing title searches. I almost laughed aloud. How many lawyers have relied on—and despised—title work? Most of the young fellows have assistants who do that now. But do any of them get to practice law in the way they thought they would when they set out on their course?

The photos showed trees in the upper reaches of the Chattooga—immense beyond imagination. A man leaned back against an old-growth poplar, eclipsed by the trunk—gave me

*pause. I'd heard tales of logging throughout the Southern Ap-
palachians. Needed lumber to feed growth—homes, factories,
mansions in Charleston, ships, everything the post–Civil War
wrought. I'd read about destructive clear-cutting, erosion—the
reason they started planting that damnable kudzu vine that's
overtaken everything it can reach. I'd never somehow seen what
we'd lost. Never really <u>seen</u> it. Massive trees, beyond imagination. Gone.*

*We never know how to move by half measures. We're
watching a shell game, certain that we've got our eye on the
thing we want until the shell is lifted, and we find what we
want still hidden behind what we thought we had.*

I wondered if the book with the tree pictures he'd been reading
was still here, or at my great-aunts' house. Or in a box in my office.
Funny he should mention title search work, when I'd been thinking
about the need to develop my lawyering-staple skills.

I put the journal down on the trunk that served as a coffee table.
It was making me think too much. Before I climbed the ladder to
the loft, I picked up a new mystery I'd gotten at the library. Somebody else's puzzles and drama would be reassuring.

Tuesday Morning

Next morning, I stopped by Maylene's for a banana nut muffin and some ice tea—my caffeine of choice, even at breakfast. No sooner had I slid into the booth than Rudy Mellin came through the door.

"A'vry, you gotta get your own hangout. You're crowdin' me here." He hesitated before he slid into the booth across from me. He twisted sideways, one leg stretched out across the booth seat. It dawned on me he'd rather be sitting in my seat, facing the door in good gunslinger style. Too bad. He should get here earlier.

"How's the sheriffing bid'ness?"

"What the hell's happened around here? Like ever'body's possessed by aliens or something." Rudy shook his head, studying the menu, though Maylene's breakfast offerings hadn't changed since the flyspecked windows were last washed. "We got a dead guy crammed in a gold mine and a woman dead at home that—Lord, I don't even want to think about that one. Quite a death spree around here, I can tell you."

"The woman dead at home, that the one you got a call about yesterday? On Liberty Street?"

The waitress joined us, and he ordered the same breakfast I'd always seen him order: coffee, three eggs over easy, bacon and sausage, buttered white toast, and grits.

"So?" I prompted him after the waitress left.

Rudy's big frame shuddered, and he lost his usual seen-it-all air for a moment. I got the sense he'd hoped I wouldn't ask, but, at the same time, he wanted to talk about it. "I tell you, that was one to give you nightmares. You remember that meningitis scare back in elementary school? They said get to the doctor if your neck started hurting and ol' Curtis what's-his-name said the spinal meningitis made your back bow up and your neck bend backwards 'til it broke and you died and we all believed him?"

I didn't remember all those details, but third-grade girls usually weren't privy to the elaborate and gruesome imaginings of boys. Sounded like the boys might have been confusing meningitis with tetanus. I just nodded.

"That's what she looked like, all stiffened up. She'd been throwing up all over the place and hadn't made it to the pot. And her face. Gawdamighty, I can't get it out of my head. Grinning like something in a bad fright movie. There she lay on the living room sofa, reeking of vomit with that frozen fright face."

"Who was she?"

"Suse Knight."

I hadn't really expected to know her.

"She was a nurse. Did those in-home physicals for insurance companies and such," he added in case it might awaken a connection or recognition for me. It didn't.

"Who found her?"

"Her husband came home from work. God help him, I wouldn't want to have that seared in my brain if I was him. He thought she'd been strangled or something. I didn't tell him that somebody strangled, with a purple face and a black tongue lolled out, looks a helluva lot better than his wife did. And I've never known one to throw up. Jeez."

That was a lot more detail than I needed with my banana nut muffin. "So you think somebody strangled her?"

He shrugged. "The ME's got it, so we might get some idea later today, maybe tomorrow. Depends on how weird things are in the rest of the state this week. That looked like a bad way to go. Real bad. Just hope I don't ever see another one."

"Say, you don't think it was meningitis, do you? Isn't that stuff highly contagious?" I was kidding him, but his eyes opened wide. I was suddenly reminded of crew-cut little Rudy Mellin in the third grade.

"I really don't think you have anything to worry about." I tried to backtrack and reassure him.

He nodded, but he still had a worry wrinkle between his eyebrows. Wherever that Curtis kid went after the third grade, I hope he decided to do something productive with his powerful storytelling skills; if the horror could last this long, look out, Stephen King.

"What about the guy in the gold mine?" I changed the subject. "What happened there?"

"A'vry, you know I can't be talking about open investigations."

That usually meant he didn't know much. I started to say, *Swell, I'll just ask Cissie Prentice.* Instead, I took another tack. "How are Jesse and her mom taking it?"

"Befuddled, I'd say. Miz Ruffin seems confused by it all. In shock, I guess. L.J. thinks it's odd she doesn't cry. From what I hear, she had reason not to cry, with him gone. I sure don't see how she got him off up there in that hole and shot him, if she's the one that did it."

"Ever have any domestic calls or complaints from the Ruffins?"

He shook his head. "Nope. Nothing but gossip about 'em."

I had finished my muffin and tea when the waitress slid two heaping plates in front of Rudy. I scooted out of the booth. "Better be getting to work, I reckon." I had likely gotten all the good information out of Deputy Mellin.

Rudy just nodded, intent now on his eggs and pork products.

As soon as I stepped out Maylene's door, a buzzing rush of noise shoved me back against the plate glass window. I hit the glass with such a crack, I feared I'd shattered it. What had attacked me? Killer bees? A blitz mugging?

A motor scooter. On the sidewalk. It wobbled to a stop three storefronts down. The passenger and the driver, both sporting pumpkin-orange helmets, stared back over their shoulders at me. The driver towered over his passenger, and I couldn't figure out how the two of them fit on such a tiny bike.

Still straddling the scooter, the driver lifted the handlebars so the front wheel cleared the ground. The passenger, with a squeal of panic, grabbed the driver, her legs flying out to either side to keep from falling off. He walked the bike around, wobbling from one foot to the other, until it was aimed right at me. Ready to take another run at me.

Then he waved. A goofy, elbows-akimbo kindergarten wave I knew well.

"Hey, A'vry!" The face crammed into the orange helmet crinkled in a grin.

Donlee Griggs.

"Hey, Donlee," I called back, hoping he would stay put and wouldn't try to get close enough for a conversation.

"We're ridin' around." He cocked his thumb toward his passenger. I swear his chest swelled with pride.

"I see that, Donlee." His passenger's orange helmet tilted and she peered around him. I couldn't make out her features, just that she was tiny and she was a girl. "You all have fun."

His orange helmet bobbed. Donlee with a girlfriend.

He revved the bike, and I almost ducked back into Maylene's door. Not that I wanted to endanger innocent bystanders. He might choose to follow me inside to continue our chat.

Donlee and his woman must have had other plans. He lifted the handlebars and waddled the little bike around toward his original destination. His girlfriend held on tight, her helmet mashed up against his back.

In an impressive cloud of blue smoke, the little scooter buzzed down the sidewalk like an angry bee, the two pumpkin heads solidly aboard.

Movement inside Maylene's caught the corner of my eye. The entire populace had gathered at the front window, craning for a view of my close encounter. Rudy was grinning, but had the decency to look a bit sheepish. The rest were laughing their heads off.

Good to be home. I knew my face was flushed with embarrassment, but all I could do was give the crowd an exaggerated shrug. Got to have a sense of humor.

As I walked away, I felt oddly sad. Donlee had found another object for his affections. The big dumb goof had trailed me around in high school. After I'd been away in school and practicing law for over a decade, Donlee had welcomed me home in November with a series of embarrassing stunts designed to win my attention and affection. At the time, half the town had turned out for the festivities and I'd felt like a fool. Now that he had a girlfriend and matching pumpkin helmets, I was struck that even Donlee Griggs had a love life while I had none. What did that say?

From Maylene's, I decided to walk the four blocks around to the post office and back to the office. Getting enough exercise hadn't been easy since I'd moved to Dacus.

I exchanged nods and casual pleasantries with post office patrons, some I recognized but none I knew. It surprised me how many people I recognized though I couldn't put names to the faces. Was my memory going bad? Or did I just think I remembered them?

As I strolled toward the junior high football stadium, I opened some envelopes. A bill for the office phone installation. I probably should have stuck with my cell phone and voice mail. Junk mail. A continuing legal education brochure.

I stopped dead in my tracks when I pulled out an envelope addressed to Miss Avery Andrews, Attorney at Law. In spidery cobalt blue ink.

I carefully slit the top open with my thumbnail and pulled out the thick sheet.

Dear Miss Andrews,

Your family has long set a standard for decorous behavior in Dacus. I'm surprised none of your family has not seen fit to advise you against your current path, but you should know that many in town question your judgment and even your morals.

Establishing your office alongside Melvin Bertram—and in the same house where he has chosen to reside—has raised eyebrows. You should realize what this flouting of convention may mean for your business here, regardless of how they choose to do things in the lower part of the state.

You need to remember that people are watching.

A friend.

The two-inch square of newspaper, carefully clipped and decoupaged to the lower right-hand corner, was an advice column about suspected high jinks between two coworkers, titled "Where There's Smoke?"

Even in the sun and wearing my wool sweater, I shivered. How dare—whoever. A friend. I wanted to stomp up and down on it. Or ball it up and pitch it in the woods. What a creepy, sneaky, disgusting thing.

I stood stock-still in the middle of the post office access road, and a car turning into the post office had to drive around me. She waved and kept driving. Nobody else was paying me the least attention. That has always been one of Dacus's most appealing traits: It was a live-and-let-live kind of place. Certainly not a place where somebody sends creepy letters rather than tell you directly—or indirectly, through careful comments to a parent or a friend. For Pete's sake, anyone could've gone to Aunt Letha and hinted that she should set me straight.

On second thought, anybody who knew Aunt Letha would hesitate to approach her with complaints about me. She might iron out the kinks in the message bearer before she turned her attentions to me. Not even Aunt Letha—or Hattie or Vinnia, for that matter—had said anything to me about setting up practice next to Melvin's office. So who was this letter writer to take sneaky shots at me?

I wanted to crumple the nasty thing up in a ball, but my lawyerly respect for evidence made me fold it carefully back in its envelope with one last shiver.

I marched off toward the office, threw the mail in the passenger seat of my car, and kept walking. I needed to burn off some of the adrenaline the anonymous letter had created.

Why did it make my skin crawl? Was it because it wasn't signed? Or because someone lumped me and Cissie Prentice in the same questionable-morals class? It was only a stupid letter. Just stop thinking about it, I told myself.

I forced my mind to Maggy Avinger's problem. I needed to come up with a workable solution that didn't involve selling her house to pay for that beautiful piece of idiocy. It really was a work of art. Harden Avinger didn't deserve that angel bowed prayerfully over his grave. By the same token, Maggy Avinger didn't deserve to be accused of his murder.

I turned at the gas station and walked toward North Main and my great-aunts' house. Where had Harden Avinger gotten the cash for that sculpture? Apparently Carlton Barner had the funds in escrow, ready to pay Innis Barker. The price tag was eye-popping, while his wife was left digging in the sofa cushions for spare change. Had he taken all their savings to lavish on himself—and to torment her? What a wonderful marriage she let herself stay trapped in.

I crunched along the heavy coating of pecan and acorn shells in front of Harrison Garnet's house. The squirrels had fed well from the massive oaks in Harrison's yard. I kept my eyes focused on the sidewalk. Something I'd read in Granddad's journal danced around the edges of my brain, had teased me as I fell asleep last night. Something that seemed to point to a solution. Then again, I sometimes dream I'm flying and I haven't yet lifted off the ground.

Innis Barker had paid for the sculpture but wouldn't get the final two-thirds of the payment until he'd engraved the poem on the statue and installed it. He had to engrave it and install it.

. . . *find what we want hidden behind what we thought we had*. A shell game. That was it. I walked faster, almost hopping. That was it. I knew how to bring the angel peacefully to earth—behind what we thought we had.

Midday Tuesday

I hadn't been able to talk directly with Carlton Barner, Harden Avinger's executor, but I'd miraculously managed to get an appointment with him for tomorrow afternoon, despite the animosity Lou Wray, his receptionist, had harbored for me when I'd first returned to Dacus. In November, Carlton had graciously offered me space in his office, but Mrs. Wray never felt as charitable about me intruding on their well-ordered office life. Now that I was safely six blocks away in the old mortuary, she'd grown more tolerant.

I paid some bills and stared at the boxes surrounding me. How to organize things when I didn't know what was in each box until I unpacked it? My grandfather's old library would be useful but, more important, it would be reassuring to have around. If I could ever get it on the shelves.

I could just unbox the books and stack them so I could see what I had, measure them, clean them, and find the right space in the two rooms of bookcases. Much simpler than what I'd been doing: putting them on the shelves, then shifting them around when I uncovered missing volumes in other boxes.

As I grabbed my box cutter with renewed resolve, the phone rang.

"Miz Andrews? This is Carl Newland Knight. Miz Maggy Avinger said to call you, said I should talk to you."

"Yessir?"

"I'm not sure what about. Just to see if you think I should do something."

"Yessir?" So much better to do your warm-up before you dial, isn't it?

"My wife . . . died. And the sheriff took me downtown, to ask me some questions. Because it was suspicious."

"Mr. Knight, if you could start at the beginning?" Hearing that his wife had just died made me feel guilty for my impatience.

"We-ell, I come home and my wife was in the den and she was dead. She had, um, been sick. All over the place. Her face looked . . . bad." The last words, he almost whispered.

Dear Lord. The woman on Liberty Street.

"The sheriff questioned you?"

"Yes'm."

"That's standard procedure in an . . . unattended death."

"Yes'm. I thought so. But . . . seemed like her questions went, um, maybe weren't so standard. I got worried."

"Not standard in what way?"

"Miz Avinger thought I should talk to you, after she heard."

"About the sheriff's questions?"

He paused, the phone silent. "Sheriff seemed to think my wife was . . . killed. She seemed to think I . . . done it. Or had something to do with it."

I wasn't sure whether the hesitation in his voice was just his way of talking or if he was having trouble talking about what had happened to his wife. From the horror scene Rudy had described, anyone would have trouble dealing with it.

"Did Sheriff Peters come right out and accuse you?"

"We-ell, no. But her questions . . ."

"Sometimes that's just her way of testing you, really seeing what you know."

Silence. "Good. I'm really sorry . . . I bothered you. Miz Avinger thought you wouldn't mind."

"No bother at all, Mr. Knight. Please don't hesitate to call, especially if Sheriff Peters has any more questions. Okay? You don't have to answer anything you don't want to, you know."

"Yes'm." He sounded uncertain. I'd seen L. J. Peters in action. I knew why he sounded uncertain, but I couldn't in good conscience offer to rush to his defense. If he hired a lawyer at this stage, L. J. would believe he had something to hide. Then she really would make trouble for him.

"Okay, then."

Poor guy. What a mess, in more ways than one.

I unpacked books the remainder of the morning. When my stomach started a faint growling, I started to make a peanut butter and jelly sandwich, but the bread looked lightly green. For lack of a quick alternative, I walked back down the street to Maylene's. I'd missed the lunch rush, so I had my pick of booths. Feeling in a healthy mood, I ordered vegetable beef soup and some corn bread, which I crumbled into the thick soup to sop up the grease that floated on top.

I ate, idly watching customers drift in and out the front door.

"Excuse me for interrupting."

A bosomy woman in tight pants and a low-cut leopard-print blouse put her hand on the table to get my attention. "Do you mind?"

Before I could respond, Lionel Shoal's wife slid into the booth and touched her not-really-blond hair to make sure the mousse still held it in place. Her creased makeup and false eyelashes completed a look that managed to look cheap, but not for lack of money.

She stuck her handful of fingernails across the table by way of introduction. "I'm Valerie Shoal. Lionel Shoal's wife. Maybe you've heard of him."

"Yes, ma'am, I have."

She nodded, pleased. "I think Lionel needs some legal advice, and I hear you're a good one to ask, that you're knowledgeable about environmental laws and all that." She waved her pale pink nails around.

I hesitated. Lionel Shoal didn't act like somebody I'd want as a client, but how picky could I be right now? I hadn't always liked the clients I'd defended in my past life. It wouldn't hurt to talk to him, at which time either of us could decide it wouldn't work. Besides, I was more than a little curious.

"If your husband has questions, he can just call me. I don't have any cards." I patted my jacket pocket as if I thought a card had appeared there, even though I hadn't had any printed yet. "But—"

"He refuses to do that. I need you to come with me to see him."

"Miz Shoal, I really can't—"

"I'm sure you know all about the explosion at Golden Cove. That's my husband's development. They can't figure out what happened, and since they can't find anyone else to blame, they're looking at him. All kinds of people are climbing over each other, investigating that explosion. I'm afraid he's in big trouble and isn't smart enough to know it."

"Miz Shoal, I'm not at all sure your husband will want to talk with me. The last time—"

"Nonsense. I hear you're the only one in town for this." She leaned across the table, insistent. "I've got a lot riding on the success of this project. In a way, it's my development, too. I've got money in this, and I don't want to get screwed over just because he's too cheap to get himself a lawyer."

Framed by fake eyelashes, her eyes were steely and no-nonsense. She glanced at my empty soup bowl. "Can you come now? I'll pay you for your time."

My first paying client of the week. Today was what, Tuesday?

"Miz Shoal, I'll talk to your husband, at your request, but only if you're the one paying the bill."

"You'll be paid." She drew up in a huff.

"No, ma'am. I'm not worried about being paid, but I can't appear to be soliciting your husband's business. I'm not allowed to do that."

She looked puzzled—and still a little huffy. "Do you want a check now?"

"I'll be happy to send you a bill—"

"Let's go, then. He's at home right now. With his office blown to bits, he's underfoot at the house. I'll take you."

I insisted on walking back to the office to get my car. I didn't want to be stranded somewhere. She circled the block and parked her Mercedes sedan in front of my office, waiting on me to pull out and follow her.

The Shoals had bought—or rented—a house at the lake, about ten miles from Dacus. My house hunting hadn't taken me in that direction; I figured it was out of my price range, and I don't play golf, tennis, or bridge, or hang out at nineteenth holes.

Valerie Shoal parked in the circular drive in front of a rambling stone and glass giant that sat alone on a promontory overlooking the lake. Must be a lot of steps down to the boat landing from here, though neither of the Shoals struck me as water skiers or bass fishing enthusiasts.

I walked up to her car as she stuck first one slender stiletto heel, then another, out her car door.

"He's home," she said, indicating the dusty black Cadillac SUV in the drive. "You can talk some sense into him." She clicked across the slate sidewalk ahead of me and unlocked the castle-sized front door.

The view swept from the entry hall out the wall of windows and across the lake to the distant hills. Maybe I needed to expand my house-hunting range. And my budget. With a rich developer for a client, a place like this might become an option.

"Lionel! Lionel, are you home, honey? I've brought somebody to meet you." She stood in the foyer, listening. "He's down in the TV room. Men. Where else? Come on."

She clattered across the slate foyer to a descending stairway. "Come on, come on. This way."

I'd let her find him. I didn't want to surprise him in his lair. Last time I'd seen Lionel Shoal up close, he'd been almost purple-faced, grabbing my arm and ordering the lot of us off his property.

"Lionel! I brought someone who knows about environmental stuff." Her voice grew a bit fainter, but not less shrill. "You need to talk to her. Lionel, for god's sake, answer me. I know you can hear me fine. That deaf act—"

Her scream set a decibel record.

I froze, startled for a split second before I rushed down the stairs.

She stood in a doorway, screaming. I didn't need to walk over to the chocolate-brown suede sofa to know Lionel Shoal didn't need my help. Or anybody else's.

The smell of vomit was overpowering. Shoal, his lips pulled back into a fright-mask grimace, was rigid, his back arched like he was trying to levitate off the supersize sofa.

Valerie kept screaming and screaming. After a moment, I turned her by the shoulders and shook her. Her head bobbled. I thought I would have to slap her, but then she quit, settling instead into a persistent but less earsplitting keen.

I led her into the hallway, hoping she'd calm down absent the sight—and the smell.

"Can you call the police?" I asked.

She kept up a low mewing sound.

"Where's the phone?" I shook her arm, more gently this time. That hit her off button, but she still didn't answer. With my arm around her waist, I led her upstairs to the panoramic view of the lake. She and the stilettos were too tall for me to steer easily.

I sat her on another bigger-than-life sofa and got her to lie down. With no cozy afghan or throw in sight, I covered her up with my jacket and went in search of a phone.

Any phone was probably artfully disguised as a knickknack or hidden in some remote-controlled recess. Finally, I found the kitchen. A wall phone, in plain sight, thank goodness.

I called the direct number for the sheriff's office, reported a dead body, and suggested that Sheriff Peters would want to come in person, along with an ambulance. Bypassing 911 might keep the announcement off the scanners and away from the Ghouly Boys, those ambulance followers who have nothing better to do than show up at car accidents, crime scenes—and explosions. I ignored my own recent entry—and Melvin's—into Ghouly Boy-dom.

Valerie was still on the sofa, staring wide-eyed at the ceiling, immobile but breathing, judging from the rise and fall of her ample chest underneath my jacket. Was she going into shock? I needed to find her something a little warmer.

I went back downstairs, where all the bedrooms seemed to be. I also had to admit to a specific curiosity, something that hadn't fully registered when I first saw it. I'd already been to the door, so one more visit wouldn't further contaminate the scene.

In Shoal's den, heavy red velvet drapes hid the windows overlooking the lake. The billboard-sized television, with the sound turned low, hosted news-channel talking heads. A quick glance at the carpet confirmed what I thought I'd seen but hadn't really understood.

Chocolate candies dotted the floor beside the sofa. Some had escaped their ruffled brown papers and rolled across the deep blue carpet. Without stepping through the doorway for a closer look, I could see what looked like the corner of a red candy box under the edge of the sofa. A greeting card illustrated with a bright bouquet of flowers lay on the end table close to the doorway: *Congratulations.* Otherwise, the room was bare of decoration. A miniature movie theater, set up for nothing but watching the large TV.

His grin, like an animal baring its teeth. I wanted to put something over his face, out of respect. Too late to get that out of my head, though.

The same vomit smell, the same contortions Rudy had described at the Knights' house. What in heaven's name? Seeing it a second time didn't make it any less horrifying.

Was it tetanus? Meningitis? Was some deadly contagion spreading across Dacus? Had L.J. thought to call the Centers for Disease Control in Atlanta? That was probably the medical examiner's prerogative. Could it have been poison? That seemed melodramatic. More likely a seizure, maybe a drug reaction. What would make someone suffer like that?

In a guest room down the hall, I pulled the puffy down comforter off one of the twin beds. Back upstairs, as I tucked it around Valerie, she blinked her eyes.

"Can I get you something?"

She blinked slowly. "In my purse."

She'd left her purse on the entry table. The cloisonné pill box was easy to find and held only one kind of pill. I got her some water, then I sat in a chair nearby and waited.

The cavalry took its time arriving. I watched afternoon shadows deepening the hollows on the hills across the lake and tried to think of anything other than what lay downstairs.

Tuesday Afternoon

I went outside to greet the emergency medical techs—an unbelievably overweight fellow and a red-headed pixie woman named El—as they climbed out of their truck.

He huffed as he lifted a giant kit from the side storage on the truck and asked, "Where are they?"

"Only one needs your attention," I said as I held the front door open for them.

I expected them to tell me to blow it out my civilian, watch-too-much-TV ear with a roll of their eyes and a full-scale rush into the crime scene to try to save Lionel Shoal. They didn't. While her partner lumbered up the long flight of front steps, El ran ahead, down the stairs and, just as quickly, was back.

"No need to mess up that scene," she said to her partner as he labored through the front door. El crossed the slate floor to the sofa and bent to assess Valerie Shoal, still huddled under the comforter. Valerie started crying as soon as El spoke to her.

The male tech, who didn't have a name badge sewn on his shirt, radioed someone. El ripped the Velcro fastener on the blood pressure cuff and lifted Valerie's arm. I waited by the front door for the cops, counting the minutes until I could escape.

I didn't know either of the first sheriff's deputies to arrive. A squint-eyed deputy—his gold name badge said T. MYERS—had to see for himself what was downstairs. He hustled back upstairs and dispatched the younger officer to ring the front of the house with crime scene tape.

"We'll handle this one as a suspicious death until someone tells us otherwise," he pronounced. He looked a little green around the gills, but he went outside, pulled a video camera from the trunk of his car, and began narrating as he walked back into the house, leaving me to play maitre d' at the front door.

The next car to arrive was driven by Sheriff L.J. Peters herself. I descended the broad front steps to meet her. She took her time getting out of the car—checking her lipstick in the rearview mirror? Doubtful. As always, when she emerged, she reflexively checked the implements hanging from her belt.

"Well. If it idn't A'vry Andrews. I mighta known."

L.J. sauntered around the front of her car, her hand resting on the butt of her gun like a Wild West gunslinger sizing up a dusty street.

"L.J." I said. I'd started to call her Lucinda Jane, for old times' sake, but that's what had always prompted her to pound me in grade school.

"How'd you end up here?" Her eyes narrowed.

"Mrs. Shoal ran into me at lunch, asked if I'd come talk to her husband."

"About?"

"A legal matter."

L.J. snorted. "I just bet he had a legal matter. He's got feds crawling up his ass and out his nose. I bet he's got a legal matter."

When I didn't respond, she asked, "So? Then what?"

"I followed her out here and we found him. Dead."

"That's convenient, how she managed to find you so you could he'p her find the body."

I wasn't going to let on to L.J., but that had crossed my mind. "Come on, Sheriff. She didn't expect to find him. She's genuinely in shock."

"So what happened? A heart attack or something? He commit suicide?"

I shook my head, trying to choose my words carefully. I didn't want to let slip anything that hinted I knew what the scene at Suse Knight's house had looked like—anything that would get Rudy Mellin in trouble or make him stop talking to me. I simply told her what we'd found downstairs.

L.J.'s eyebrows shot up as soon as I described the rictus grin, but she didn't say anything. She recognized the similarities. She reached to lift the yellow tape that now blocked the entrance to the front steps. I wondered where all these deputies had learned about running the two-stage perimeters I'd seen them use first at the explosion and now here. Camden County must be coughing up some money for training.

"Excuse me, Sheriff." The deputy who'd run the tape and now stood guard at the edge of the broad, sweeping staircase, grabbed the tape so L.J. couldn't lift it high enough to step under. "I'm sorry, but Officer Myers hasn't finished the preliminary video inside—"

L.J.'s expression seared the words shut in his mouth.

"I'm the sheriff."

"Yes, sir—ma'am. But—"

"But what?" L.J. barked.

The poor kid was just trying to do what he'd been taught: protect the scene, even from your superior officers and the politicians who set your salary raise pool. Now he was learning what only experience can teach: who's the boss.

L.J. ducked under and let the yellow tape drop back into place behind her.

"Sheriff," I said, "is it okay if I go now? I didn't touch anything but the door knob and the phone. If they need prints or a statement or anything, you know where to find me." I'd been fingerprinted when I applied to sit for the bar exam, so I assumed my prints were still on file. It was easier to be helpful.

We locked eyes a moment, then she shrugged.

"Give the dep'ty here a statement." *Dep'ty* dripped with sarcasm. "I do know where to find you."

The rookie deputy looked disapproving of my reprieve, but he pulled out his notepad and took down my answers to his questions: where had I gone inside, what had I touched. He wrote everything. Slowly. I kept my answers short. He soon ran out of questions, much to his frustration.

I gave him my phone number and my office address. "Near the courthouse on Main Street, down the street from all the other lawyers," I said to reassure him that I was easy to find.

I left, grateful to be gone. I couldn't quite get the smell of vomit out of my nostrils or that tortured grin from my mind. I felt guilty leaving Valerie alone, but she had gone to sleep, snoring softly, before L.J. arrived. Sitting around felt like a death watch. I'd let L.J. do what she gets paid to do, and Valerie knew how to reach me if she needed me.

Numb from the adrenaline and the raw emotion, I didn't want to take the direct route home. I turned onto the road that wound around the lake. I would just drive. As had become my habit, I studied the houses and tried the neighborhood on for size. The lake had been flooded thirty or so years ago by the power company, to cool its nuclear reactors. For a time, T-shirts proclaiming I'M FROM CAMDEN COUNTY, I GLOW IN THE DARK were all the rage. At the time, according to Dad, locals couldn't believe any idiot would pay $1,500 for a lot on a red-mud-banked lake when good farmland was going for a couple of hundred dollars for a full acre. Now the lots were worth hundreds of times the investment, and the houses with their multi-peaked roofs and massive expanses of glass were still inconceivable to most of the locals.

The lake development had attracted snowbirds, retirees from up north who nested much to themselves, with occasional forays to Dacus grocery stores and to the *Clarion*'s letters-to-the-editor page.

Locals could afford to come here and fish, though the cost of a six-person motorboat was a major expense for many of them. Most who skimmed the deep blue water in speedboats had no idea they flew over watery graves and the once-great capital of the Cherokee Indians. I'd grown up knowing about the controversy sparked by damming the Keowee River, but I was too young to have known the deep green valley buried under the water. I'd known nothing but this lake and only stories of the families, including ancestors of mine, who'd settled and farmed the valley for generations. No sense of nostalgia tugged at me as I drove past the houses, and nothing here felt like a possibility of home for me.

The road back to the main highway was curvy and empty of traffic, so I hit the accelerator. Speed would blow carbon out of my carburetor and maybe the numbness from my brain.

A deputy's car, running too far over the centerline, met me in a curve. Both of us jerked our steering wheels sharply right, and I kept moving, not giving him a glance.

In my rearview mirror, I saw him do a one-eighty in the road and come up behind me fast, his blue lights flashing.

What was happening around here these days? All these road patrols. For Pete's sake. I pulled to a stop on the first side road and fished for my driver's license.

To my surprise, Rudy Mellin climbed out and marched to my window.

Both hands on my car roof, he leaned down to face me. "What'd I tell you 'bout slowing it down?"

I smiled, I hoped winsomely. "Sorry."

"Let me see your license."

I handed it to him, very politely. He carried it back to his car.

I waited a beat, then crawled out and strolled back to his patrol car. Should I beg? Show some dignity? Punch him? I swallowed the bit of irrational anger I felt.

"Come on, Rudy. You aren't really going to give me a ticket."

Rudy had his head bowed, studying the screen on his little on-board computer. After too long, he tilted his head up, eyeing me from under the broad brim of his hat. "Checking your priors, Miz Andrews."

I wasn't going to humor him by begging—or tick him off by pointing out he had been driving over the white line.

He handed my license back to me. "And having a good laugh at your license photo."

I didn't rise to the bait. "Headed to the Shoal house?" Not even worrying about my insurance premiums had distracted me from the images I'd been trying to outrun.

"That where you been?"

I nodded.

"I'm not in too much of a hurry, if it's what I think it is."

"Trust me, it's exactly what you think it is." We both were quiet a moment, each with sobering images in mind.

"Any idea what killed that lady you found yesterday?" I asked, still hoping for some explanation that wouldn't make it so scary.

He shook his head. "Autopsy's not finished yet, far as I know. Took her to Newberry for that one."

He sat with one leg out the door, his body half-turned in the seat. I propped my fanny against the rear door of his car, and we studied the trees and the red-mud road bank opposite us in a companionable silence for a moment.

"Did you all track down the saucy lead on that dynamite you were chasing?"

"Jeez. You wouldn't b'lieve that one. 'Bout the time I think I've seen it all."

"They the ones that blew up Shoal's office?"

"Naw. Dynamite was used, but no connection with these two. Hard to b'lieve how much dynamite is wandering around loose. Strictly bush league, this bunch. Her boyfriend wanted a stick or two to go fishing. Nowhere near enough to blow up those two houses."

"You're not joking."

"Wish I was. Wanted to take it up to the lake, get a whole bunch'a fish at once."

"This was worth selling her virtue?"

"Virtue?" He snorted. "She had method to her madness. Seems her boyfriend spends all his time fishing. She figured if he'd get the fishing done faster, he'd have more time to spend with her. Don't you hate it when they start figuring."

"Romantic fish dinners at the lake? Movies from the video store? Wow."

Rudy gave another sharp snort. "Naw. She wanted sex. Seems he was always too busy fishin' or too tired from fishin' and not interested enough in foolin' around."

"She traded sex for dynamite . . . so she could have sex." And these people can vote and have children.

He shook his head. "Good thing for him she didn't get her hands on a couple of sticks. Sooner or later, he'd've ended up with it lit under his house trailer, whatcha bet?"

I could only shake my head. "So what else you been doing?" He knew I meant *How'd you missed being first on the scene at the Shoal house of horrors?*

"Chasin' that gahdam pig."

"Catch him?"

He shook his head. "This is what my life's come to."

"Comedy. Drama. That pretty much sums up life. Sounds like you've got it all." I smiled down at him. He wasn't smiling back. "What's with the pig?"

He sighed. "Some lady spotted it, over behind the elementary school. So I went to check it out. Damn thing weighs prob'ly two hunnert pounds and moves like—I don't know what."

"A greased pig?"

Again with the look.

"So what's this pig doing that you all got to chase it down?"

"From the size of it, what it's doing is eating."

"Big, huh."

"Big as any hog you've ever seen."

"So why's it important to catch it?"

"Danged if I know. He ate greens outta one lady's winter garden. Mostly, though, he stays to hisself. Folks seem worried it'll freeze to death. He looks pretty well insulated to me."

"That'd be sad, though, if he froze to death."

"Not near as sad as grown men tearing through the bushes after a two-hunnert-pound pig that could set a land speed record at a greyhound track. That's what's sad."

Rudy and most of the other deputies weren't built for speed, but I refrained from comment on that.

"They waiting on you at the Shoal house?" Nice as it was to stand on the roadside shooting the breeze, one or both of us needed to get to work.

He sighed. "Not really. Everybody else already rushed up there."

"Including L.J."

"Best way to wreck a crime scene is to have one that needs studying."

"The rookie was trying."

"They always do." He swung his left leg into the patrol car and reached to pull the door shut. "Slow it down, okay? We don't need any more headline-making death scenes."

I saluted, but I didn't promise anything.

Tuesday Afternoon

I got back to the office intending to unpack more boxes, but the ringing phone gave me a reprieve from setting to work.

"Avery? Valerie Shoal." The voice on the other end was barely more than a whisper. "I've been lying here thinking. What happens if somebody dies without a will?"

Uh-oh. My brain crowded with responses, most of them uncharitable thoughts about a fresh widow whispering into the phone about her dead husband's will while the crime scene guys took photos downstairs.

"The state has rules that provide for distributing assets between spouse and children," I said.

"Like the wife?"

"Yes, ma'am."

"And any children he has?"

"Yes."

"So, like, if he's not divorced . . ."

"The wife and children split the assets, with the wife getting half." Even sedated, Valerie was all too aware of what was going on around her.

"Shit," she said, slow and slurred. The phone clicked off.

A real lawyer would calculate how many minutes that phone call had lasted, to tack them onto the bill. I still had trouble thinking in terms of operating in a businesslike manner. I also had sense enough to figure any bill sent to the Shoal residence now might be hard to collect on.

As I hung up the phone, I noticed the light blinking on my answering machine and punched the button.

"This message is for Avery Andrews. This is Tim McDonald. My organization has recently relocated to Camden County, and we're interested in obtaining legal counsel. We wanted to set up a meeting here at our headquarters at your earliest convenience. Please call."

I scribbled the number on the notepad beside the phone, thus far the only island of organization in my sea of uncertain transition.

Nice. A paying client. Someone with a headquarters instead of someone headquartered on a bar stool at Tap's Pool Room, from whence had come the few court-appointed, small-time criminal defense cases I'd handled since coming home.

I wasted no time dialing Tim McDonald's number. I waited through ten rings and was about to hang up when a husky, impatient voice answered.

"Hello." No receptionist's cheery greeting.

"Tim McDonald?"

"Yeah."

"This is Avery Andrews. You called my office?" Strange way to run a company headquarters.

"Yeah. Can you come here to meet with us? We may need a lawyer, to handle some things for us. We'd like to interview you."

Unconventional. Maybe a sensible way to make a decision about an important relationship, but also odd.

"Certainly, Mr. McDonald. When would be convenient—"

"Right now."

Past unconventional and odd to downright rude.

"No. That's not possible. I——"

"This afternoon?"

Was his rudeness born of urgency? Ignorance? Or was it just his style. "I could fit you in tomorrow afternoon. Where is your office located?"

"Office. That's a good one," he said. "Nothing so fancy. We're set up at the old Yellow Fork Camp. You know where that is?"

"Up on the mountain?" Somebody had to be playing a joke, but I didn't recognize the voice. "Mr. McDonald, you understand I charge by the hour for my time, including travel."

"See you when you get here."

My mouth was open, but I had no chance to pin the time down more precisely. He hung up.

What kind of business was he setting up at an abandoned summer camp? He didn't sound like the camp counselor type, but what made sense on that site except another summer camp? Gone were my visions of playing corporate counsel to a high-tech start-up or similar rising star. Instead I had an abrupt, barely communicative guy with a hick drawl and few social skills. Probably didn't have enough business savvy to know he should come in to a lawyer's office. Lucky for him, I didn't have enough to do to turn down a paying client—and I planned to go up the mountain to my cabin tomorrow anyway.

I couldn't get that dim, dark-blue room out of my mind. That face, Shoal's body rigid in an electrocuted pose, like a tortured wax museum creature. Things like that just don't happen in a small town. That refrain kept echoing, things like that don't happen. Except in books.

I wandered through my two office rooms, trying to focus. Mindless physical labor would help. The leather and the weight of each volume I found unexpectedly reassuring, carrying with it predictability and precedent.

Before I could cut into another taped box, the phone rang again. I almost didn't answer, fearing it might be another call from a slightly sedated Valerie Shoal.

"Avery? Maggy Avinger. I've been going through some things here at the house. Last thing you need, settling into a new place, is more junk, but I found a few things you might enjoy. Some books, a couple of snapshots of your grandfather, and a table for your new prayer plant."

"How sweet." Here I was knee-deep in book boxes, but who says no to books or family photographs? "Thanks. When would you like me to pick them up?"

"Could you come now? I confess I have an ulterior motive. I could use some help moving a few things."

"Sure."

The address she gave me was only a few blocks from my office. I was surprised to find Maggy Avinger's house full of packing boxes.

"Oh, didn't I tell you? I'm downsizing. Moving to a smaller place. Amazing how much stuff one collects in a lifetime."

I could only nod in agreement.

"So much stuff," she said. "And how little of it one really needs—or even enjoys."

She led me into her dining room and indicated an elegant little wrought-iron table and a small carton. "A plant stand. And some books—local interest, mostly. Thought you might enjoy them. Or feel free to pass them on. And here"—she offered me a manila envelope—"are some pictures I came across, most from church functions over the years. That's a wonderful photo of your grandfather, presiding over some event," she said as I slid the photos out of the envelope.

I recognized the look on his face all too well—his get-me-out-of-here expression, though most who saw him probably took it to be nothing more than his austere reserve.

"Thanks. And thanks for the table. That will be the perfect height."

"Just make sure there's a plastic liner in the basket to protect the tabletop. Look through these other books and help yourself. They're all headed to the library book sale." She waved at the built-in bookcases as she led me through a sitting room and into the kitchen.

"I hope you don't mind my ulterior motive. I just need help loading these boxes into my car. They're not terribly heavy, but I just can't manage them and the door and the steps all at the same time. Mrs. Fry said she'd have the museum open tomorrow and could accept them. I didn't want to miss her."

Three open cartons of glass jars, some dulled with dust and some shining in blue, green, and amber, covered her kitchen table.

"What interesting bottles."

"Indeed." She lifted a rich blue bottle for me to admire. "My dad was quite a collector, much to Mother's dismay. All manner of stuff has been stored out in the back shed for years. I started wiping them off, but decided the museum folk could handle the dust better than I. They may just pitch everything in the trash, for all I know, though Mrs. Fry sounded genuinely interested in having them."

With both hands, she lifted a large alabaster mortar and pestle from the table. "Father got this from the old Schmidt Pharmacy, when it closed."

"How beautiful!" Years of use had both scratched and polished it. "What did your dad do?"

"Farmed, mostly. Later on, he was part owner in the Feed & Seed. Putting to use his chemistry degree, I guess. If you could just put these boxes in the backseat of my car, I'd appreciate it. Then I can catch Mrs. Fry first thing tomorrow." She stood on the back stoop to hold the wooden screen door for me as I made three trips to her car.

"Is there anything else I can move for you?" I asked.

"No, that's quite enough." She led me into the sitting room. "Do look through the books. They've all got to go."

Against my better judgment, I couldn't resist. Running my finger along the spines of her neatly shelved old bestsellers and a section of cookbooks, I found a lovely set of children's classics in small leather bindings: *Treasure Island, Tom Sawyer, Huckleberry Finn, Peter Pan, Sherlock Holmes,* the Alice books.

She noticed when my finger stopped there. "I'd be delighted if you'd take those." She sounded thrilled. "Those were my childhood favorites."

"Are you sure—"

"I'm tickled to know you'll have them, Avery. It's so hard to ask for help, and I can't tell you how much I appreciate it. Please take these as my thank-you. Knowing you'll enjoy these means so much, more than you know."

"They're beautiful. Thank you."

I added them to the box she'd already packed for me. "Where are you moving to? And when?" I had to ask, since she hadn't volunteered.

"I'm not quite sure yet. Just trying to get things sorted through. You know that always takes longer than you expect."

I certainly did. I gathered my box of gifts, something to add to my office full of boxes.

"Oh!" She set down the wrought-iron table when we stepped into the front hall. "Do wait. Before you go."

She bustled back toward the kitchen, leaving me in her entry hall with the box balanced on one hip. In a wave of relief, I realized she hadn't mentioned her husband's eight-foot angel. For the first time since she'd come to my office wanting the angel gone but refusing to deal with the epitaph's threat, I was happy with her reluctance to talk about it. It gave me time to talk to Carlton Barner about whether my bright idea would work before I mentioned it to Maggy.

Looking around her front rooms, I was amazed how she maintained order in the midst of her move. I could see subtle signs of change only if I looked closely. The dark square on the flowered wallpaper where a picture once hung. The scant decorations on the sideboard in the parlor. Coming from the chaos of my office, I stood in awe. How did she manage it?

A mahogany secretary stood in the entry hall on delicate turned legs. That's what I needed to manage my incoming mail, a station like that, with baskets to sort items. In the stack of mail, my idly wandering gaze caught sight of cobalt writing. I froze.

Peeking from beneath a grocery store circular. A sheet of creamy

paper, the corner of a clipped and pasted news article, and the familiar poisonous blue ink.

I heard Maggy's footsteps approaching. Should I say something
to her, let her know she wasn't alone? What could the letter writer
possibly see in Maggy Avinger that needed nettlesome correction?
This wasn't the same writing on the banana pudding recipe Mack
had gotten. Had somebody else already found out about the angel?

"I'm coming. Just one minute." She called from the parlor.

I should keep my nosy self out of her business and my mouth
shut. I certainly hadn't told anyone about my note. Why would she
want to talk about hers?

"Took me forever to find the right box. I wanted you to have
this."

She held a foot-square box stuffed with packing paper. "I'd best
carry it to the car for you. You have all that other stuff."

"Thanks——" My tone carried a question.

"It's the mortar and pestle Father bought," she said. "The
Schmidt Pharmacy was down the street from your office. I want you
to have it."

"Maggy. I can't——"

"No argument." She crossed the few steps and opened the front
door. "You are the one to keep it. I saw it in your face. I insist. It'll
make a nice addition to your new office, from an old professional to
a new one."

Flabbergasted that she would entrust me with such an heirloom,
I offered no argument. She ushered me and my gifts to the car, then
waved good-bye from her front porch.

I understood Maggy's need to part with her possessions. At some
point in any move, you realize you have too much stuff. You give up
finding it a good home and just want it to find its way down the
doorstep. I had too much stuff, yet here I was hauling more orphans
home. Beautiful orphans, though.

As I unloaded the boxes and table from my car, I couldn't get my
mind off the letter on Maggy's hall stand. My letter and Cissie Pren-

tice's had intended to correct what might be seen as not-so-youthful indiscretions, a nudge toward a more circumspect lifestyle. Whatever could someone have found wanting in Maggy Avinger's life?

If Harden Avinger's poisonous joke had leaked to our poison-pen writer, I'd—do what? I sputtered indignantly in my head, aware of my impotence. Of course it had leaked. Harden Avinger had wanted it to.

I kept coming back to how creepy that spidery blue ink was, as if the blot spread across the page and then across my mind. Who knew Cissie and me and, at the same time, would be too timid to confront us directly? And who knew us and Maggy? I hadn't asked Maggy about the letter. She was a forthright person. If she wanted to talk to me about it, she would. Maybe I should tell her about mine.

I figured the letter writer was older, her moral benchmarks a bit Victorian. Her language was old-fashioned, and her cobalt fountain pen ink on vellum painted a different picture than if she'd used a roller ball and lined notepaper.

Someone I knew but couldn't see was watching me from the shadows. I wanted a chance to explain myself. Why, I couldn't say. It was just creepy.

Did it unsettle me because I'd wrestled with my own qualms about this move, about this office, about Dacus? She—whoever she was—didn't know how much I hate being told I couldn't do something. I set to work moving into my office.

Wednesday Morning

After I'd gotten back from Maggy's, I worked late on my office, cleaning and putting books on the shelves. I placed the rich leather-bound children's books in a place of honor near my desk, so I could see them and smile. At first, I'd displayed them on a shelf in the front room, but then thought about some kid with a snotty nose and no respect for my books getting hold of them.

I'd also moved the mortar and pestle to several spots before finding it a home atop the oak filing cabinet between the oversized windows in my office.

That was my problem—always trying to find a good spot when I should settle for good enough.

I'd ended up sleeping on the leather sofa in my office and helping myself to the shower in the extra bath upstairs. Fodder for another note, if the poison-pen writer spotted my car in the office lot overnight.

I hadn't seen or heard Melvin all night, and he wasn't around in the morning. Even though he came and went without reporting in with me, it was unusual for him to be gone overnight. Business trip, I assumed. Or maybe he'd found himself a girlfriend. Him and Donlee.

Buried behind a box and the contents I'd emptied on my desk, the phone rang.

"Miz Andrews? Carl Newland Knight here."

"Mr. Knight. How are you?" The mental image of Lionel Shoal's body gave me a 3-D version of the memories Carl Newland Knight had of his wife. I now felt an odd bond with him.

"Well as can be expected." He paused. "I hate to bother you again, but—I was going through some stuff here at home. I found something. Somebody needs to see it. I didn't know what to do with it."

"What did you find?" I sympathized with him, but his stammering, quiet helplessness lit a flicker of caution in me. I didn't want to be drawn in. I couldn't hold his hand through his entire grief process, as he sorted through and dealt with each of his wife's possessions.

"It's . . . hard to describe. It's a letter . . . and a newspaper article."

Uh-oh. "In blue ink?"

The line stayed silent a moment too long. "How . . . did you know?"

"Could I see it?" Before my brain got too far head of reality, I should make sure it was the same kind of letter Cissie and I had gotten. And Maggy Avinger.

"Sure. I'll bring it . . . to your office. I just didn't know . . . what to make of it. I'm leaving now. Soon as I hang up."

Before I could finish tidying a place for us to sit, the worn leather strap of horse-cart bells I had hung on the knob to announce visitors jangled loudly. Mr. Knight came in.

From his hesitant voice in our phone conversations, I'd expected a small, mousy man. The Carl Newland Knight who appeared in my front room had spent more than a little time lifting weights and probably had played high school football. Basketball, too, given his height. His head was shaved smooth and his thick neck sat on hulking shoulders.

"Miz Andrews?"

"Come in, come in. Have a seat. Mr. Knight, I want you to know how sorry I am about your wife."

His eyes clouded over and, for a moment, I thought he would cry. His grief was palpable and hard to face.

Without a word, he handed me an envelope addressed to Mrs. Carl Knight and settled into the tufted wing chair, which was a snug fit for him.

The thick paper felt all too familiar, the short newspaper clipping precisely pasted in the lower right corner below the cobalt blue ink.

"Paternity Test Scam Saves Deadbeat Dad Dough." The clipping looked to be from one of those grocery-checkout tabloids. The article profiled a man in New York who avoided paying child support for eleven children by supplying substitute blood for his paternity tests. Eleven children with nine different women. That was scary enough, without the letter on which the article was pasted.

The message in blue ink was chilling.

Dear Mrs. Knight,

Innocent children suffer while you help fornicators and adulterers escape their due. You have been warned and yet you persist. The time for warnings has passed. You will get your due.

I reread the message before looking at Carl Knight. "I'm not sure I understand."

He sat stock-still, but began blinking furiously, whether from nervousness or to keep back tears, I couldn't tell. He found the words only with great effort. "Suse is—was a nurse."

I nodded.

"She—I hate to say this out loud to anybody. Swear to God you won't tell."

"Mr. Knight, you're here to consult with me. Whatever you say is confidential."

He pinched the bridge of his nose to keep the tears at bay. When he spoke, his voice was stronger.

"Suse did that. Helped men fake . . . their tests. She offered to help them. For money."

"How'd she do that?"

"She . . . had her own business. Doing physicals for insurance companies or . . . some home health work. She went to people's houses. Sometimes a lawyer would ask her to come draw blood. For a court case. She just got this idea. She wanted more money than her regular work could pay."

Carl talked about wanting money as if that didn't quite make sense to him. Or maybe it was her willingness to sell her soul that didn't make sense.

"How do you know? About her activities." I was starting to talk with maddening pauses myself.

With his head bowed, he studied the floor. I doubted he was counting the dust bunnies on the dark wood. "She . . . used my blood . . . sometimes."

"How many men did she help out?"

"I don't know. They paid in cash. And she spent it. Who knows how many." He didn't intend that as a question.

"Did anyone else know what she was doing? Besides her clients?"

He shook his head. "I only know for sure one case. The lady kept insisting. She made him get retested, with a witness at the blood draw. She wouldn't take no for an answer. She . . . knew he was the father. Suse got a little worried about that one. I don't know what the lady decided to do."

"Where else would she have gotten blood, other than from you?"

He shrugged. "She was a nurse."

I studied the note and the spidery writing.

"What have the police told you about your wife's death?"

He began blinking furiously again.

"They've been very close-mouthed. One of the deputies finally told me. They think she was . . . poisoned."

"Poisoned." I said it softly. He seemed so fragile, despite his bulk, that I felt I needed to be gentle.

He nodded. "She'd eaten some candy. I don't know . . . where she got it. But it was there."

I forced myself to take a deep breath. "A box of candy? Chocolates?"

He blinked and nodded. "The sheriff thought I did it. But I haven't bought any candy. Not this candy . . . from California or somewhere."

They would check his credit cards and online purchases, which meant they hadn't found any connection yet between him and the candy or he wouldn't still be walking around free.

Chocolate wrappers and pieces of candy scattered on blue carpet. Poison. That suspicion had crept around the corners of my mind at Shoal's house, but I hadn't wanted to acknowledge it to Rudy, or even to myself. Now I had no choice. I couldn't quite believe Carl had anything to do with his wife's death. After what I'd seen at the Shoals' house, the candy was a good bet.

"Did your wife know Lionel Shoal, by any chance?"

He shook his head. "I don't think so."

"He's a real estate developer. New in town. Maybe she knew his wife, Valerie Shoal?" I tried to prod his memory.

More head shaking. Someone from the sheriff's office would soon be back asking him the same questions. They would check other avenues, too, looking for connections.

I kept watching him. Was this all an act? Could he really be this shaken? Had he sent the letter—or letters—to deflect attention from himself? That seemed far-fetched, though not without precedent. But how could he have known or cared about me or Cissie or Maggy Avinger?

I didn't see a guy who looked like a walking ad for anabolic steroids sending poison pen letters written in dainty, spidery ink.

A chill thought struck me: Suse Knight's poison pen letter had proven truly poisonous. Which cast the news clippings and the poison pen letters in a new light.

"Have you mentioned this letter to the sheriff?"

"Uh-uh. I just found it."

"Does the sheriff know about your wife's . . . extracurricular activities?"

He hesitated. "I . . . don't know. The sheriff didn't ask anything about it. Until I found this, I . . . didn't think anything of it. I thought Suse . . . just got sick with a virus or something."

"What did she do with the money she made?"

He shook his head, with a slight frown of disgust. "I accidentally saw the receipt. For her boob job. She didn't ask me before she went and did that. And she gambled. Her and her friends, they go over to Cherokee. To the casino. Guess she thought she had to have more. To play with."

"Mr. Knight," I said slowly, still turning over all the permutations in my head. "Your wife isn't the only one who got a letter like this. Other people have received them. I'd advise you to take this to the sheriff." This was a murder investigation, not something he could pretend never happened.

He looked surprised. "About . . . my wife? Other people got letters about my wife?"

"No, no. I'm sorry. Not about your wife. About themselves. But this is more than a coincidence. Sheriff Peters needs to know about this, and about your wife's . . . side business."

I'd spent too much time around Carl Knight. I had to stop stuttering through my sentences.

"If you think so," he said, obviously reluctant to invite Sheriff Peters's attentions. I completely understood his reluctance.

"Mr. Knight, I'm not ordering you to go see the sheriff. I certainly won't volunteer the information myself without your permission. I'm just advising you that it might help figure out what happened to your wife."

L.J. needed to know about the letters. She had murders to solve. I expected she'd get a warrant to search the Knights' financial records and personal papers, checking for motive. At least I assumed that was the way things would happen. What did I know?

He looked at the note I still held. "Can you take it to the sheriff? For me?"

My turn to pause. "Sure," I said finally. "If you'd like me to."

He nodded. "Sheriff Peters is—can be—hard to deal with."

Tell me about it. At least she wouldn't try to slam hulking Carl Newland Knight up against a brick wall.

"I'd be glad to," I said. "Do you have your wife's business papers, showing how she'd set up her practice? Her tax returns, things like that?" Carl might be more at risk from an irate, defrauded mother who'd been denied child support suing him than he was from L.J. I needed to know if Suse set herself up as a corporation or a limited liability company, how much malpractice insurance she carried, and whether the policy covered intentional acts, which I doubted. Her death might actually protect Carl's assets, depending on how her business affairs were arranged.

"I also need to get you to sign a contract, showing that I represent you as your attorney and that you understand the fee structure."

He nodded, looking uncomfortable. This was the part of solo practice I wasn't handling well—the details. Specifically the money details, charging people for my time. It didn't feel so intimate when someone unknown to me in a far distant part of my giant law firm sent out my bill for me. I just filled out a time sheet and went about my lawyering business. Asking people for money was hard.

I went into the next room and shuffled around in the jumbled desk drawers until I found the sample representation agreement I'd gotten from Carlton Barner.

Carl Newland Knight signed the agreement, happier once I'd explained I wouldn't charge him for the initial consultation. Technically, this was his second initial consultation, the first being over the phone, but neither of us pointed that out.

After he'd gone, I slipped the letter and envelope he'd brought into a larger manila envelope. A DNA match from the envelope flap was the kind of miracle that only happens on television and the letter had been handled by at least two people, but just in case a crime lab could use some magic methods. I wanted to minimize the damage.

I pulled my own letter out of the side table drawer where I'd stuck it and put it in its own protective envelope. I needed to see if Cissie Prentice still had her letter. The more the cops had to work with, the better.

Poisoned. The reality was much scarier than Curtis what's-his-name's grammar school tales of meningitis run amok.

Had Lionel Shoal, by a frightening coincidence, received his own annotated news clipping? I wasn't about to call Valerie Shoal to find out. L.J. Peters could do her own addition: one plus one plus one.

Wednesday Morning

I couldn't get Cissie on the phone, so I stuck Carl's letter in my desk drawer. To get my mind on something other than spidery blue handwriting, I walked down the street to buy the latest edition of the *Clarion* so I could study the real estate ads.

Maybe it was the crick in my neck from sleeping on the office sofa or the oppressive junkiness of my office, but I had an overpowering urge to try another nest on for size. The cabin, as much as I loved it, was proving a bit remote and primitive to live in full-time.

The first thing to catch my eye wasn't an ad for the ideal fixer-upper but Noah Lakefield's front-page article on Dacus's murder spree.

Seeing it all itemized in black and white, in neat, narrow columns, Dacus's crime wave inspired awe.

Three Suspicious Deaths Stun Camden County

Officers in the Camden County Sheriff's Department have been challenged as never before by three mysterious deaths within a week.

Sheriff L. J. Peters acknowledged that the deaths of Len Ruffin, Suse Knight, and Lionel Shoal are all under investigation and all currently classified as suspicious in nature.

On Sunday, Len Ruffin's body was found in an abandoned mine shaft during a "plant rescue" operation at the new Golden Cove luxury home development above Lark's Rest Campground. The body was discovered by a group of volunteers working to save endangered native plants threatened by the construction.

The day after the discovery of Ruffin's body, the Golden Cove office and a model home valued at $800,000 were damaged in two simultaneous explosions. The explosions are under investigation by federal Alcohol, Tobacco, and Firearms (ATF) agents.

Late Sunday evening, the body of Susan "Suse" Knight was discovered by her husband at their home. The circumstances of the death made it unclear whether she died of natural causes or foul play. Her remains were transported to the state forensic pathologist's office in Newberry for further study. A Sheriff's Department source says the death is being treated as suspicious.

On Tuesday, the body of Lionel Shoal was discovered at the Shoals' lakeside home by his wife, Valerie Shoal, and local attorney Avery Andrews. The victim owned Shoal Properties, the company developing Golden Cove. Shoal's death is also being treated as suspicious, and investigators are awaiting the medical examiner's report.

One focus of the investigation, according to sources, is the development of the luxury mountain resort Golden Cove. The discovery of Len Ruffin's body at the Golden Cove site and the subsequent death of the site developer, Lionel Shoal, have investigators looking for possible connections.

"It is much too early in the investigation," said Sheriff Peters, "to be jumping to conclusions. True, there are some coincidences here. But that may be all we have—coincidences."

While the Sheriff's Department continues its investigation, three families plan funerals and wait for answers.

Very dramatic ending, Noah. I'd have to personally thank him for giving me billing in the article. I was surprised Mom or Aunt Letha hadn't already called me.

A second front-page article also carried Noah's byline: "Pet Pig Continues to Elude Sheriff."

Noah had better be careful with so many of his headline-grabbing stories poking fun at the sheriff. In part because her mom named her Lucinda Jane and in part because she took after her daddy and her shoe size reached thirteen double-wide at a young age, L.J. doesn't have much of a sense of humor. Noah didn't want her grabbing a handful of his curly hair during a traffic stop gone bad—and he sure couldn't do much as a reporter in Dacus if his "sources in the sheriff's office" suddenly dried up.

Despite more sightings than Elvis, the runaway pig continues to elude one of the biggest man—um, pig hunts in Dacus history.

"I haven't seen anything like this since 1963, when Elbert Stump and his brother took off running with a Chevy full of 'shine and a whole county full of deputies in a heat after him," said Pudd Pardee, head of the county's Rescue Squad. "I was a kid then, but it was big news."

Life on the run hasn't been all bad for the pig many are calling Bambi, after the former Playboy bunny who went on the lam following her murder conviction.

"She looks well fed," said Mabel First, whose winter vegetable garden was raided by Bambi. "And she sure can run. I had no idea a potbellied pig could move that fast. She's about the same size as a couple of those deputies, but she sure leaves them in the dust."

"Bambi" is a hundred-plus-pound Vietnamese pot-belly pig, a breed often adopted as pets. "Sadly, though, many people are not responsible pet owners," said Amy Cole, Camden County Pet Protection president. "We're afraid someone couldn't care for this pig after it reached maturity and set it out. Too often owners don't do their homework. They think their cute little piglet will always stay small and cuddly. Their pet pig isn't so cute when it outweighs the other members of the family."

Night temperatures will dip below freezing this weekend, giving searchers a sense of urgency.

"Pigs such as this aren't suited to forage on their own and they are sensitive to cold temperatures. We need to find her before something bad happens."

Anyone spotting the runaway pig is asked to called the Sheriff's Department at 555-1957.

I wish I could have seen L.J.'s face when she read that article—seen her from a safe distance, of course. Noah Lakefield's reportorial talents were certainly enlivening the pages of the Dacus *Clarion*. He might soon be escorted to the county line in the dark of night by a couple of burly guys wearing holstered handguns, but until then, he was adding some sparkle.

I wandered onto the office's porch and sat in one of Melvin's rocking chairs to read. It didn't take long to peruse the newspaper's classified ads; the whole paper wasn't but twelve pages long. No new real estate offerings popped out at me. At this early stage in my search, asking my family for the name of an agent was too complicated; my mom would want to know why I couldn't stay with them. I went inside to call the company with the largest real estate ad.

I asked Missy Jones, the chipper woman who answered the phone, if she could show me what was available. She sounded so excited, she must have been levitating. She invited me to come right down to her office.

I still hadn't seen or heard from Melvin, so I locked my office and the front door. We needed some kind of sign on the door, maybe one of those BE BACK AT cardboard clocks. Then again, we needed a lot of things to be a proper place of business. Should I be worried about Melvin? We also should work on some ground rules. I needed to know when to worry.

The Upstate Realty Company office was in an adorable dollhouse on the opposite end of Main Street from Melvin's grand Victorian. The front door opened directly into the dollhouse's single room. Inside, two desks faced each other, and two women stood in the center of the small room, chatting. Not much else would fit inside.

The perkiest-looking of the two greeted me. "Avery Andrews?" A forty-something-year-old woman with artfully streaked blond hair and an expression of permanent surprise offered me her hand.

"Yes. Missy?"

"So nice to meet you. If you don't mind waiting—"

The other woman, older, in a subdued pantsuit with short gray hair, carried an expensive but much-worn handbag over her shoulder. I realized she didn't work here.

"I'm sorry. I didn't mean to interrupt. I'll wait outside."

"No, don't go." The older woman, the one I took to be another customer, reached out her hand as she studied me with grave interest. "You're Avery Andrews?" She studied me intently.

I nodded.

"I'm Alex Shoal," she said.

"Shoal?" Not a common name, at least around here.

"Lionel Shoal's wife." She paused, giving her pronouncement time to reorder things in my brain. "I understand that comes as a surprise to people in town," she said.

"Um, yes. I'm afraid it does."

"As I was just telling Ms. Jones here, it comes as a surprise to me, too, to find I'm not the only Mrs. Lionel Shoal in town."

"Yes, ma'am. I can see how . . ." I let my sentence trail off.

"Actually," she said, "I was hoping to meet you, after I saw your name in the newspaper article this morning. I can't believe we've run into each other like this."

Dacus is a small town, but not usually this small.

"We could talk after you finish your business here," I offered. This was bound to be more interesting than looking at Dacus real estate offerings.

"No, we were finished, but I don't want to interfere. You've come to see Ms. Jones." Alex smiled at Missy, who had been watching us as if we were her favorite soap opera.

"Missy and I can always talk later, can't we?" I said.

Missy's perennial smile narrowed a fraction as she watched a couple of potential clients prepare to swim off the hook. I doubted the Upstate Realty office was jammed to capacity very often.

"Missy, I'll call you for an appointment—and give you a little more warning next time." I gave her what I hoped was a conciliatory smile. She still looked disappointed, maybe because she would miss out on the next installment of the drama.

"Thank you for your help, Ms. Jones. You've been most gracious," Alex Shoal said, shaking Missy's hand.

Alex and I stepped out onto the dollhouse-sized porch.

"Is your office far?" she asked.

"The other end of town."

"Suppose we sit in my car a moment. Do you mind?"

A brown Mercedes with some age on it sat parked at the curb.

The interior was spotless and the front seat almost as spacious as a sofa. The sun warmed the interior. Alex slid in behind the wheel and turned to face me. She had wide, intelligent brown eyes outlined with delicate smile wrinkles.

"I'm not sure where to begin, except to say I'm curious," she said.

"About?"

"The other Mrs. Shoal. If you don't mind me asking."

Her expression was pleasant and pained at the same time, but she was too gracious to call attention to how awkward this was for her.

"I don't really know her. I first saw her last Sunday, in a local restaurant with your—with Mr. Shoal. They were new in town and were pointed out to me. Then she came up to me, at lunch on Tuesday. Wanted me to talk to Mr. Shoal, about a legal matter."

"A divorce?" Her throaty, smooth voice didn't falter.

I hesitated. It wouldn't hurt to tell her. "No."

"What's she like?"

A natural question. "Very . . . different from you." Polar opposites, I wanted to say.

"In what way?"

I shrugged, studying her. Was it worse to know or to imagine? "Please understand, I don't know her. Our interactions were limited."

"Is she young?"

"No. Though she . . . dresses young." Hard to add and subtract makeup and attitude, but I calculated that Valerie and Alex were likely very close in age. I couldn't see why Lionel Shoal had moved on from this quiet but classy-looking lady to Valerie. One could never quite know about couples. Maybe he'd been shopping for younger and got fooled. More likely, from what I'd seen, Valerie had latched on to him, and it wasn't for his sex appeal.

"Does she look cheap? Don't answer that. I'm sorry. That's not fair to you."

I shrugged; it felt disrespectful to Valerie whatever-her-name-was to say it aloud.

Alex Shoal looked past me out the car window, her hands folded in her lap. I had admired her cultured restraint. Maybe it was the easy way the tiny wrinkles on her face had outlined a warm smile in Missy's office. Maybe it was her Lauren Bacall voice, or her deep brown eyes tense with pain. Whatever it was, I liked her, and my heart hurt for her.

"I knew something was up," she said, her tone still matter-of-fact. "I just didn't dream it was this. Everyone kept hounding him, the newspaper, the creditors. He left Phoenix to make a fresh start. A new project, a new place."

She gave a bitter laugh. "I should have known. I guess the

biggest surprise is how stupid and blind I am—have been, for years. You work to build a marriage, keep it together . . ."

Her composure cracked. Tears turned her eyes liquid, but she didn't bother fumbling for a handkerchief. She just let them fall.

"Twenty-five years. Two children. Countless moves, always just ahead of the creditors. Always another pot of gold at the end of another rainbow. Rainbows fade quickly around Lionel, but I kept believing they were really there."

"I'm so sorry, Mrs. Shoal."

She blinked as if she'd just remembered I was there. "What stuns me most is my own stupidity. Looking back, dear God, who could be such an idiot? His father died recently. As soon as he got his inheritance, I should've known. For the first time ever in our lives, he finally had money, after all the get-rich promises and schemes."

Her shoulders rose and fell with a shaky sigh. "You know what he told me? That he had to keep the money in a separate account, in his name, for tax reasons. Wouldn't give me enough to pay off even one of the credit cards or the back rent. Said we could take care of it all at once, after the estate was settled. That was a lie, wasn't it? To keep me from getting anything in a divorce, wasn't it?"

Her tone had become insistent with a tinge of panic.

"I don't really know anything about Arizona law," I said.

Her gaze was intent. She knew I was hedging.

"Yes, ma'am," I said, "that was likely what he had in mind."

The tears fell in a flood. She gave one wrenching sob, as if it had been torn from her chest. Her carefully constructed dam burst.

"I . . . can't pay. He's taken . . . everything I had. This car . . . is all I have left of what my daddy left . . . to me." She sobbed, her face twisted with hurt and fear.

I didn't know what else to do. I leaned over and put my arms around her. Even with the steering wheel in the way, she turned and buried her face on my shoulder and cried like I've never heard anyone cry.

If Missy looked out her real estate office window, she'd likely decide not to sell either of us a house in a decent neighborhood, given such a penchant for questionable public displays of affection.

It took several minutes for Alex Shoal to cry herself out. As the sobs became less racking, I fumbled in my jacket pocket for a tissue and found a clean one.

"I'm . . . so sorry." She blew her nose and reached under the seat for her purse and more tissues. "I'm so sorry."

"You're entitled. Lord only knows." I patted her shoulder and leaned back to allow her to regain her dignity.

"Are you going to be okay?"

She blew her nose and nodded.

"I know you've got a lot to work through. My office is straight down the street, on this side. A mauve Victorian with a wraparound porch. There's no sign, but you can't miss it. Please let me know if there's anything I can do to help." I talked fast, wanting to offer her help and get out of her way at the same time.

She nodded, holding a tissue to her nose, her eyes closed.

I really needed to get some business cards printed. This was no time to fumble around for a scrap of paper to jot down my phone number.

As I left Alex parked at the curb, Missy waved hopefully at me from her office window. I waved back, but I couldn't bring myself to go talk about real estate.

On the walk to my office, I decided on a detour to the newspaper office. I needed an update on the latest breaking news.

Midday Wednesday

The note on the *Clarion*'s front counter said, "Leave your work order in the slot or come back at 1:30," and was signed "Alice."

Rather than head up the creaky stairs to see if Dad was in his office, I scouted around downstairs among the crowded machinery and paper-littered worktables and found Noah Lakefield at a desk against the back wall. The best I'd hoped for was getting his cell phone number from Walter, the editor, or his wife Alice, also known as the ad sales department and office manager. But here he was in person. Not much of a workspace for the ace reporter, tucked away alone with the hardware. Not that Dad's office upstairs was fancier, just better organized.

I rolled an office chair with a lopsided back over to join Noah at his desk.

He looked faintly irritated at the interruption and squinted like he wasn't quite sure who I was. He'd been engrossed in his computer screen. I understood. I hate having someone blunder in when I'm concentrating on a project.

As recognition dawned, he punched a button to bring up a blank screen, raked his fingers through his tangle of curls, and turned to face me.

"What kind of warm welcome is this?" I said. "No hi 'ner nothing?"

He didn't frown, but he sure didn't smile.

"Sorry to bother you," I said, "but where else could I go for the latest news?"

"About?"

"The Dacus death spree. By the way, liked both your articles. Especially the one about the pig. I'd be careful about speeding or spitting on the sidewalk, if I were you. However, except for the Sheriff's Department, everyone is enjoying it mightily."

He thawed enough to offer a small smile of acknowledgment. I didn't know what prompted his mood, but I would ignore it and assume it had nothing to do with me until further notice.

"What do the cops know that they aren't broadcasting?"

He shrugged, his expression reserved.

I offered him a tantalizing tidbit to thaw him out. "Have you talked to anybody who saw Lionel Shoal's body?"

He raised his eyebrows. "No. You?"

"I was there. Anybody mention any funny coincidences?"

His bushy eyebrows knitted together in a frown and he shook his head.

"Hey, I didn't come here to do all the talking," I said to give him a playful nudge.

His eyes narrowed. "What, you going to get your daddy to make me talk to you? Why don't you ask him what's going on?"

"Because he wouldn't know." His sharp tone set me back on my heels, but I kept my voice even, the better to draw him out.

"No shit," he said.

"Whoa. What's that all about?"

He sized me up for a minute, maybe surprised I'd agreed with him. "Pardon me for saying it, but your dad doesn't know shit about the newspaper business."

"That's a news flash? Everybody in town knows that. Dad knows that, in case you didn't know. That's why he pays people who do know the business."

He studied me. I struggled to hold my temper, feeling protective of Dad. Who does this guy think he is? And why the attitude, out of nowhere? I put on my best impassive negotiator face, though I wanted to punch him.

"So—why?" he said, his arms outstretched in frustrated supplication.

"He retired early. The paper was about to fold. He's a mechanical engineer, the paper had a bunch of old machines he could keep running. He's singularly uninterested in local gossip, but he dearly loves machine grease. Made sense to him. Seems to me you have a job thanks to that. So?"

He shook his head in resignation. I didn't ask what frustration had led to his outburst. Whatever it was, he could work it out. My dad didn't need me defending him, even though I had to admit I was struggling not to.

So why had this talented hotshot accepted a job at this little half-time newspaper, half-time print shop? Best wait and ask him when he wasn't so defensive—and when I wasn't just about ready to smack him.

"Like I said, I didn't come here to do all the talking. You want to swap stories, or shall I leave you to your computer screen?" And your little hissy fit.

He took stock for a moment. "Ruffin, the guy in the mine, didn't die of natural causes. He was shot six times with a Browning Nazi-Belgium nine-millimeter."

"Wow, how'd they trace the gun?"

"They didn't. The gun was found with the body."

"Good detective work there. Any idea whose gun?"

"Naw. A rare make, guys brought them home from World War II, but they're sold now at gun shows and such. They've ruled out suicide or accident.

"Nothing about the scene is similar to the death of Suse Knight.

Can't find any connection between Knight and Ruffin. Can't find any connection with the explosion at Golden Cove. Thought they had a lead on that one, some woman who offered a blow job to a highway department employee—"

"In exchange for some dynamite."

He looked surprised. "Not some. Just one stick. How do you know about that?"

"I've got my sources." I couldn't keep up our game of information one-upmanship. "Is that the funniest thing you've—" I broke up, laughing.

Noah fought it but couldn't help himself, despite his pique. Once he got started laughing, neither of us could stop. We laughed until we both teared up.

"I've heard the fishing's good around here," he said, wiping his eyes.

"Only if you get there before her boyfriend shows up to net his limit—and everybody else's."

He took some time to catch his breath and get back to his story. "They can't find any connection between that dynamite and the explosion. Suse Knight's death also appears unrelated. At first, they feared she'd contracted some deadly disease, even called in the CDC. Her face was contorted, her muscles spasmed so severely they couldn't get her laid flat on the stretcher. She looked like something out of a horror movie."

I shuddered as my own mental images of Lionel Shoal's body replayed, the stuff of nightmares.

"Again, no connection. Lionel Shoal, of course, is involved with Golden Cove. They can't find any means or motive for him blowing up his property. No relationship with Len Ruffin, other than Ruffin's body being found on Golden Cove property. And no relationship at all between Suse Knight and Ruffin, Shoal, or Golden Cove that anyone can find."

"Except that Lionel Shoal and Suse Knight died the same way."

He sat forward, his eyes wide. "What?"

"Lionel Shoal's face was distorted and his back arched and

frozen, just like Suse Knight's. Suse had been throwing up all over the place. So had Shoal. Looked like he'd been eating candy."

"A box of chocolates?"

I nodded.

"The kind in brown paper cups?"

"Yep. They were spilled all over the floor."

He smacked his palm on the desk. "That's exactly what they found around Suse Knight's body." He rolled his chair toward me in his excitement. "I knew these things just couldn't be coincidence. They had to be related."

"But you still have all the bits that don't fit. Like a giant puzzle with pieces from different boxes. An odd connection here and there, but no picture. You don't even have any edge pieces to frame it in."

"There's one edge piece," he said. "Suse Knight and Lionel Shoal were both poisoned. Strychnine."

"Huh?" So they had narrowed in on it already.

"A toxicologist in Charleston recognized it immediately, from the grotesque faces and rigid muscles. Apparently they both got megadoses. Suse Knight had a box of chocolate candy. A square red box of liqueur chocolates."

My brain raced around, trying to connect the dots. "But there are still more pieces that don't fit than do."

He shrugged. "That's what makes it a good story."

"And a scary one."

We both sat, lost in our thoughts.

"The sheriff have any suspects in sight?"

"The sheriff?" Noah's lip curled, his snurlish attitude back in a flash. "You're kidding, right? What a joke she is."

I was tired of his sarcasm. "Guess they do everything better where you come from. That why you didn't stay? It was too perfect, so you had to move on?"

Even if I, too, thought L.J. was a joke, she was our joke. He hadn't been here long enough to earn the right to make fun of her.

I expected him to come out swinging. Instead, he blinked, gave a halfhearted shrug, and looked away. I'd hit a soft spot. Hmm, the newsman had a story. I didn't have time to dig for it, at least not today.

"I got to run." Best let him get over whatever had him in such a stew. I rolled back the chair I'd borrowed.

"Oh, I almost forgot." I turned back. He was probably the best source. "You know anything about somebody opening the old Yellow Fork summer camp, up on the mountain?"

"No." His tone said, *And why should I care?*

"A guy called today, wanted to meet with me. I hadn't heard that anybody had bought it, until this Tim McDonald called."

"Tim McDonald?"

I nodded.

"Where is this place? Yellow Fork?"

"Up the mountain, past where the road splits."

He scribbled himself a note, retreating back into his preoccupied universe.

"Okay, then," I said.

I left him sitting in the clutter and confusion of the *Clarion* and walked the block to Carlton Barner's office in time for my appointment. Everything huddled around the courthouse: the newspaper, the lawyers' offices, the Law Enforcement Center. Quick commute time.

Most of the Dacus lawyers had offices in converted houses of differing sizes and styles within walking distance of the courthouse. The Barner Law Firm was housed in a single-story bungalow, with painted cement steps, a wooden porch, and a familiar come-home feel.

While Lou Wray didn't exactly welcome me, she didn't snarl or ignore me, which had been her normal greeting during the couple of months I'd camped out in a back office. This time, she didn't even make me sit in the waiting room. She escorted me to Carlton's small conference room, usually reserved for real estate closings, and even offered me coffee.

"No, thanks, Mrs. Wray. I appreciate it." If she was extending an olive branch, I wasn't going to whack it off. "How've you been?" I didn't know enough about her to ask about her family.

"Fine," she said, stopping in the doorway. "And you?"

"Fine. Thanks for asking."

I smiled. She nodded primly and left. Détente.

I grabbed a blank legal pad off the credenza and scribbled an outline of the points I wanted to make with Carlton. The more I'd thought it over, the more I liked the solution I'd come up with for Harden Avinger's final resting place. Now I just had to convince his executor of its genius.

Carlton breezed in and proffered his hand. Even though he wasn't scheduled for court, he wore a tightly knotted tie and blue blazer, his long delicate gray pants carefully creased, not a hair around his bald dome out of place.

I didn't waste any time. "Carlton, I've got a proposition, a solution that both honors Mr. Avinger's wishes and saves Mrs. Avinger from undue embarrassment."

Carlton cocked his head, attentive but noncommittal.

"The letter he left specifies that the epitaph be engraved on the monument. Doesn't mean the epitaph has to be visible, does it?"

His lips pursed with skepticism, but he waited for me to explain.

"What if Innis Barker engraves the epitaph as written, then covers it with a more appropriate—and less libelous—epitaph."

"I . . . don't know." Carlton leaned back as if moving away from me and my proposal. At least he was going to give it some thought.

"If she'd actually done something to harm him," I said, "that would be one thing. But I haven't found anyone who says she did anything but take good care of her husband throughout their marriage."

I didn't report the consensus that Carlton's client had been a jerk of monumental proportions. "Surely you don't want to be party to his last tragic joke."

He sucked in a slow lungful of air and let it out. "A'vry, I'm going to have to think about this one." He shook his head. "There's the letter of the law and then there's the spirit. I . . . don't know."

"Carlton, you've known both Harden and Maggy Avinger. There's also just doing what's right."

"We can't be absolutely certain something didn't—that he didn't know something we don't."

He couldn't bring himself to accuse her.

"Both his own doctor and the hospice nurse who was with him when he died said unequivocally that he died of a disease process, that there was no way he was poisoned."

Carlton studied the toes of his wingtips at the end of his outstretched legs.

"Let me think about it."

That was abrupt. "Fine." I'd hoped for a resolution, but I'd settle for anything short of an outright no.

On the short walk back to the office, I thought about the Avingers and the Shoals, about marriage and the end of marriage, and suspicion. Did L.J. have any suspects? Was Alex Shoal on the list? If she wasn't, she certainly would be once L.J. got wind of Lionel's double life—or double wife. I could see why Alex Shoal might want him dead, but she'd had to track him down. Did she find him and send that box of chocolates? Was her surprise at where and with whom he was living a ruse for my benefit?

In any event, it didn't make sense that Alex Shoal would send chocolates to Suse Knight. Surely Lionel had been old enough not to have to fix any paternity tests, at least old enough to know where babies came from and take precautions.

If his wife—his real wife—had killed him, somebody ought to give her a button. Could what he'd done to her, forcing her to live hand to mouth, squandering her father's money, hiding his inheritance from her, leaving her in debt, could that constitute domestic abuse? Interesting little legal puzzle, since a South Carolina statute lets a convicted spouse killer serve only one-fourth the sentence if she—or he—can show abuse. All pure speculation, though.

Something far from speculation: I needed to get those anonymous letters to L.J. The more I wandered around the edges of all that had happened recently, the more I wanted to back away from the edge. I needed to track down Cissie Prentice and get her letter, too. The more they had to work with, the better. The less I had to do with it, even better.

Wednesday Afternoon

I found an apple in the office's communal refrigerator. Something Melvin had bought, so I'd have to remember to replace it. That and some peanuts would tide me over until supper. I also grabbed a gallon-sized plastic bag from among the various sizes Melvin had neatly stored in a drawer.

Cissie Prentice answered her phone on the second ring and seemed relieved when I said I wanted to pick up her letter. Poison letters, as I'd begun thinking of them.

"Oh, gawd, Avery. Please. Get the thing out of my life. After you told me I should hang on to it, I stuck it in a drawer and haven't looked at it again. But every time I walk by that cupboard, I know it's there. It gives me the creeps."

"Will you be home later this afternoon?"

"Sure, until my tennis game."

As I hung up, I wondered what Cissie Prentice did when she was at home. Thanks to one or more of her earlier divorce settlements, she didn't have to work and could hire a maid.

As I gathered my satchel and whatever else I'd need so I wouldn't have to return to the office, I heard a familiar toodle-oo from the hallway.

Great-aunt Hattie, followed closely by her younger, more padded sister Vinnia, appeared in the door.

"Avery, honey. Have you time to talk a minute?"

"We were talking, coming home from a meeting at church— Oh, were you leaving? We—"

"—decided to see if you were free for a bit."

"We need to talk. Do you have time?"

"—some advice. It'll just take a minute." Vinnia finished up the tumble of words. They stood side by side, so familiar and yet so out of context. From the strained look on Vinnia's soft face, they obviously hadn't come to admire my new office.

I had to reexcavate two chairs for them.

"What's up?" I asked as I rolled my chair around the desk to join them. They sat in two mismatched side chairs, Hattie's sensible lace-up shoes planted firmly on the floor while Vinnia, shorter and plumper than her lanky older sister, had to perch on the edge of the chair so her low-heeled navy pumps could reach the floor. Vinnia and I were both height challenged.

"Don't look so worried, dear. It's not bad news. Are you sure you have time?" Vinnia emphasized the word "bad" in a way that drew my attention. As usual, we both turned to Hattie for the details.

Hattie eyed me in that direct, no-nonsense way that had tamed many a high school biology student over her decades of teaching. She'd been retired twenty years; her legend endured for a reason.

"We trust this conversation will be confidential. We need legal advice, Avery."

My imagination offered a rush of possibilities: a traffic ticket? car accident? Aunt Letha punched someone at the church meeting they'd just left?

I looked at Vinnia to see if her usually expressive face revealed more than the sharp angles of her older sister's face did. Vinnia just smiled back at me, placid.

"Uh, sure," I said. "What do you need?"

"We need you to look at Father's will and our brother's—your grandfather's—will and tell us exactly what our rights are."

"Your rights?"

Hattie pulled thick bundles of papers from the outside pocket of her walking jacket. She didn't offer them to me immediately. Instead, she studied me as if she had something to decide. Maybe whether to trust me.

"We need to know . . . in what way we own the house."

"O-kay." I wasn't following her.

"Avery, honey," Vinnia leaned forward conspiratorially, her hands clasped in her lap. "We really need to keep this quiet. We don't want this to cause any trouble. We're not even sure yet, well—" She shrugged.

"Whatever you say here is completely in confidence. If I can't help you, we'll find—"

"Oh, no!" Vinnia cut me off. "There mustn't be anyone else. We—"

"That's enough." Hattie gently reasserted command. "Avery, we want to know if we can sell the house, or our part of it. We wondered who really owns it. You must know, though, that Aletha refuses to hear any of this. She's vehemently opposed to any such change. You understand."

I certainly did. Aletha, my great-aunt Letha—Hattie's and Vinnia's older sister—was an awesome force who had served, after their mother's death decades earlier, as the family matriarch. Hattie's easy assumption of command came from years as a teacher, but her skills were no match for the naturally superior and equally well-honed skills of her older, larger, more imposing sister.

"Why do you want to sell the house?"

Vinnia made conciliatory patting motions with her plump, pink hands. "Now, we're not sure we do. We're just—"

"Looking at our options. We're not young anymore. We have to think about the future."

Not young, true, but in my life, my three great-aunts had always been tireless constants, and when it came to changing any of those constants in my life, I was with Aunt Letha; I just didn't want to hear any of it. None of it.

"But what—"

Hattie read my unanswered question. "We're looking at some long-term options. Maybe an apartment or cottage in one of those new retirement communities."

"Ava moved into one. It's all the way over near Clemson," Vinnia explained. "They have a nursing facility if you need it, and someone cleans your room if you want, and they even cook your meals and come looking for you if you don't show up."

Sort of like the county jail, except with old people, I thought. Out loud, I said, "Sounds kind of—regimented. Why do—"

"We're looking at several places. It would just be nice not to have to worry about maintaining that rambling old house."

"Ava has the cutest little apartment with a patio and flowers." Vinnia beamed.

I shivered. I wanted to put my hands over my ears and hum and stomp my feet so I wouldn't have to hear any of this. I had lived in cute little apartments with patios and a condo with a balcony. The thought of their bland sameness absorbing the rich lives of my great-aunts distressed me.

I tried to keep a look of professional openness on my face. "What do you have there?" I indicated the bundled papers Hattie still held. Three thick sheaves of paper, each folded in thirds, were bound with rubber bands.

"Our father's will." She handed it to me ceremoniously. "And our brother's will—your grandfather's. And the deed to the property."

I accepted them each in turn and held them, making no move to unbind and open them. To lawyers, wills are usually matter-of-fact, though on occasion they offer interesting intellectual puzzles, attempts to navigate the arcane rules of trusts and estates while accommodating the to-be-deceased's wishes to reward or punish loved ones. When the document in your hand marks the last will and testament of a grandfather in whose legal footsteps you found yourself tottering like a toddler, it was no longer predictable or arcane. I could almost feel his hand on it.

I stared at the folded papers a bit too long. These ladies had known me all my life; their silence hinted that they knew some of what I was feeling. After all, they were surely wrestling with their own uncertainty.

"Aunt Hattie, Aunt Vinnia." I hoped I sounded professional. "I'll read these over, see what they say, see how the property was transferred."

"Avery, understand we don't like going behind Aletha's back. We've talked to her about this. Rather, we've tried to talk," Hattie emphasized. "Aletha just makes a rude sound and marches out of the room."

Vinnia nodded, her brows knit together.

"I understand." Boy, did I understand. Aunt Letha was a force of nature.

"We just need some information. We're not set on any course. We got to thinking and realized how little we know. Father passed away and left the house to Avery, as the oldest and only male child. When he died, Aletha took the lead in getting his estate probated, and neither of us had any reason to pay attention to how the ownership was divided."

My grandfather—and my namesake—had died when I was in law school.

"Yes, ma'am." I wanted to say, *Listen, Dad will keep doing all your home repairs. I'll come bring your meals. You can't leave.* But that's not why they'd come to my office. They were treating me like an adult. The least I could do was return the compliment. Even if my brain was screaming *But I don't want things to change. Not this much.*

"Are you going to Lydia's opening night on Friday?" I needed to change the subject.

"Absolutely," said Hattie as they stood to take their leave.

"We wouldn't miss it," said Vinnia, slipping her flower-embroidered purse onto her arm. "We talked about having dinner for everyone before the play, to celebrate, but your mother wisely pointed out that Lydia and Frank would be too distracted to enjoy it. So we'll do something Sunday, after church."

"Great," I said, escorting them to the front hall.

"You still have an awful lot of work to do here, don't you?" said Hattie, surveying the jumble of boxes and paper and teetering stacks of books.

I could only nod.

"It's so nice that Avery's books will have a good home now," said Vinnia, beaming. "They were packed away too long." She leaned over and clasped my wrist in her warm hand. "He would be so pleased."

"I hope so," I said, almost in a whisper.

My office phone started ringing before we could spend more time getting misty-eyed.

"We'll talk to you later."

I waved goodbye and stepped back into my office.

"Avery. Noah Lakefield. Forgot to ask when you were here. Something I'm working on reminded me. Would you be willing to be my tour guide? At your convenience, of course."

Wow. Didn't see that coming. Maybe my visit had jostled him out of his peculiar mood. "I'll have to dig around," I said. "See if I have a pith helmet and a whistle. What you got in mind?" My voice sounded a tad sarcastic, even to me. Noah didn't seem to notice.

"The Chattooga River. I've watched *Deliverance* on that old movie channel. Here I am, so close. I ought to see the icon itself."

"Uh, sure." How to explain to him that most folks around here despised James Dickey, his book, the movie, and Ted Turner for broadcasting it incessantly? And how to explain that you couldn't just go *see* the river the way the movie showed it? There wasn't an overlook, and it wasn't a Disney ride. I didn't say any of that.

"Great," he said. "Tomorrow morning work for you? I'll pick you up."

"Uh, sure, I can do tomorrow. But I'll have to meet you." I'd planned to stay the night at the cabin. I could spare a little time to show him his icon before I had to head into town in the morning, but I wasn't about to first drive all the way back to town to pick him up. "You know the little store right before the crossroads, where the road forks toward Cashiers and Highlands?"

"Yeah, I think so. On the left?"

"Eight o'clock okay?"

"Fine with me," he said. "Oh, by the way. Sorry about what I said earlier, about your dad. I've just—work's got me distracted right now."

"Sure." What else could I say? He'd have to fight his own battles at the paper. That wasn't any of my concern, I had to keep reminding myself.

Cissie was going to give up on me if I didn't hurry. While I was talking to Noah, I'd turned off lights and my computer. As soon as I hung up the phone, I hefted my satchel, hoping I'd stuffed in everything I'd need for my out-of-the-ordinary afternoon and morning appointments.

Cissie peeked through the lace curtain as soon as she heard me climbing the steps to her cottage. Cissie's English flower garden, wicker porch swing with ruffled cushions, and her affection for her inherited English rose tea service seemed at odds with her very postmodern attitude toward love and marriage—and sex. I'd known Cissie long enough to know what most people didn't: She had a stack of romance novels hidden in her bedside stand, and she dreamed her prince would one day ride in and sweep her off her feet.

So far, she'd kissed a lot of frogs. She'd done lots of things with the frogs. They'd all stayed frogs.

"A'vry! I've been waiting and waiting. Wherever have you been? After you called and mentioned that nasty letter, it was all I could think about. I know it's just sitting there in that drawer, oozing venom like a snake. I'm not even going to touch it. You'll have to get it."

I was glad she stopped for a breath.

"Do you have a gallon-sized freezer bag?" I knew I'd forgotten something—the plastic bag I'd gotten out of the office kitchen.

Cissie looked puzzled.

"To store it in, in case there are any fingerprints."

I followed Cissie through her effusively floral sitting room to her tiny, immaculate kitchen. Even though I could never live with this many flowers and ruffles and bows, somehow I liked Cissie's house. It felt doll-like and ordered and bright.

"Here." She pulled a bag from a tidy drawer. "The letter's in the cupboard, in the parlor. Just get it out of here."

She fluttered her hands as if to dispel smoke, shooing me ahead of her.

"A'vry, did you know Len Ruffin, the man they found dead in that gold mine? Did you know he got a letter, too?"

I turned to her, with the cupboard drawer only half open.

"He sure did. You realize what that means? Somebody didn't like him, somebody killed him. That's just . . . frightening."

Cissie didn't know how frightening. She didn't know about Suse Knight's letter, or mine. I turned quickly back to my task so she couldn't see my face. I slid her wrinkled letter into the plastic bag, trying not to smudge anything it might hold.

"I've had my hands all over that thing. It's probably got tear stains on it. It scared me so. It . . . hurt." Her voice broke. "I probably ruined anything on it."

"I don't know that L.J. will be interested, but just in case it might be useful." I shrugged.

Cissie gave a gentle snort and brushed a loose strand of golden blond hair behind her ear. "L.J. Peters investigating something like this. Rousting drunks, I can believe. But—" She huffed again.

I held the plastic bag by one corner, careful not to let the letter shift about inside. I gave Cissie a quick hug.

"Don't worry about it, okay? But do take precautions."

"Don't you worry. I'm locking myself in here. Until Jeff comes."

"Jeff?" I raised an eyebrow but didn't say, *Not the preacher, I hope.*

She gave me her catty-sly smile. "You haven't met him. He's new in town. Lives out on the lake. His wife died and he sold his business and moved here. Didn't want to be around sad memories."

I didn't ask why he'd left the good memories behind as well. Cissie would be too busy treating him to some new memories to worry about that.

I stepped onto the porch and heard her latch the door behind me. She peeked around the lace curtain and waggled her fingers bye.

Time was too crunched for me to run by my parents' house. Tomorrow, though, I'd make a point to get my .38 and concealed-carry permit out of the lockbox in the top of my old bedroom closet. Unlike Cissie, I couldn't hide in my house and wait for my tennis partner to show up, so I needed to follow my own advice about taking precautions.

Wednesday Afternoon

Visiting Cissie's orderly—if overly floral—cottage shifted my thoughts again to my free-floating homelessness. Better to think about that than the bagged letter I carried gingerly to the car between thumb and forefinger.

I backed out of Cissie's drive and turned toward the Law Enforcement Center. The sheriff's minions could decide what to do with Cissie's letter—and mine. *Dang.* I forgot to unearth it and bring it with me. And Suse Knight's. How could I have forgotten them? Too much distracting me as I left the office.

The narrow circular road through Cissie's neighborhood had steep pitches and forced me to drive slowly—which was fortunate, or I might not have stopped in time.

I couldn't decide at first what it was. The animal minced across the road in front of me on its skinny legs, amazingly nimble considering its heft, its back as high as the car's hood.

Bambi, the potbellied pig. After she crossed into the wooded area at the side of the road, she half-turned to study me, her tiny eye glittering. She offered me that small smile pigs have frozen at the corner of their mouths before she sauntered into the undergrowth of someone's naturally landscaped lot. *Run, Bambi, run.*

Should I call the sheriff's office to report the sighting? Wait to watch the deputies thrash around in someone's rare shrub and wild-flower collection? Was Bambi really in much danger from cold weather or predators? Maybe from cars, judging from my near miss, but she looked well fed and content, as only a pig can.

I felt a little guilty, but I opted not to do my civic duty. I didn't immediately report Bambi's whereabouts. Even though I was running late for my meeting with Tim McDonald, I drove back to the office, found my letter, got Suse Knight's out of the desk drawer, and went to deliver all three letters into the hands of law enforcement.

My reward for not calling ahead: Rudy was out. The kid at the front desk managed to look both bored and officious, neither of these becoming attitudes in somebody who's head hadn't grown to fit his ears and whose neck didn't fill the collar of his uniform shirt.

"Can you call him? I have something he'll be interested in." I stood holding my gallon-size plastic bags, the edges pinched gingerly between two fingers.

"I can see that Deputy Mellin gets whatever." He halfheartedly extended a hand to accept the bags.

"No-o. I need to see him." I stood there, stubbornly frozen in place. I wasn't about to hand this insolent teenager—he looked about fifteen—letters chastising me and Cissie for bad behavior. It would be embarrassing enough to relinquish them to Rudy. At the same time, I didn't want to leave here with them. I wanted them out of my hands, literally.

Junior Cop Boy just stared at me.

"Is there somebody here from crime scene investigation that I could talk to?"

He rolled his eyes and lifted a phone receiver, murmured into it, waited, murmured some more, and finally turned to me. "Lester Watts can see you. End of the hall, to your right."

Lester, who had been designated the crime scene photographer after a car accident left him partially disabled, didn't seem any happier to see me than Junior Cop Boy had been, but I felt better about handing the letters over to him. He'd been a cop so long he'd had any judgmental tendencies worn off him. He scarcely raised an eyebrow, just said he'd talk to Rudy and get them processed for prints.

I left the Law Enforcement Center and raced up the mountain, figuring I wouldn't meet any boy deputies with radar guns that late on a weekday afternoon. Just past the country store where I'd arranged to meet Noah Lakefield tomorrow, I took the left fork. Farther up the road, the directional signs I'd expected to see for Yellow Fork Camp were gone, and I missed the turn. I retraced and, on the next pass, found the rutted and potholed road through the woods back into the old summer camp.

The arched wooden gateway at the end of the road still rustically spelled out YELLOW FORK CAMP overhead in silvered-gray wood slats. Cabins and recreational buildings still stood in a tired circle around a red clay common area, the color the dirt around here turns once any dark topsoil is blown or worked away. A couple of old pickups and a faded red SUV were parked alongside a building fronted by a deep porch. I drove toward that building, since the trucks represented the only signs of life.

As soon as I opened my car door, I heard a loud shout, so I followed the sound behind the buildings where the old ball fields gently sloped toward the lake.

In the middle of what had been the softball field, three towering wooden masts, looking fresh and dark compared to the weathered gray and tired red of the rest of the camp, rose from recently dug red-clay mounds. A man with a shaved head, his black pants stuffed into combat boots and muscles straining his black T-shirt, barked orders at a raggedy group.

He had his back turned to me, so I couldn't understand his words, but his six listeners were giving weak imitations of standing at attention. In their oversized jeans, wrinkled shirts, and ball caps, the four guys were giving poor imitations indeed. The two girls weren't even trying. One, in her tight jeans and even tighter T-shirt, had her arms crossed trying to keep warm in the weak March sun. The other girl had her hands crammed deep in the pockets of her windbreaker.

All six listened as the bald commandant strode back and forth in front of them, one hand held at parade rest behind his back, the other rhythmically whacking his leg with a baton.

"Miz Andrews?"

I jumped, startled by the voice in my left ear.

"I thought you knew to come to the office." A short man with gleaming white hair and an unlined face fixed me with surprising blue eyes.

"Tim McDonald? Avery." I offered him my hand.

His handshake was curt, almost dismissive. "Glad to meet you." He turned us toward the sagging building with the deep porch and away from the field. I wasn't that easily deterred.

"What's that?"

"A test run for one of our executive training camps. We'll be bringing business executives here for team building and motivational retreats." He spoke with well-rehearsed salesmanship as he led me back toward the camp buildings.

I nodded, glancing over my shoulder. Undoubtedly some of the business types forced up here by well-intentioned bosses or sales departments would react with the same faked attention the twenty-somethings were currently showing the drill instructor.

Our foot treads sounded loud on the curled wooden floor boards, and the door stuck a bit in its frame as Tim McDonald ushered me inside.

Nothing in the office looked ready for an influx of well-heeled business executives. It wouldn't have withstood the arrival of a few Brownie Scouts on a day trip. A scarred desk and two sofas were shoved against the wall, and several slatted armchairs with the cushions in tatters were stacked on top. The only pieces in use were six webbed lawn chairs in unexpected primary colors and a rickety folding table holding a few rolls of blueprint paper.

A door at the back of the room, opposite where we'd entered, swung open, and I glimpsed a well-lit shop reminiscent of my dad's at home. Inside, a man wearing a face shield fed a length of pipe into a shrill saw blade. At least they were working to get this place in shape.

The newcomer closed the shop door behind him, cutting out most of the noise, and joined us.

Tim did the honors. "Avery Andrews. Mitch Eggles."

Mitch Eggles looked about fifty. Over his bushy woodsman beard, his dark eyes studied me. He nodded but didn't offer a handshake. Tim turned a couple of the bright lawn chairs to face a third, which he indicated I should take.

In my previous life, my clients had come to me knowing who I was and what I could do. Clients hadn't interviewed me. Well, they probably had, but it never had this flavor of an inquisition.

I sat facing Tim and Mitch, waiting. I had to admit I was curious. As I had explained to Tim on the phone, I charged by the hour. They'd wanted to see me on their turf, so this was their game and their dime.

The two exchanged subtle glances, the webbed lawn chairs creaking slightly with any movement.

Tim said, "Miz, um, Avery, we wanted to meet you face-to-face. So we could all . . . take each other's measure."

I refrained from nodding. Women nod to say, "I hear you." Men nod to say, "I agree with you." I returned Mitch's silent steady stare. I didn't want him to think I agreed with anything yet.

"Our organization is in its start-up stage," Tim said. "We'll need a lawyer to help with certain legal details. You know the kinds of things—deeds, setting up our organization, the usual things businesses do."

We all sat a moment. I still didn't nod.

"We also might need a lawyer who is good in court. We've heard you are. Not all lawyers who do routine paperwork can handle a lawsuit. Least, that's what we understand."

"That's true. You suing or being sued?"

"Being . . . Well, neither one. We just want to be prepared. Should the need arise."

As Tim talked, I kept an eye on Mitch, who stared back from out of his bushy beard and eyebrows like a wolf in a den.

"What kinds of situations do you anticipate? Liability lawsuits because someone was injured? Or—" I left the question for him to fill in the blanks.

He dodged. "We understand you represented—or counseled— the Posse, or individual members of that group."

That took me by surprise. I would've described it as Max and members of the Posse motorcycle gang counseling me, or better yet, using me as an errand girl to send messages to the sheriff back in November.

"I'm really not at liberty to discuss other clients' business. I'm sure you understand." I could dodge questions, too.

Tim nodded, accepting that as only right. Mitch sat forward.

"So, young lady, answer me something. Do you think that once law enforcement has named someone as a person of interest, that that person is probably guilty?" His eyes bored into mine.

I blinked, surprised at the question and surprised when Melvin and his wife's murder popped into my mind. "Cops can make mistakes, sir. That's why we have courts of law—and defense attorneys."

Mitch's beard parted to ask another question, but when Tim put a hand on Mitch's arm, he closed his mouth. Mitch's lips worked in and out as he settled back in his chair, still watching me. I watched back. Even though Tim was doing most of the talking, Mitch was the one to contend with.

"Avery, I can't thank you enough for agreeing to come here to meet with us," Tim said, both palms on the plastic arms of his lawn chair, signaling the end of the interview. "Make sure I have your correct mailing address. We'll send a check for the time you've spent this afternoon."

Huh? I took the hint and stood, trying not to look befuddled or too new at this small-practice lawyer stuff. Should I ask for details? Assume this was an audition? I did need to clear up one thing.

"Tim, Mitch. I hope you understand this doesn't mean I agree to represent you. With all due respect, you haven't given me much information about what you need done. I'd want to make sure my skills would be the best match for you."

I didn't want to scare off potential clients—especially if they mailed their check as promised and it cleared. But this operation had some question marks around it. Mitch and his almost-mute stare, for one.

Tim nodded as he led the way to the warped front door. "Certainly, certainly. I'm sorry we can't be more specific right now. You know how it is with start-ups. We just wanted to make sure we knew who to call, if and when the need arises."

The cupped and weathered floorboards on the porch creaked under our steps. Tim must have read my thoughts. "We have a lot of work to do before we host our first training group, that's for sure." His hand hovered protectively at my elbow, to make sure I made it safely down the stairs. In the sunlight, I was again struck by how youthful his tan face and crystal-blue eyes looked, despite his shock of silver hair.

"That's true of any new business, isn't it?" I said, thinking of my own stacks of books and the old Victorian's suspect electrical wiring.

As Tim escorted me toward my car, a loud bellow from the drill sergeant drew my attention to what I could glimpse of the converted softball fields. The instructor had the kids scaling the wooden towers on ropes. This crew was a personal injury lawsuit waiting to happen. An even more likely risk was Sergeant Bilko popping a blood vessel while yelling at those kids. I hoped Tim and Mitch had workers' comp insurance.

Tim closed my car door for me, took a step back, and waved goodbye. I drove slowly toward the camp gate and watched in my rearview mirror until he disappeared onto the shaded porch.

Once out the gate, I alternately watched my rearview mirror and studied the woods on the left side of the road. Best I could tell, the road circled fairly close around behind the camp buildings. If so, I should be able to see the softball field—yep, through a break in the trees.

I eased my Mustang to the side of the road and hoped the slight embankment and the thick undergrowth hid the engine noise from the ball field below—or the absence of engine noise, when I cut it off. I left my door open and scrambled up the three-foot embankment to get a better view.

The still-cold March air, with its low humidity, carried the random barked orders from the man in black fatigues. The two girls and one of the guys stood on the ground, holding ropes for the three young men who were at different stages of scaling the thick wooden poles.

I've never rappelled or rock-climbed, so I wasn't sure what I was watching, but it looked as though each wore some kind of sawtooth boots and climbed using a combination of his own strength and that of the kid on the ground roped to him. Another thick rope ran between the three, from one pole-climber to another. Redundant safety systems? That was good.

The guy climbing on the center pole lagged six or eight feet behind the other two when they made it to the top of their poles. Having Sarge directly below the center pole screaming up at him didn't either calm him or encourage him. I wouldn't want Sarge staring up at my fanny, screaming. Remind me not to sign up for summer camp here.

The kid lost some ground thanks to the yelling, but he finally attained the pinnacle.

I expected the three to rappel down. Instead they clung to the top, intent on some task. Sarge barked more orders, unintelligible from my vantage. They appeared to be fixing the thick rope that linked them to the top of each pole.

The guy clinging to the pole on the right yelled across at his companions, what sounded like a count to three. Then what I'd taken to be a thick rope unfurled. It whipped loudly as it rolled open, turning into a black banner at least two stories high. A plain black banner. No message, just an impressively large black canvas swaying slightly at the edges.

I didn't hear Sarge congratulate them. Maybe his praise fell like the gentle rain of mercy.

Before the kids could rappel down behind the banner, I picked my way through the scrub brush and down the embankment to the car. I waited until I had driven a few yards down the road before I closed my oversize car door, not wanting the sound to attract attention.

Corporations paid for a lot of strange things in hopes of gaining a competitive edge. I could only wish Mitch and Tim and Sarge Whosit all the best.

Wednesday Night/
Thursday Morning

I'd piddled around the cabin, picking up fallen tree limbs in the winter-weedy yard, and sweeping and dusting inside. The cabin was solitary, and darkness closed in solid, first among the pine trees and hardwoods edging the clearing, and eventually tight around the cabin itself. The few security lights dotted around the other lake cabins muted the stars. There would be no moon.

I settled in, as was my occasional ritual, with peanut butter, Mom's blackberry jelly, loaf bread I kept in the freezer, and some ultrapasteurized milk from the cupboard.

I ate sitting sideways in my favorite stuffed chair, my legs hooked over the arm, my plate under my chin, and one of my grandfather's battered leather journals propped open on my knees. I felt in need of a visit with him.

I thumbed back to a spot where I'd left off a couple of days earlier. Over the ridge behind the cabin, my grandfather's land nestled against the national park. The ire in his words surprised me, as he ranted about the government landgrab, buying mountain property for pennies on the dollar to piece together the national forest.

Even though I knew the Southerner's distrust of government ran deep in him, he'd always been a reverent respecter of nature. He'd even tipped into his journal a now-yellowed news photo of a man standing in front of a poplar tree trunk, a photo likely taken before he was born, before these forests had been logged almost to extinction by men who had to feed families off tough land. Trees are, after all, endlessly renewable, they thought. No need to worry—until erosion carried off the topsoil and the need for timber and pulpwood outpaced long-term tree growth. Four grown men standing together would have barely blocked the trunk from view. No more trees that size, certainly no poplars.

> One of the loggers who helped scalp this land was also the one who encouraged the government to buy what became the wilderness area in western North Carolina, one of the few virgin stands of timber left. So-called forestry experts say trees need to be cut to keep the system healthy, to open up for new growth. Amazing that the forests here did so well before we started "managing" them. Ought to be left alone now.
>
> Never any mention of the men who lost their family homesteads or their livelihoods. Bet they'd rather not be managed, down the hill in some textile mill, any more than the trees needed to be managed.

I thought of the road cut in to Golden Cove and all those towering trees and the tiny delicate plants and birds' nests and squirrels. As stewards, we don't manage well.

I read awhile, and eventually nodded to sleep in the chair.

Despite stumbling to bed after midnight, I woke early, freshened up, and gently guided my grandfather's vintage Mustang convertible over the rutted dirt road from the cabin. I viewed the thick woods around Luna Lake with a new eye, the perspective from my grandfather's almost one-hundred-year span, a perspective of unresolved conflict over what to protect and how.

At Pop's Place, I had just finished topping off my gas tank when Noah arrived. Miraculously, his cumbersome vehicle didn't turn over as he whipped into the store's parking lot. The car came to rest in a faint cloud of dust near the gas pump, sun glinting off the big silver canoe.

"Hi!" He yelled and waved as he climbed out. "Do you think it'll be okay if I leave my car here? Or should I follow you?"

"We can ask." Thank the good Lord he wasn't planning on me riding with him. Or using that ridiculous canoe on the river.

He held Pop's wooden screen door open for me, and music greeted us. All eyes inside turned to study us as we came in. No one missed a beat, literally. No emotion. No greeting. Just stares.

Here in Pop's Place, the regulars assembled on a rump-worn sofa and assorted chairs to pick or strum an instrument or tap a foot in time to the music. It didn't take them but an eyeblink to recognize us as nothing more than paying customers, thereby worth not another look.

Noah stood frozen, staring and listening, a tentative smile on his face as if he'd landed among an alien race with whom he hoped to make friends. I watched Noah and could see Pop's Place afresh, through his eyes. The wood shelves and creaky uneven plank floor sanded by decades of shuffling feet. The neatly stacked but dusty merchandise. No fast-food franchises or day-bright fluorescents in this roadside store. Worn, comfortable, slightly oily smelling. And loud with live music.

This morning's gathering was small, only four players and a couple of full-time listeners. Plenty enough to fill the low-raftered building with banjo, guitar, and mandolin music. On the weekend, the crowd would spill out the door, weather permitting. Some singers might come to join in, a couple of clog dancers on the fringe of the crowd perhaps. Between now and then, the players would ebb and flow, depending on who got off work or whose wife would let him out of the house. Most times, though, Pop's had music. Authentic mountain folk music or bluegrass or twangy old Nashville country or tub-thumping gospel.

I'd watched for Noah's reaction because, only a few months earlier, I myself had been surprised by my own reaction. When I'd first walked back in here, after being away practicing law in Columbia and Charleston, I'd been surprised. Not surprised to find music here, but surprised to realize I had never found it anywhere else but home.

This wasn't the only place around Dacus where folks gathered to play music. Far from it. Friday or Saturday night square dances at the state park or over in Dillard, Georgia. Wednesday night or Sunday afternoon gospel singings at churches. Family gatherings around the piano. Heck, even school bus trips where most of the kids knew the words to "The Old Rugged Cross" or "That Good Ol' Mountain Dew," a silly ode to moonshine, not a soft drink jingle. The surprise had been realizing I'd never found casual communal music anywhere else but home.

The circled players studied the dusty threadless rug at their feet, focused on the changing leads in "Rollin' in My Sweet Baby's Arms," a Doc Watson favorite.

The grin spread on Noah's face, and he looked like he planned to join them. I took his elbow and steered him toward the door. It might look impromptu, but there were rules. Damn cinch Noah didn't know what they were and didn't know any better than to sing or get in the way of somebody's fret arm.

"That was great! Who are they? What was that song?" Noah practically danced toward my car. "I should do an article."

I didn't break it to him that *National Geographic* had already done one, back when he was in grammar school.

When I'd asked if we could leave his vehicle, the guy at the register had just nodded. Wait'll he got a load of Noah's dual-habitat amphibimobile parked beside his store.

"Is it some kind of club?" Noah asked.

"Whoever shows up plays. Pretty much anytime."

"Wow." Noah slumped into the Mustang's low seat and stared

back at the store as I pulled away. "They're good enough to go professional."

"A couple of them are professional, I guess you could say." Good enough, sure. Them and dozens more around here who'd grown up listening to, then playing with their grandfathers or aunts.

"Lots of folks around here save their music for pleasure and work jobs to pay the bills." I didn't try explaining that to some around here—probably most of those guys' wives—making music, like painting or writing or reading, was a waste of time, unless it was in church. Just living required too much effort for such frivolity. Granddad always said it was the schizophrenia of being both Scots and Irish, dour and fun-loving.

As I turned left toward the fish hatchery, I asked, "Any part of the Chattooga in particular?"

I took the first curve fast. Noah reached for his seatbelt—a lap belt that hadn't been factory issue when this car rolled off the line in the midsixties.

"Something I would've seen in the movie. You know, *Deliverance.*"

"Sorry. You'd have to be on the river to see that, farther down on Sections III and IV." I knew the scenery he was talking about. Roads didn't reach most of the famous views. Thank goodness, else they'd already be ruined by stampeding tourists.

A glance in his direction confirmed that he was disappointed. And maybe a little nervous about how fast I was driving.

"How about I take you to one of my favorite places. You can see the river up close." No way I wanted to fuel the male fantasy that James Dickey—durn his hide—had fed with his alcohol-fired imagination four decades back.

Fifteen minutes later—about the time Noah realized I knew this road well enough that he could relax his stranglehold on the door handle—I turned off at the brown U.S. Forest Service sign to the hatchery.

I was forced to slow down as the shoestring road doubled sharply back on itself and we climbed down past thick laurel hells, dropping steeply into a deep-cut valley that registered the state's lowest temperature nearly every morning. Even twenty miles an hour is fast if the curve is sharp enough.

We pulled into the heavily shaded, damp green parking area buried deep, as if we'd descended into a hidden land.

We climbed out and could feel how much the temperature had dropped. "You need a hat or anything?" I asked as I put on my earmuffs. I don't care if they look goofy; I hate cold ears.

"Uh, no. I'm fine." He had on a flannel shirt and a sleeveless down vest. He looked cold to me, so I handed him an extra knit hat—what we always called a toboggan—from the jumble of stuff in my backseat.

"The fish hatchery's to the right. We can see the trout they're raising to stock the river. Or we can go see the river first."

Noah stared around him, his thumbs hooked in his jeans pockets. He looked surprised—or awed. Whether by the cold or the massive trees or the dripping quiet, I couldn't tell.

"The river," he said.

Even in March, the undergrowth was dense and green, so the path's opening from the parking lot wasn't easy to spot, even though a signboard stood beside it, complete with a map and rules for campers. I didn't stop to read it.

As we strolled along the path, Noah craned his neck and studied treetops that almost disappeared from view.

"Do you have trees like this in Vail?" I asked. "I've never been."

"We've got ski slopes and fake Swiss chalets and local people who can't live there anymore because the taxes are too damned high." The anger in his voice was old and only a bit worn. "Nothing like this." His voice trailed off, and he kept studying the treetops, the loamy dark soil, the evergreen undergrowth.

Scattered at intervals along the trail, wooded bowers hid lichen-crusted picnic tables. As we turned the last bend, I prepared to dramatically present his first glimpse of the river.

"Dang." I stopped dead. Where was the bridge? Only concrete pyramid-shaped pillars stood in the water, showing where the footbridge across the river once stood. "The hurricane. I forgot all about . . . I thought they'd rebuilt it."

"Hurricane? This far inland?"

"Gulf storms often don't blow themselves out until they hit the Appalachian chain." Flash flood warnings meant something in a land of steep hillsides, fast water, and few escape routes.

"Gosh, Noah, I'm sorry. I—This is the only way I know to the trail that follows the river." I felt like an idiot. Some local expert I was.

"This is the Chattooga?" He sounded hesitant, not wanting to ridicule and, at the same time, not wanting to fall for some kind of prank.

"It's the East Fork. One of the quieter parts." This sure wasn't what he had expected. This section wasn't one of the rocky tumbling torrents that could bend a metal Grumman canoe around a boulder. This was trout-fishing territory. Below us, the trees bowed over the river, framing it; the water flowed noisily over rocks; the sound and smell of air and earth and water surrounded us completely.

"We can double back. There must be another trail around to El-licott's Rock." The water sounds were so loud I had to lean in close to be heard. And this was the gentle section.

He shook his head absently, absorbed in his surroundings, taking it in.

"No-o, that's okay. This is good. We can sit here a minute." He looked at his watch. "I didn't realize how long a drive it was. I'll need to head back to town before long. I forgot to tell you about that, didn't I? I got sidetracked back at the store. There's a press conference I should attend at the nuclear power plant. Can we just sit here a minute?"

Odd change of plans, but okay with me. We both perched on the blunted concrete pyramid on the riverbank and stared down into the water glistening over the rods.

"So, how does this compare to home?" I asked.

He sat quiet a moment, thinking. "It's greener. Of course, we have fast-moving water, and rocks. But not quite this sound. Or the dank smell. I can't—It's hard to describe. It's . . . claustrophobic."

I raised my eyebrows. Not the awed, poetic tribute to my homeland I'd expected.

"There's so much . . . stuff. It closes in. You can't see the open sky."

Now that he'd put it in words, I realized what had seemed skewed when I'd first visited the Rocky Mountains. I thought a recent and terrible windstorm had felled all the trees that lay like Pixy Stix on the ground, but people just stared when I asked about it. I finally realized what was missing: They had no thick green undergrowth to gracefully shroud the downed trees, to allow them to rot away unseen.

"Guess it is odd, compared to home. These squatty old mountains must seem puny, compared to the Rockies," I said.

"No, just different." He kept studying everything intently. "Darker. Like something could sneak up on you." He fell silent.

Talking about home didn't seem to interest him, so I foraged around for another topic. "Any more news about what killed Lionel Shoal or Suse Knight?" That was a topic that had probably occupied his attention as much as it had mine over the last few days.

"No. Autopsy reports won't be complete for a few weeks. Toxicology can take a while."

"Things certainly move faster on television."

He snorted, probably thinking, *And everywhere else outside this godforsaken state.*

"Any more ideas about a link between Shoal and Ruffin?" I asked.

"Nope. Neither one of them had a lot of friends, I can tell you that. And when it comes to Len Ruffin, nobody has trouble speaking ill of the dead. Except his wife, who is too mousy to say much of anything."

"How about Shoal?"

He shrugged. "A developer one step ahead of irate investors in several states. Oh, and one step ahead of a wife he'd robbed and left holding the bag while he shacked up with a silicone-enhanced replacement who's angry because she miscalculated his net worth. What more can I say?"

So Noah had found the real Mrs. Shoal. I hated to think of Alex being exposed or embarrassed any further. I knew I couldn't protect her, and after what she'd been through, could it really get any worse?

"And Suse Knight?"

He broke his focus on the river to face me. "You could fill me in on that one," he said. "I understand you're representing her husband."

I didn't bother wondering how Noah had found out about Carl Newland Knight's visit to my office. Dacus was, after all, a small town. I looked up, studying one of the towering hardwoods, not wanting my expression to inadvertently give away anything that might hurt Mr. Knight. One of my very few clients. I wondered what his friends called him.

"No comment, counselor?" He was still watching me.

"No comment."

"I'll take that as a yes, you're representing him."

I graced him with what Melvin calls my go-to-hell smile.

"You sure ask a lot of questions, counselor, but you don't supply many answers."

"I'm the one who told you how Lionel Shoal died. That's a pretty important connection, plenty for you to work on."

"Work on, yeah." He snorted. "Not much to print."

What had started as just idle conversation about Dacus's murder mysteries had gotten a little heated. I wasn't sure if it was me or something else eating at him, but Noah tripped into irate mode easily. Might as well lob him a question I was really curious about.

"You ever gonna tell me why you came to Dacus?"

He bent over, plucked a piece of straw grass, and began twirling it between his fingers.

"A job," he said. "What's your excuse?" The last was a jab, not a question.

"My family is here."

"That's not necessarily a reason to stay somewhere—or return.

Especially when—" He shrugged and turned back toward the water, deciding not to finish his thought.

I listened to the water bubble over the rocks. That alone was reason enough to come home, though this was the first opportunity I'd taken to enjoy it since I'd been back.

Noah checked his watch. "You ready to head out?"

"Sure." I dusted the leaf mold off the seat of my jeans. I had work to do, too, though I'd rather have spent the day hiking along the river to Ellicott's Rock. No need to argue with Noah. He was entitled to both his bad mood and his opinion.

We walked in silence, and I soaked up a few last smells and sounds.

As we pulled out of the damp, deep green parking lot, I said, "I'm sorry about our hike, about the bridge and all."

"No, that's okay. This was fine. It gave me a feel for the place. Just what I wanted." His voice was quiet, and he stared at the deep forest on either side as the car made the steep climb out of the valley. No sign of pique or bad mood. Just silence, a silence I chose to take as companionable. After we turned onto the main highway, he wrestled a notebook from his hip pocket and scribbled a few notes to himself as I sailed the last few miles down the mountain to where we'd left his car.

At Pop's Place, I waved him on his way, his ridiculous canoe contraption swaying as he pulled onto the blacktop. Strange fellow, that Noah Lakefield. Inside the store, I grabbed a pack of peanuts and a Coke. The musicians were taking a break.

Before I headed toward town, I clipped my plastic cup holder to the window frame—such amenities were not standard equipment on 1964 autos—and poured my peanuts into my Coke bottle. Always a treat in a glass bottle, and combining the two made it easier to drink and drive—and think—on curvy roads.

I kept playing victim association games in my head. There had to be some connection between the spate of odd deaths. Particularly Lionel Shoal and Suse Knight; they'd died in such a similar and gruesome way. But what could be the connection? In Suse Knight's case, an irate mother-to-be could have come after her for helping a shiftless boyfriend dodge a paternity bullet. I could see a woman being frustrated and angry enough to kill, knowing who the father was when the blood test said otherwise.

Did Suse Knight fake a paternity test for Shoal? Was that a connection? Seemed unlikely, given his age, though South Carolina's former senior senator sired children into his seventies. Anyway, I didn't see Valerie giving him enough leash to fool around on her. She'd have been wearing his ears on a necklace if she'd caught him running around.

What about Len Ruffin? Had Suse Knight faked a test for him? Had some irate pregnant lover killed them both? Hard to imagine. From what I'd heard of him, sowing misery close to home was his strong suit.

None of the three victims were easy people to mourn, but Ruffin, in my book, was the least likely to be missed. Anybody who'd hurt a child, his own daughter. Courts see similar cases with depressing repetition, but, despite the practice they get, courts offer poor protection, especially from parents. If Jesse had been my daughter, I might have considered killing him myself. But if the Ruffins were like-mother-like-daughter in the mousy-quiet department, could Mrs. Ruffin have suddenly turned into a tiger to defend her daughter—and herself? Unlikely. If she had, it would have been in a fit of passion, and he'd have been found dead on the kitchen or bedroom floor. If she had stuffed him in the mine, surely she wouldn't have let her daughter go on the plant dig, knowing he was there.

Of the three victims, Ruffin might be the one that most needed killing, but his was the murder that made the least sense. It didn't fit the pattern. How had Ruffin's body ended up stuffed in an abandoned mine? Wouldn't an autopsy show if he'd been killed in town, driven up the mountain, and dumped in the mine? Had somebody in Lionel Shoal's operation found him snooping around on the site? Had Ruffin discovered something Shoal wanted hidden, and been killed on the spot?

None of that made any sense. The only thing I knew for sure

about Ruffin was the one thing I couldn't forgive him. And the two people who were now safe from him seemed the least likely to have killed him.

Shooting somebody and stuffing him in a hole was an up-close and personal act. Poison was a cruel, impersonal, long-distance kind of murder. Maybe the poison candy deaths were the only related ones. Where had the candy come from? I certainly hoped L.J. had called in experienced help. Could she get the state crime lab and the FBI involved? When it comes to doing her job, L.J. tends to know when she's out of her league. I'll give her that.

Poison candy. From my dimly remembered legal reading, I recalled a product tampering case, a Victorian-era murder where a woman mailed her lover's wife a box of arsenic-laced chocolates. Surely, after anthrax letters and terror threats, no one would eat candy that came in the mail. Or would they? A beautiful box with a scrawled note. They would think it came from someone they knew. Which it probably had. That's what made it so very scary.

Poison-pen letters, poisoned candy. Was there a connection? That thought made my head spin. This whole thing had too much the flavor of an English drawing room murder. But in those, nothing more than a dainty line of blood trickled onto the hearth rug. No vomiting, no tortured contorted bodies. Lionel Shoal's face, that horror-house grin twisting his mouth, was seared into my memory. I wished I'd only heard about it, without the memory enhancers of smell and fear.

Forget about linking the victims. Who was capable of killing them? Someone unknown? Unlikely. These murders were intimate and personal.

The vengeful part of me would like to think Alex Shoal and Len Ruffin's wife had finally come to their senses and exacted their revenge. Highly unlikely. And what about Suse Knight? I couldn't see Alex Shoal sending Suse a box of poisoned candy to draw the police off her trail. If Alex had been that kind of woman, Lionel Shoal would've been dead a long time ago.

Who blew up Golden Cove? Did Lionel Shoal decide to destroy

it and leave town with his investors' money? If so, where were the screaming investors? Even if he was about to do a bunk, why go to the trouble of blowing up his buildings? Maybe the dynamite trail the police were following would lead somewhere. Melvin might know about the investors. I'd have to remember to ask him.

My speculations carried me all the way down the mountain to town. I turned left off Main Street, picked up the mail at the post office, and sat in the car sorting through it. Mostly junk. Notice of a South Carolina Bar Continuing Legal Education seminar. I needed to get some hours in, so I wouldn't be cramming at the end of the year. A good excuse to go to Columbia for chicken-fried steak at Yesterday's.

From between the sheets of a supermarket circular slid a familiar vellum envelope. I stared at it in my lap, at the careful blue script of the address.

My stomach knotted. I raised my hands, my body drawn back as if the envelope might strike.

Breathe. I needed to get this to Rudy. I couldn't open it, though I wanted to know what it said. This would be the first letter the lab had gotten intact. In case it might offer new forensic information. I scooped the envelope gently into the newspaper circular, laid it on the passenger seat, and turned toward the Law Enforcement Center.

Thursday Morning

"No way can we open it," Rudy said. "Lester Watts and I talked it over yesterday, after you brought those other letters in. The documents lab in Columbia will have to open it. We shipped off those you brought and the others we had just this morning. We'll send this one along to join them."

I hadn't thought about it needing to travel all the way to Columbia.

"You sure you can't just gently slit it open and take a peek?" I asked, only half joking. "You could wear gloves."

Rudy just sucked on his toothpick.

I knew better, but I had to ask. I should've opened the danged thing before I surrendered it. How embarrassing might it be? After all, none of the letters had been Rotary Club testimonials for the recipients.

"I'll have them fax a copy of it as soon as possible." Rudy's consolation prize to me for being a good citizen.

Best I could ask for. "Wait a minute. Did you just say 'the others'? There were other letters, besides the three I brought in?"

"Yep. We got a few calls over the last weeks, people said they'd gotten these weird letters. Tame stuff, so we didn't follow up. After all this other started happening, we went back to them. Two ladies let us have their letters to be tested. The other just wanted to file a complaint, but she didn't want anybody to read her letter. Not much we could do with that."

"What did they say? The ones you got."

Rudy rolled his eyes.

"Okay, that wasn't fair." I wouldn't want him broadcasting the contents of my letter to whoever asked.

"Trust me," he said. "It was tame stuff. Along the lines of telling them to stop gossiping."

"Wonder why they kept their letters," I said, mostly trying to figure it out for myself.

Rudy's look said, *So why did you?* If he'd gotten an anonymous letter, he wouldn't have that look.

"Another question: Where did the candy come from?"

"Candy?" Rudy's eyebrows went up in mock surprise, as if he didn't know what I meant.

"Oh, come on. The candy at Lionel Shoal's and Suse Knight's."

He dropped his pretense. "From a shop in Atlanta. Handmade specialty chocolates. No record of them shipping those to Dacus, but lots of people from here drive to Atlanta to shop, and lots pay cash." He sat on the edge of his desk, his toothpick planted at the corner of his mouth.

"Was there a note or anything with the candy?"

"We found the wrapping in the trash at Shoal's. Upstate South Carolina postmark. Mailed with regular postage stamps—too many stamps, to make sure it got there. Found a congratulations card on the side table. Signature was just a scrawl, could've said anything."

"What about at Suse Knight's?"

"No wrapping anywhere. Must have been thrown out. Did find

a thank-you card lying on the living room coffee table, so the cards look like more than a coincidence."

"Congratulations and thank you. He probably thought somebody was congratulating him on Golden Cove, and she thought a grateful client had sent her a gift. That would be enough to lull them into eating the candy." I shivered, a sudden chill.

"Yeah, I thought it was dumb to eat something that just showed up in the mail," said Rudy, nodding ruefully. "That could explain it, though."

I pride myself on being cautious, alert to scams and random danger, but I could see myself opening a special box of chocolates that came with a "welcome to your new office" card. Another chill ran up my back.

"I'd better get back to work," I said.

Rudy heaved himself off his desk and walked me the two steps to the hallway. "See you later."

As I entered the office's kitchen door, Melvin's voice greeted me from the recesses of his office. "Quite a way to run a business, showing up early afternoon without a word."

I veered left, into his office, and plopped down in his soft leather client chair. Not that clients ever came here. His investment clients lived all over the country. I don't think he had a single one in Dacus who could drop in for a visit. Lucky Melvin.

"I'm not the one who disappeared for a couple of days without a word," I said.

"Muddy sneakers? And jeans?" Melvin dimmed his computer screen and settled back in his chair. "Please be careful of the rug."

Sure enough, dark brown river-trail mud caked the side of one shoe.

"Sorry." I checked the bottom of my other shoe, to make sure it was clean, and tilted the errant one so it wouldn't get on his probably genuine Persian rug.

"Some of us have work to do," I smarted back. "We don't just sit at a computer managing investments."

"You certainly do have some work to do." His smile was wry. "I'm considering setting a BEWARE—DEMOLITION ZONE sign in front of your door. Maybe we should rethink the French doors. So many windows, such a clear view."

Ouch. He was kidding, but he was also right. "Some of us, as I said, have real work to do."

"Such as?" His smile was still bemused.

"Delivering evidence to the sheriff's office."

I hadn't told him about the poison-pen letters. Melvin had started out as a client in November, but he was becoming a friend and father confessor. I'd been too embarrassed to tell him about my first letter—it hadn't been very flattering, to either of us. Facing him now, I had to acknowledge to myself why I hadn't told him. The intimacy implied in the letter made me uncomfortable. I knew, from a long history working in an office full of men, that maintaining platonic friendships meant carefully maintaining boundaries. I hadn't wanted to cross any boundaries with Melvin, especially since our physical boundaries, as we set up our offices, weren't fully defined. But he deserved to know about the letter.

Dear Lord, had he gotten one of his own? That thought jolted me. I hadn't considered that.

My expression must have shown my surprise at that thought.

"You okay?" he asked.

"Um, yeah." Best to dive right in. "Several people—including me—have gotten anonymous letters."

I paused to see if he'd volunteer anything. He patiently waited for my story.

"It's the weirdest thing," I said. "You wouldn't think something like that would be so . . . frightening, but it is. Really scary. Not knowing who sent it. Or why."

Melvin leaned forward, his arms folded on his immaculate leather blotter. "These letters aren't . . . threatening, are they?"

"More like repent-or-else letters. The *or else* wasn't spelled out. Still . . ."

With a simple nod, Melvin let me know he didn't think I was crazy. "Whoever wrote you must have known you'd take it to the police. You're a lawyer, after all."

"Maybe," I said, feeling my way along an idea taking shape. "Maybe he or she didn't care whether I took it to the police."

His fingertips formed a contemplative tent as he listened.

"I didn't," I said. "Take it to the police. Not right away. Mine was kind of personal. It scolded me for moving in here. Said it wouldn't look right."

"Because?" He tried to control how much surprise showed on his face. "Because my wife was murdered?"

"No." It hadn't dawned on me that Melvin was sensitive about his own skeletons, things he knew people still gossiped about. "No. Just some, I don't know, antiquated sense of propriety."

He snorted. He'd grown up here. He knew what I meant.

"Guess there's really no criminal penalty for writing that kind of thing, is there?"

I'd not thought about that. "No. I . . . guess not."

"Without a threat or something, I mean."

Or something. Two dead people had gotten letters. That was a powerful "or something." I didn't want to dwell on that. I didn't feel free to tell him about the other letters. They had been shared in confidence.

Melvin changed the subject for me. "So where've you been playing in the leaves and mud?"

"Huh?"

He looked at the top of my head. "Leaves. Or leaf. In your hair."

I combed my fingers through my tangled hair. *Sheesh.* Deputy Mellin hadn't even bothered to tell me.

"Up on the river. I introduced Noah Lakefield to the Chattooga."

"Noah?" An odd note sounded in his voice.

"The new reporter at the newspaper. You met at the explosion."

"You took him on the river?" Melvin sounded almost—what? Territorial? Surely not jealous.

"Oh, gosh, no. We just went to the hatchery. Stupid me didn't know the bridge hadn't been replaced, so we didn't go far. Besides, he's from out west. Thick green cove forests seem to spook him a bit. I didn't think about going on the river. I haven't done that in ages."

"Want to go?"

"You raft?" Buttoned-down Melvin issuing spur-of-the-moment invitations? To go rafting?

"Kayak, usually." He said it with the disdain kayakers reserve for rafters. "But we can go with a raft group, if you'd rather. You free tomorrow?"

"Uh, sure. I think so." My short walk in the woods had whetted my appetite for getting outside. But what happened to chiding me about my eyesore office? Was I more surprised by his sudden out-doorsiness or his spontaneity?

"I'll make arrangements and get back to you. You going to stay up on the mountain tonight or at your parents?"

I mentally scrolled through what I had planned for today and to-morrow. Precious little with any income-generating potential.

"I'll probably stay in town tonight." I'd promised to bake cook-ies for the community theater's opening-night festivities. My niece Emma would be helping me or, more likely, bossing me around. "I can meet you here at the office."

"Great."

I never dreamed Melvin did anything more back-to-nature than walk to his Jeep. Maybe the hint of spring in the air and my mention of the river had stirred up a primal urge to return to nature.

I shut myself in my office. The clutter was getting to me, but I couldn't seem to make the unpacking go quickly. Or go at all. Too many interruptions.

I pulled out the file folder where I'd stuck the papers Aunt Hattie had given me. In my former big-law-firm life, my assistant used to type lovely file folder labels for me. Then she got a gadget that made labels. Looking at my almost undecipherable scrawl, maybe I needed to get a gadget. Making labels could distract me, keep me from reading these wills. Or thinking about what they might mean.

I hadn't spent any time reading wills since I'd finished my trusts and estates class in law school. I'd even had a friend draw up my own will, simple as it was. Even though I wouldn't admit it to anyone, opening these stiff, formal papers that were too close to home intimidated me.

Once I forced myself to start reading, it all appeared straightforward. My great-grandfather—Aletha's, Hattie's, Vinnia's, and Granddad's father—had bequeathed his various properties to his children. The house on Main Street—the family homeplace—was given to my grandfather as the "oldest and only surviving son." That wording gave me pause for a moment. Had there been another son? I'd never heard of one. The three sisters had been given some farm property and stocks and money. Granddad had been the residual legatee, the one who received anything left over after a few small gifts to charitable organizations, which included the Dacus First Baptist Church.

All pretty predictable. The boy gets the house. Great-granddad must have been a bit progressive. Not only had all my great-aunts attended college, they'd also received income-producing property at a time not far removed from when women were treated as property themselves.

I next opened the last will and testament of Avery Hampton Howe, my grandfather, which detailed his specific bequests. The cabin to his only child, my mother—which surprised me. Everyone in the family used it, and I'd never thought about who owned it. The house on Main Street had gone to Aletha, Vinnia, and Hattie in equal shares. The deed registered the house according to his wishes: The three sisters owned the house as joint tenants with right of survivorship. Each held an equal share which, upon the death of one, would pass to the survivors.

All very straightforward. Not like the wills we'd studied in class.

No violations of the rule against perpetuities, no defective witnesses. Simple and clean and valid.

The textbook wills that, over the centuries, had presented dramatic courtroom clashes held no real passion. Holding these wills, I realized a last testament is only an intellectual exercise when the transfer involves property you've never spent the night in and people you've never eaten Christmas dinner with. This one, for me, was difficult to critique, and quite powerful. Too close to home.

My grandfather—my idol and the reason I'd gone to law school—had done what his father had done: passed the family homestead down to those in the best position to use and care for it. Both men had relied on familial feeling and good sense to dictate how their heirs chose to live—and die. All had worked predictably well, right up until Ava whatever-her-name-was moved into a cute little retirement village apartment.

In order not to complicate the situation for his sisters, much younger than he was, my grandfather had left other property to my mother and had not included her as one of the joint owners of the home place. The three great-aunts could dispose of their house as they saw fit—as long as they all agreed.

How should I counsel Vinnia and Hattie? Technically, they shared ownership of the house equally with Aletha, but that didn't offer an easy solution. Aletha could buy them out, but I doubted she could pay enough to buy them a cute little retirement-village condo. Also, as the oldest of the three, Aletha was the one most likely to need nursing care first. A mean thought flashed to mind: *Maybe that's why Hattie and Vinnia are thinking about clearing out.* Nobody would relish caring for Aunt Letha.

I really wanted to talk to Mom or Dad, but I had to keep this family issue to myself.

One thing I couldn't bring myself to contemplate was my family no longer living in that house. I needed somewhere to live. If somebody had to buy out Aunt Hattie and Aunt Vinnia, maybe I could. I shuddered as the reality of that dawned. Roomies with Aunt Letha?

To distract myself from that thought, I unearthed my laptop. Between baking cookies with Emma tonight and rafting tomorrow with Melvin, my social calendar seriously cut in on my work time. Even with scant few paying clients, I still had a lot on my to-do list.

I started with Dot Downing's file. Despite several attempts using different search words, I couldn't turn up a South Carolina case that dealt directly with setting aside a land transfer because of fraud by a buyer. I clicked through plenty of case summaries in which sellers defrauded purchasers, but I couldn't find even one in which the buyer had done the defrauding.

Surely other swindlers and shysters had used similar schemes to filch valuables from unsuspecting, good-hearted people like Dot Downing. Once they were caught, was the legal outcome so predictable the cases were never appealed? That would explain why my South Carolina case search wasn't turning up any appellate reports.

If half of what I understood about Dot Downing's case was true, we could easily prove fraud in the inducement. Fraud typically means proving a willful deceit or "guilty mind," which described nicely what I'd seen of Lionel Shoal's dealings. Proving fraud should entitle Dot to set aside the contract; she would return anything she'd received and Shoal's estate would return anything he'd taken.

The problem lay with those splintered ruins at Golden Cove—and the ruins Shoal had left of his private life, especially Alex Shoal. If the transaction was reversed and Dot got her land back, Shoal's company or his estate—whoever had ownership of the development—could claim Dot owed them for improvements made on the land. Not that I personally would call road cuts, grading, and bombed-out buildings "improvements." Would damage such as loss of native plants and destruction of wetlands count as a set-aside, a counterbalance to any claimed "improvements"? It certainly should. Questionable improvements versus irreversible damage. Easy calculation, to my way of thinking. I'd have to make a Columbia law library visit; my database access here was limited.

The other complication was where had Shoal gotten the money to pay for the construction? That would also take more digging.

I decided to work on a problem that felt closer to a solution. If I hurried, I could see Innis Barker before he closed. First, I dialed Carlton Barner's number and was a bit surprised when Lou Wray asked if I could hold a few minutes while he finished with a client. Sure, I'd wait on hold. Much better than waiting for an unlikely callback on a question he didn't really feel comfortable answering.

I moved papers from one stack to another on my desk until I heard Carlton's familiar deep drawl.

"A'vry? How are you?"

We exchanged some obligatory pleasantries before I asked what we both knew was coming.

"Carlton, can I tell Innis Barker to go ahead with the monument, with the alterations I suggested?"

I could hear the hesitation in his voice before he drawled a long, slow, "We-ell." I should have gone to see Carlton in person. It's too easy to say no on the phone.

"Carlton." I rolled his name out smooth and thick and sweet. "You know it's the only right thing to do. Harden Avinger's wife did nothing but nurse him patiently through an awful illness. The whole town knows Maggy Avinger for her good spirit and how she cares for people. She deserves to be protected, and his memory doesn't need to be tainted by one crazy joke he didn't think through. All of us have pulled harebrained stunts in our lives. None of us—not even Harden Avinger—would want to be remembered for a stunt just because we had the misfortune of making it the last and most permanent thing we ever did."

Carlton was quiet a moment, either to make sure I was finished with my speech to the jury or to think through his reply. "You've got a point there, A'vry. We bend over backward to honor dying wishes. But if he didn't have time to rethink it . . . you've got a point there."

"Any reason we can't honor the letter, if not the spirit of his request?"

"No-o. No, I suppose there isn't."

Whew. "How about I bring something by for your signature, so I can take it over to Innis? Or you just want to call him?"

"I'll just call him. That'd be easiest."

"I'm sure you'll want to okay whatever epitaph goes on top of the old one, as the executor. I'll talk to Miz Avinger about what she suggests. This'll let a couple of people rest in peace, don't you think?"

"I'm sure it will." He sounded convinced. He would probably rest easier, too.

Good thing I didn't have to go by Innis Barker's. I was cutting it close picking up Emma at school, and I didn't need a lecture from my punctilious six-year-old niece about the importance of keeping to a schedule.

Before I left, I called Maggy Avinger's number. When she didn't answer, I simply told her answering machine I had some good news and I'd talk to her later. I wanted her to draft what she wanted on her jerk of a husband's tombstone, but an answering machine message wouldn't be the best way to convince her to accept the angel. That was a conversation we really needed to have in person.

Emma climbed into my car, her thick red-gold hair in two braids and her knobby knees poking out from under her denim skirt. She had to struggle to pull the long, heavy car door shut, and she was too short to see comfortably out the windows, but she seemed as delighted as I'd been, when I was her age, to take a spin in the Mustang.

"Too cold to put the roof down today, Short Stuff." I pulled into the line of traffic leaving the grammar school. Lord love the moms who did this every day.

"No time for pleasure riding," Emma said, unzipping a giant binder. "I have a list for the grocery store. We need to stop there first."

A certain amount of anal-retentive-obsessive-compulsiveness— or what used to be called fussiness—runs in my family. Two proud hereditary lines came together, culminating in the fifty-pound Attila the Hen sitting beside me.

"Yes, ma'am." What else could I do? I turned toward the grocery. "What's on the list?"

"Things to make cookies." I could feel the eye roll, even though I didn't turn to witness it. Did mild perturbation cause some disruption in the cosmos, or was I so conditioned to be a source of disappointment to Emma that I could sense it without seeing it?

"So, how many packages of cookie dough you figure we need to get?"

"Packages?"

"You know, those sugar cookie rolls. You got something to decorate them—"

"No, no. No rolls." She had both hands up in a dramatic *Halt, who goes there* fashion. "No, no. We're making something good. This is to raise money. Besides, the people who attend this thing will need something to look forward to, believe me."

Emma had a plan, so I just pushed the buggy as I was told. She filled it with oatmeal, walnuts, chocolate chips, and sugar, softly humming Ko-Ko's "I've got a little list" refrain all the way to the checkout line.

"I love that song." Maggy Avinger's cheerful voice startled both Emma and me from our reveries. "Are you in *The Mikado*?" She smiled down at Emma's serious face.

"No, ma'am. My mother is. She's Yum-Yum."

"Oh. How fun."

I knew from Emma's solemn stare she was thinking, *The cookies will be good, but not the performance.* Fortunately, all Maggy would see was a quiet, polite child.

"Are you going to the performance?" I asked.

"It's one of my favorites. I hope to make it this weekend, but I'm not sure yet."

"I left you a message on your machine. Maybe we can talk today?" I caught Emma reminding me with a glare that I had work to do today. "Or tomorrow?"

"Sure. I'll give you a call." Maggy smiled down at Emma. "Bye, now." She left us at the checkout line.

I paid the cashier, hefted the sacks, and followed Her Imperiousness out to the car, marveling at how someone so short could be so much like my mother—or, horrors, like her Great-great-aunt Aletha. Baptists really should take another look at that reincarnation thing.

We went to Mom's house to bake the cookies because, as Emma explained to me, that kitchen had double ovens. About the time I began to believe she was a miniature adult instead of a kid barely out of kindergarten, she reminded me by dropping a glass measuring cup into a bowlful of sifted flour, leaving herself wide-eyed and powdery white.

After some trials and errors, we got a system that worked. The timer binged, signaling another batch could go in, while another could be lifted off the sheets to cooling racks.

"So what don't you like about *The Mikado*?" I asked as I slid a cookie sheet into the oven.

"Who said I didn't like it?"

"You said the people would need something to look forward to."

"Yeah. Intermission. And these cookies. Have you heard these people sing? The men aren't good at all." She shook her head, solemn.

I joined her, lifting cookies to the cooling racks.

"It's the least we can do," she said, "to thank them for supporting the theater, by having some really good snacks. Don't you think?"

I couldn't argue. If it was an act of gratitude and recompense we were engaged in, then I wouldn't begrudge the small fortune I'd spent on top-grade cookie ingredients.

"I've got a little list, I've got a little list, hm-hm-hm, who never will be missed," she sang to herself in a bell-like voice, pitch-perfect. The mixture of her little-girl delicateness and the Aunt-Letha-like words of the song about settling scores made me shudder just a bit. One thing I could say about my family, they breed true.

Our well-oiled and orchestrated cookie-baking machine churned out several dozen really good chocolate-oatmeal-walnut cookies. Under Emma's watchful eye, I only managed to sneak a couple. I didn't remind her, as I took her home, that I'd be back at her grandparents' house later to spend the night and she wouldn't be there to guard the cookies. I didn't taunt her. She was, after all, a kid. A kid who would find some way to thwart me.

"Emma, I was thinking you might like to spend the night up at the lake cabin with me sometime."

"Sure, Aunt Bree." I smiled inside. She hadn't used her toddler nickname for me in a while. She wrestled her backpack-on-wheels from the floorboard of my car to her driveway. "The cabin would be fun."

"Great. We can take the canoe out on the lake. Or go hiking."

"That would be fun. It's too early for bugs. I hate bugs." She gave the car door a mighty heave and waved goodbye. I watched as she rolled her backpack up the sidewalk and I waved at my sister Lydia when she opened the door for her.

I'd gotten Emma home well before her bedtime, but I was pushing up on mine, if I planned to join Melvin tomorrow for a trip down the river.

Friday Morning

On the way back to my parents' house after taking Emma home, I picked up the voice mail message Melvin had left while I was playing chef's assistant: "Be ready to leave from the office at 8:00 A.M. Wear clothes that dry easily. No cotton. They'll provide wetsuits. Remember you'll want a change of clothes, unless you plan to ride home wet. In which case, we're taking your car. But you aren't driving."

Did he think I'd never been rafting? Of course, I probably would have forgotten not to wear cotton or, I hated to admit it, that I'd need dry clothes.

Melvin came out the back door at eight o'clock sharp, just as I climbed out of my car.

"Whoa," I said. He continually amazes me.

"What?"

"I've—just never seen you dressed like that."

"Because we've never gone to the river." He wore baggy long

shorts and a body-hugging mock turtleneck made of some space-age fiber.

"Guess I'm just used to your button-down look." I didn't want to let on, but what really surprised me was how buffed-out he looked in that shirt. When did he work out?

"Don't you have any sports sandals?"

I wrinkled my nose and shook my head. "I hate sandals." Then I noticed what he was wearing.

"They'll loan you some booties with your wetsuit, but you won't like them. What kind of socks do you have on?"

I looked down at my sneakers. "Athletic socks?"

He shook his head, obviously disappointed in me from head to toe. He climbed the stairs, unlocked the back door, and disappeared inside. I pulled my gym bag from the backseat, wondering what else in there wouldn't pass inspection. Admittedly, I hadn't rafted in a while, but had there been this many rules?

Before I began to wonder if he'd abandoned the adventure altogether, Melvin reemerged, locking the door behind him.

"Here's some wool socks, so your feet won't freeze."

"Wool?" I accepted his offer. They didn't feel as scratchy as I feared, but they were still scratchy.

"Wicks away moisture. Unless you like getting hypothermia, your body heat slowly leached away by soggy cotton socks."

He threw our gym bags in the back of his Jeep wagon while I climbed in the passenger seat.

Melvin's not exactly a stodgy driver; he just drives like someone whose vehicle may flip over in a sharp curve, which is probably why he hates riding with me.

A leisurely forty minutes later, he parked at the edge of a graveled lot and we climbed the weathered steps into the outfitters' shop. I found myself swaggering a bit, *Yea-uh, I know what I'm doing. I've got wool socks in the car.*

Melvin had asked, on the drive up the mountain, how much rafting I'd done.

"Some," I said. I didn't confess that my only river excursions had been lazy floats down the French Broad with groups of high school or college friends.

Those had been magical experiences. I'd tried to block out the chatter and squeals and pretend I was the only one there, suspended on a glistening river cut deep into hills dotted with more shades of green than the eye could consider.

Once, I'd watched a hawk float on currents high overhead, suspended and circling with no more effort than it took to hold his wings ready to accept the air, a sense of isolated freedom. I still remember my irritation when the raucous horseplay from another raft broke the spell. An angry irritation. Odd how strong it still felt.

"Okay, we're checked in." Melvin joined me on the porch. "We get a safety lecture and our gear back there."

We dutifully filed into a back room and took our seats on the wooden benches with others who would be in our group. More people than I expected in March. Not until the lead guide started her safety lecture did I realize what I'd signed on for.

"This is some of the most exciting and scenic whitewater anywhere. Today you'll be rafting Section IV, the most challenging section on the legendary Chattooga River. You'll encounter a series of Class Four and Five rapids, maybe some approaching Class Six. We've had a lot of rain, and the water is high today."

Class Six rapids? The roughest navigable rapids. Melvin must have misunderstood my level of expertise. I thought we'd signed on for gentle Section III not Section IV. Certainly not Section Four with flood waters. Talk about performance anxiety. I'd never done a whole day of Class Fours and Fives.

I listened to the familiar instructions: Keep your hand around the paddle's T-grip handle at all times so you won't accidentally smack your raft mates in the nose; if you fall out, float feet-first downriver so your feet don't become entrapped, forcing you underwater until you drown; wear your helmet so you won't bash your brains out on rocks you can't see coming; listen to your river guide unless you'd like to hike out or be lashed to the bottom of the raft with bungee cords. She really didn't say that, but her tone said she wouldn't countenance anyone getting stuck under a boulder and drowning in a hydraulic on her watch.

Everything felt familiar: the bright yellow rafts, the dingy white paddles, the clammy wetsuits, which were akin to wearing a giant bowling shoe. Plastic helmets hadn't been required on my first raft trips. Then somebody—a raft company lawyer, an ever-watchful government official, who knew what helpful soul—said we had to wear them, to keep our heads from cracking like raw eggs. If we encased ourselves in enough bubble wrap, maybe we could completely eliminate the need for a raft.

For me, the most unfamiliar part of this trip was that little knot of anxiety. Was it because this was the roughest river I'd ever rafted? Was I afraid of getting hurt? Afraid I wasn't physically ready to tackle such a challenge? For certain, I was afraid of making a whopping fool of myself in front of Melvin, the kayaker taking a step back into the baby pool for my benefit. No way I wanted to fall out of the raft or get myself caught in some newbie embarrassment.

As the recycled school bus carried us to the river put-in, Melvin chatted up some of our fellow rafters. I stared out the window, cuddling my plastic helmet to my life-vest-covered chest and trying not to smell my faintly mildewed wetsuit. When we arrived, I climbed out of the bus feeling like a stunt double for the Creature from the Black Lagoon.

Once we were on the water, my anxiety was quelled in the familiar movements of paddling and hard-backs and all-forwards. This section of the Chattooga didn't allow much time to look for hawks overhead, and it lacked the open vistas and sweeping valleys of the French Broad. This was a hard, fast river, with dramatic rock formations and dark forest close on each side.

Our raft guide sat behind us, using her paddle as a rudder, planning how we would approach each rapid. The intensity of the flow could alter dramatically in just hours on a river this steep, and she knew the quirks that even subtle changes in water flow would create in each bend and drop.

She and the other three raft guides often shunted us into an eddy just before a rapid while they climbed a rock and took the river's measure. I tried to look with her eyes at the water shoving over and around rocks, but I couldn't pick the right path. I'd have to ask Melvin about the difference in kayaking and rafting. How would you know how to tackle this river? Who in his right mind ever first thought to paddle down it?

For lunch, we beached the four rafts, and the guides pulled sandwich fixings, hummus, and Oreos from the plastic pails that had bounced down the river with us all morning, lashed in back of the rafts.

I carried my paper plate and cup of water and climbed to a rocky perch from which I could watch the river and pretend I was here alone.

Locked in by the high rock walls and the thick trees, the sound of the water over the rocks drowned out thought. Unfortunately, it didn't drown out the voices of the two middle-aged couples who gathered at the base of my roost.

At first, I didn't pay much attention, but as they finished their sandwiches, their conversation got louder and more insulting.

"—looking for our mountain home. We've been to visit so often, we've just decided we need to own a piece of it," said a woman, her accent sharp and nasal.

"Hope that doesn't mean you have to fill your front lawn with yard art." The other female Yankee accent screeched with laughter at her own joke. "Did you see the houses on the way here? Junk all over the yards."

"Obviously no rules about parking your car in your front yard," a man offered.

"Or every car you've ever owned. Saw one with a tree growing up around the engine block."

"If you don't find a house with a formal living room, you can always put your sofa out on the front porch like they all do," said the screecher.

The whole group guffawed at that one.

"I'm just glad I could talk Gladys into this raft trip. She was convinced we were going to run into one of those retards or wild men."

"Yeah, you talk all brave. Don't tell me you haven't been trying to see into those trees or up on those cliffs."

Gawd, I hate James Dickey. I quietly scooted to the edge of my rock and sat on my haunches, perched above them.

"I've been listening," said a man whose belly strained his wetsuit. "I haven't heard anybody squealing like a pig."

"Yet," said the other. The laughter was weak. I picked that time to nudge a tiny granite pebble so it grated along the boulder and bounced down beside them. One by one, they looked up. I just stared down, not saying anything.

That shut them up. A dead hollow stare. The little group broke up quickly, gathering their picnic leavings. One of the women hazarded a backward glance at me. Out of embarrassment? Or fear? I just stared back.

After they left, I slid down the rock, about the time Melvin strolled over to join me. He stooped to pick up a napkin and some potato chips they'd left behind.

"That wasn't very nice of you," he said with a familiar wry turn at the corner of his mouth.

I just glared up at him.

He laughed. "Forget the carpetbaggers. Enjoying the river?"

I nodded. Why let them ruin it? Still, I shuddered to think they were here scouting out their new vacation homes. Them and thousands more like them, flocking to eyesores like Golden Cove. And here on the river, where I'd hoped to escape from thoughts of interlopers and change.

"Why don't they just stay home?"

Melvin laughed again. "I figure the nice ones do. They just send us the ones that can't get along with anybody up there."

I had to smile at that. We stood watching the water.

"It's so—sparkly," I said. "Like it's alive."

"It's the mica."

"Huh?"

"That's what makes it so bright. The mineral muscovite, a type of mica."

"Hmm. Little sun mirrors, huh."

He nodded, as if in approval.

The river had saved the best for last: Five Falls, with Corkscrew and Crack-in-the-Rock and the rest tumbling one after another, dropping two hundred feet in a mile.

We emerged into a slow-moving, swimmable stretch, calm and quiet, where we hooked the rafts together. A tiny motorboat came from downriver and towed us along sluggish, skinny Lake Tugaloo, and we carted the rafts to the bus for the forty-minute ride to base camp.

In the shower room, the lunch buddies gave me a wide berth. I gave them more silent stares, just for good measure. Maybe they'd decide to migrate elsewhere.

As I settled into the deep leather seats of his Jeep, I asked Melvin, "Did you enjoy it?"

He shrugged. "Yeah, I did. It was a different experience. But I liked it."

"Tamer than kayaking?"

He nodded. "That describes it. Not as solitary, not as immediate, I guess. Or as personally challenging. But it allowed time to relax and enjoy the scenery. Not so mentally demanding."

We lapsed comfortably into our own thoughts. I could see how Noah Lakefield, coming from Colorado, found the thick undergrowth claustrophobic, and how those Yankees might find what they don't understand to be stupid or frightening. To me, it just felt like home. My sense of contentment with it surprised me.

As the road began to flatten into Dacus, I checked my watch. Uh-oh.

"You going to see *The Mikado*?" I asked as we turned into the office driveway.

He shook his head. "I heard about that. Some local group?"

"My sister's singing in it. She's Yum-Yum." I claimed my duffel bag full of wet clothes. "My niece said the men weren't very good and the guy who's playing Poo-Bah acts all swishy."

"Now there's a recommendation. You're going?"

"Opening night. Couldn't miss it."

"Not wouldn't miss it, I notice, but couldn't."

"Yep."

"Have fun. You'll be in the office tomorrow?"

I hadn't thought that far ahead. "Probably." I waved goodbye. According to my watch, I was in for a lecture from Emma if I didn't hurry.

Bittersweet news awaited me at home.

Friday Evening/
Saturday Morning

The front page of the Dacus *Clarion* lying on the kitchen table stopped my headlong rush for a real shower and a change of clothes.

Bambi's Run Comes to an End

The Vietnamese potbelly pig at the center of a massive police search was captured without incident at 4:49 P.M. on Thursday. She had been nicknamed Bambi by her concerned and growing number of supporters in the community.

Local resident Red Paren looked out his kitchen door and saw the pig in his garage eating from his dog food bowls. "She [Bambi] had apparently come out of the woods looking for something to eat," said Paren. "Pigs'll eat about anything, but I hear she's partial to dog food."

Paren closed the garage door, trapping Bambi and ending a weeklong, citywide pig hunt.

"My dog was in the house raising a ruckus about something, so I happened to look out and see her. First I thought it was a bear, that big rump bent over nuzzling in the corner of the garage. Then I recognized her. I just mashed the door closer quick like. She didn't try to run or nothing. She's a right sweet pig. I'm glad she's safe now."

Bambi was taken to the county animal shelter.

"She'll be examined and quarantined for a time. Then we'll set about finding her a home," said Amy Cole, county Pet Protection president. "Several people have expressed interest in adopting her."

I was both sad and relieved that Bambi's desperate bid for freedom had to come to an end. With all the publicity, she would certainly find a home.

I pulled on a black suit and purple sweater, put on mascara and lipstick, and managed not to make Mom, Dad, and Emma, who were waiting on me, late for the opening curtain. Emma's dad Frank was helping backstage, so she sat with us. She kept cutting her eyes up at me, biting her lip to keep from laughing whenever any of the men sang.

When Ko-Ko sang with Poo-Bah of his list of enemies, the lyrics had been rewritten to include nominees drawn from current headlines. The list brought chuckles from the audience. I bent down and whispered in her ear. "He is a bit prissy."

She arched her eyebrows with an I-told-you-so look.

At intermission, as we stood and stretched, Emma announced, "I told you the men couldn't sing very well." Fortunately she whispered. Not that anyone would have disagreed with her candid assessment. No amount of false praise could change the painfully obvious.

The refreshment stand in the lobby—nothing more than a lunch room table set up with baked goods, giant bottles of soft drinks, and an ice chest—was busy.

"Bet our cookies are already gone," said Emma.

People crowded around the table, and I couldn't see what offerings remained.

"That's what we get for having such good seats down front," I said, handing her some dollar bills. "See what you can find us."

Emma knows how to pick good treats.

I waded through the lobby toward the relative calm of the wall farthest from the refreshment table.

"Avery? Avery Andrews?" A pudgy guy who looked familiar waved me over to join a small group.

"Howie Mason. You might not remember me since I'm not wearing garden gloves. Ha!"

Or a panicked look on your face. The guy who'd run downhill after discovering the body in the mine. "From the plant dig. Hi," I said.

"Avery's new in town, aren't you? She was up on the mountain that day. I was just tellin' these folks about our adventure."

I nodded to his friends, not bothering to explain how new I wasn't. I'd never seen Howie Mason before or since the plant rescue, and hadn't been introduced that day. Apparently my newness in town and his role as discoverer of the body had been all the introduction we needed.

"Boy howdy, that was something that day, wadn't it?"

I nodded, remembering too many disquieting scenes the last few days.

"Yep, one minute, I'm minding my own business, the next minute. Whee-oo. Wisht I'd just stayed down the hill that day."

A thirtyish brunette with big eyes and several rings sunk into her fleshy fingers asked, "Just how did you come to find him?" She looked interested in anything Howie had to say.

"Guess it was better me than some of those older ladies up there, huh, A'vry? Though I didn't think so at the time. The lady in charge of the project sent me up the ridge to scout how far we were from an old logging spur. I wadn't wild about hauling myself up that hill, I can tell you. But it sure didn't take me long to make it back down."

"Was he just laying there?" the other woman in the group asked. A bit younger than my parents, she and her husband seemed as anxious as the young woman with the beringed fingers to hear the gory details.

"He was head first in this big crack in the hillside. Or that's what I thought it was. Who knew that's what a gold mine looked like? His legs had bloated, all tight in his pants. He looked like he'd been blown up with a tire pump. Thank Gawd I couldn't see his head."

Emma picked that moment to return bearing two wrapped Rice Krispies treats and a drink. Bless her. "Our cookies are already gone," she announced.

I murmured an "excuse me" and slipped away before I heard any more details. I already had plenty of mental pictures from that day, and those I'd been trying to erase.

Emma and I wandered down a deserted side hall and sat on the stairs, getting marshmallow sweet on our faces in companionable silence. Or relative silence. Emma absentmindedly hummed her new favorite melody, "I've got a little list."

"Your mom's doing a good job as Yum-Yum," I said as I licked my fingers.

Emma nodded. "That wig she's wearing weighs a ton. I don't know how she keeps from snapping her neck or tipping over the edge."

That would be something to distract everyone from the men's singing in the second act. We dusted our rumps, washed the sugar off our faces in the water fountain, and filed back to our seats.

After the performance, I spent the night at my parents' house. My dreams kept me busy reliving the day: rafting and singing and a handful of rings and mountain roads and Emma, all in an improbable jumble. I woke early on Saturday, planning to leave a note and slip out the back door, but I can never get up before Dad does.

"Want some coffee?" he asked as I tiptoed into the kitchen. He'd already read and refolded *The Greenville News*.

"Sure. Anything worth knowing about?" I nodded toward the newspaper.

"The usual." He poured me a cup from the thermal carafe. "You talked to Hattie or Vinnia lately?"

"Uh, no. Well, not lately. Why?" I opened the refrigerator and bent to look for cream so he couldn't see my face.

"Your mom was wondering. They said they had something they wanted to talk to you about. Just wondered if they caught you."

I shrugged, my face hidden behind the refrigerator door. I'm an awful liar. No way I could even casually mention they'd been to see me, but I couldn't convincingly deny it, either. He didn't change the subject.

"Something's up with those three, though Lord knows what. Aletha has her nose out of joint, all snippy, and both Vinnia and Hattie are acting smug and self-righteous. Whatever it is, looks like two against one. Never seen the three of them have much of a sibling spat. Figured they'd fought all that out years ago. Letha, she takes on the whole town, all comers, but she's always left her two sisters alone. Figured it was 'cause they wouldn't rise to the bait. Looks like they may have taken her on, though. Odd."

Was he fishing for information? Probably my imagination. That really wasn't like Dad. I kept my eyes down, pretending I was reading the news headlines upside down. I had to escape before Mom got up. I had never withstood one of her cross-examinations. "Did you see this?" Dad tapped one of the headlines as he turned the paper toward me.

Protest Thwarted:
Radicals Arrested at Nuclear Plant

CAMDEN COUNTY. Plans by the radical Environmental Protest Alliance (EPA) to disrupt a press conference at an area nuclear facility were interrupted when police arrested protestors at two separate security roadblocks. The roadblocks were set up by a joint federal, state, and local law enforcement task force to protect a press conference announcing the plant's first successful test of MOX reconstituted weapons-grade plutonium at the plant.

The use of weapons-grade plutonium has sparked international debate and controversy. Power company officials would not comment on whether additional security precautions are being taken at the facility. "Security remains our top priority," said Sandy Gillen, company spokesperson. "Today's arrests are only one example of our efforts."

The Environmental Protest Alliance is part of a loosely defined underground of protest groups dedicated to "uncivil disobedience." The EPA has claimed credit for two high-profile incidents in the last decade: a research lab bombing in California, protesting animal research, and an arson fire that destroyed a ski lodge in Vail, protesting the further destruction of high-mountain animal habitat.

Names of the six taken into custody have not been released. Witnesses described them as two females and four males, all young and all dressed in black. The police also impounded two vans.

The FBI named Timothy Lee McDonald and Mitchell Eggles "persons of interest" in the continuing investigation. Both men have ties to the Environmental Protection Alliance.

"Wow," I said. "We've hit the big time."

"Did you notice the byline?"

Noah Lakefield. I stared for way too long.

"Our new reporter," Dad said.

"Yeah. Wow. That's—great."

Dad didn't pay any attention to the weak note in my voice. "Yep. He's working for the Greenville and Atlanta papers, as a stringer."

"Really." And working as a police informant, too? Four guys and two girls, dressed all in black. Headed to a protest. I wondered what they'd carried in their vans. Ropes? Climbing cleats? A large black banner they'd planned to unfurl in front of press conference cameras? One that now had some sort of slogan on it?

I got up to wash out my coffee cup. "I've got to get going. Too much goofing off yesterday. Those boxes aren't unpacking themselves."

Before yesterday, I'd never heard of the Environmental Protest Alliance, though I liked the takeoff they'd done on the federal government's EPA, the Environmental Protection Agency. Too much coincidence that they showed up here, training at the old Yellow Fork Camp, about the same time Noah appeared in town? And those fires in Vail that Noah had talked about? Again, too much coincidence. No wonder he'd had to hurry over for the press conference yesterday. At least he could be first on the scene to get the arrest story and byline, even if the protest failed.

I needed to talk to Noah Lakefield, ace reporter. What kind of game did he have afoot? Best to think through my facts first, not go off half-cocked. Most stories had at least two sides, as I knew from years of interviewing clients. But if Mr. Lakefield was involved in any shenanigans that threatened my dad or his paper, I'd see that *The Greenville News* had a new story: "Local Reporter Suffers Grievous Bodily Harm."

At the office, I found no sign of Melvin or his SUV, so he couldn't provide me a handy excuse not to work. I pushed Noah out of my mind for the time being, slumped into the armchair I'd brought from my Columbia condo, and reached for a legal pad. Too many loose ends blowing in the breeze. I needed to see them lined up in front of me.

1. *See Maggy Avinger about angel and new epitaph—*
   —Follow-up with Innis Barker.
2. *See Hattie and Vinnia*
   —Consider offering to buy their interest??

How could I do that, without talking to my parents and to my sister Lydia? And what about Aunt Letha? All too complicated.

3. *Finish research on land sale set-aside for Dot Downing.*

That was a straightforward item. I just needed to finish pulling up cases, jot some notes, and decide how best to proceed.

Like a lightening bolt, it hit me. Had going to the Shoals' house with Valerie constituted a conflict of interest? I hadn't thought about that. She'd wanted me to talk to her husband about the criminal suspicions mounting against him, but that conversation hadn't happened. He was dead. Technically, I'd had no client contact with him and had learned nothing that would affect representing Dot in setting aside her land transfer.

Technically, too, Valerie wouldn't have any claim on the property if she and Lionel Shoal weren't married. However, Valerie seemed the kind who would do her best to establish a claim. Who could have dreamed such a complicated twist of interests, all with people I knew?

What about Alex Shoal? She hadn't retained me, either, but she's the one who potentially stood to lose the most. Likely no way to get her inheritance back for her, especially if Shoal had used her money to build the model home and office. On the other hand, if Shoal had given Alex's money to Dot Downing as a down payment, it could be returned to her if the transfer was set aside. That could work out well for Alex—if Lionel had paid any down payment or earnest money, that is. Who knew what shell game Shoal played.

Alex Shoal could use some cash, and she wasn't in a financial position to contest the loss of the bargain in the land deal. To do that, she would have to pay Dot Downing the rest of the contract price and then take on the responsibility of completing the development. Alex was probably less interested in possible profits from land speculation and more interested in immediate cash.

I wanted to handle Alex with respect, which might be a problem if the only way to protect Dot was to bring a fraud or misrepresentation claim against Lionel Shoal's estate.

That ugly phrase "conflict of interest" reared itself again: Did my conversation with Alex Shoal create a conflict? I'd need to fully disclose my contact to Dot Downing. I couldn't let my sympathy for Alex Shoal get in the way of representing Dot's interests. I suspected Alex would be happy to get out from under any obligations on that land sale, but, in any event, I would be scrupulously open with both Dot and Alex.

My biggest fear was that Lionel had borrowed heavily against the property and that other investors—probably a bank—would swoop in to take both Alex's money and Dot's property.

How difficult would it be to follow the money?

—*Check with Dot Downing about money, etc., from Shoal.*
—*Check whether liens filed against Dot Downing's property.*

Sheesh, this small-town law practice stuff could get complicated in a hurry. Too many intertwined interests, too much tiptoeing around others' interests.

Valerie Shoal, the pretend wife, likely wouldn't make things easy. Did she know she wasn't legally married? In South Carolina, any claim she made wouldn't go far since the state frowns on adultery and other licentious behavior. Valerie wouldn't be pleased, but judging from the questions she'd asked earlier, I suspected she had a good idea where she stood.

In fact, depending on how Shoal arranged his financing, Valerie might end up being the only person harmed by Lionel Shoal's death. Most everybody else he'd come in contact with stood a chance of redeeming something from the mess he'd created. I doubted Alex Shoal would agree with my assessment; she had stuck with him through all manner of lies and abuse. Love is a strange thing.

Musing on Lionel Shoal's demise brought to mind another item:

4. *Follow up with Carl Newland Knight.*

My one client with paying potential. I needed to ask Carl whether L.J. had backed off and focused her crack investigative talents elsewhere.

What about the third in the trio of deaths, Len Ruffin? Had they formally released a cause of death yet for any of them?

While my computer was booting, I called the Sheriff's Department. I planned to leave a message, but Rudy picked up my call.

"Now that's service with a smile," I said. "Personal service, and on a Saturday, no less. Thought you'd be over guarding the nuclear plant or rounding up black-suited radicals."

He snorted. "No way in hell. Too much paperwork. I got enough gahdam paperwork of my own, I can assure you. Paper everywhere. For what, I ask you?"

As I cradled the receiver against my ear, I studied my own office and could only murmur my sympathies.

"I called about one particular piece of paper, Rudy. Any word yet on what was in that sealed letter I brought by?"

I was dying of curiosity, but given the focus of the other letters I'd likely be dying of embarrassment after I, along with Rudy and the entire Camden County law enforcement network, learned the letter's contents.

"They faxed a copy from the state lab. That's only one of the many freakin' pieces of paper cluttering my desk and ruining my Saturday."

I heard shuffling and heavy breathing.

"Here." He sounded triumphant. "Damndest thing, A'vry. Somebody wanted you to know Lionel Shoal had smashed hisself out of a fortune."

"Do tell." *Huh? No embarrassing critique of my behavior?* I was relieved—and curious. "Is it like the others, with a newspaper clipping?"

"Uh-huh." Rudy began reading, trying to decipher the old-fashioned inked handwriting.

Dear Miss Andrews,

In trying to destroy the wetlands and gain sympathy for his development, Lionel Shoal likely destroyed a fortune in large crystals and valuable precious and semi-precious stones.

The land over which he hauled his heavy equipment sits on a rich quartz vein. In addition, just on the other side of the hill, the explosion at his model home collapsed a nearby abandoned mine which was likely the easiest, most accessible entrance to the vein.

Greed makes one stupid. Help Dot Downing realize whatever may be salvaged.

"Wow. What's the article about?"

"Lifetime Search Yields Fortune—Finally. Local Man Discovers Giant Crystal Worth Thousands."

"Where?"

"Hiddenite, North Carolina. Apparently this guy's seen as something of a fanatic. Spent hundreds of thousands of dollars digging and looking."

"Funny, I was just reading about him. Persistent fellow."

"Even blind hogs find acorns ever' now and then."

"You think Lionel Shoal blew up his buildings?"

"Don't know."

I had mental pictures of Shoal that night at the explosion site, rude and pushy, angering everybody around him. Was he trying to divert suspicion, trying to look innocent and uninvolved by acting bad? "Did Shoal have any military experience?"

Rudy took only a blink to see what I was hinting. "Don't know." He was silent. Had they not thought of investigating that option, to see if Shoal knew how to blow things up? Or was Rudy just not letting me in on their secrets?

"Of course, he was a real estate developer," I said. "He might have learned how to handle dynamite sometime in the past." I had trouble picturing Shoal rolling up his sleeves and getting his own hands dirty. He seemed the type to want a get-rich-quick guide rather than a hard-work how-to manual.

Another possibility popped into my mind. "Rudy, do you have those environmental protestors there, in your jail?"

"Naw, the FBI transported them to Greenville, so they could be arraigned in federal court on Monday. We had quite enough nonsense from reporters for the few hours they were here, I can tell you."

"Any hint that they've been playing with dynamite?"

Another silence. Something else he couldn't or wouldn't talk about.

"You think the letter writer is right, about the damage to the crystals?" I asked.

"Who knows? This article talks about how fragile these deposits are, how blasting or heavy equipment can ruin them. That'd be something, wouldn't it."

Ironic. And sad, especially for Dot Downing.

"Says here the Hiddenite vein is akin to the vein that runs through these mountains. That was gold-mining country, too, you know."

After too much pause, waiting to see if he had any other nuggets, I said, "Thanks, Rudy. I was curious about that letter."

"I'll bet you were," he said, his attention drawn away from treasure hunting long enough to let me know that he knew what I'd been curious about. He'd seen the other letters.

"Why'd you get this, do you think?" Rudy rustled the paper. "Why not send it to Miz Downing?"

"Um. Good question." I hadn't thought about that. "Maybe because I represent Dot. I don't know."

The letter surprised me. All the others had a scolding, schoolmarmish tone, telling the recipient to straighten up. Lionel Shoal was beyond scolding, so why not write Dot and tell her what she might own? Or Alex? Or even Valerie? Why write me?

"Aren't you going to ask about the other letter?" Rudy interrupted my reverie.

"What letter, Rudy?"

"The one the SLED investigator found while going through Len Ruffin's papers."

"One of these letters? With a news article?"

"Yeah, Sherlock. We've all managed to notice the unique identifiers. Difference was, Ruffin's letter wasn't so nice. It told him to keep his hands and, I quote, "everything else," off his daughter or, and I quote, "I'll bury you where you won't be found. Abusing your wife is bad. Moving to your daughter is unforgivable, in God's eyes and those of any decent human being. Only death stops a monster. Prove me wrong.' "

I felt as though the breath had been sucked from my lungs. "So all of them got letters. All the ones who died."

I didn't realize I'd said it out loud until Rudy spoke. "And some others. You and Cissie Prentice, you got letters. I knew she was a bad girl, but you, A'vry? Tsk-tsk. You got two letters, and neither one of them about your penchant for speeding. What'd'ya think that means? Besides that you're special."

"Well, we know not everybody who got a letter is dead."

"Still not a club that'll be able to hold many meetings. No offense."

"Thanks for reminding me." I hadn't turned the heat on in my office, and I realized I was huddled inside my jacket.

"Be careful, A'vry." Rudy's voice grew uncharacteristically serious. "At least until we get this figured out. Then you can go back to bein' as bad as you want to be with that Melvin Bertram." His seriousness hadn't lasted long.

"Thanks."

We hung up, and I went to check the locks on both the front and back doors. Too early to try Maggy Avinger again, so I started clicking through computer searches, double-checking what I'd already done on the land transfer question. I had found a South Carolina statute that rendered any land transfer made to "defraud and deceive" a buyer "utterly void," but no specific statute protected the seller. Maybe I could use the criminal statute that made it illegal to obtain a signature or property—including real property—by false pretense. Under that statute, when the property was worth more than five thousand dollars, the criminal punishment was a fine of not more than five hundred dollars or more than ten years in jail. Five hundred dollars? What a joke. When I stopped to think about it, though, Lionel Shoal's sentence had ended up being much longer than ten years.

Because I was thinking about him and because the cursor on the computer kept blinking while I stared aimlessly at the screen, I typed "Lionel Shoal Phoenix" into the search line. The articles that filled the page were not a complete surprise. I clicked the first: "Developer Leaves Investors with Empty Hole." A housing development gone bust, and Shoal just gone. The short article quoted several irate investors. What had Alex Shoal said? Something about the newspaper hounding him? An understatement, no doubt.

I skimmed through the article quickly and was about to click to the next when, at the bottom of the page, the reporter's name stopped me cold.

Of course. How could I have missed it? Part of me wanted to laugh out loud. Dad had been right. Noah Lakefield had moved here from Phoenix, not Vail. The other part of me felt icy mad. If some stupid game he was playing caused my dad any kind of grief, I'd lash him in that freaking canoe and push him into his iconic river, by way of Raven Cliff.

I dialed the *Clarion* office. No answer, of course. Saturday. I scrambled around, looking to see if I had his cell number. Had he given me his number? I'd track him down, even if I had to call Walter at home. Best take a deep breath and cool off a bit, though.

I believe in coincidences, though I doubted that Noah and Shoal both turning up in Dacus was really a coincidence. Now that I thought back, it certainly could explain why Noah pulled a Clark Kent and disappeared so quickly the night of the explosion—and earlier, when Shoal started ranting at the plant dig. Shoal showed up and Noah vanished. Whatever Noah's perfectly rational explanation was, it had better be one that didn't embarrass my dad.

I took a deep breath. Focus on your list, Avery.

From whatever direction I approached it, fraud was prohibited. The problem was how to prove it, how to establish the "guilty knowledge." I was making this harder than it had to be. This wasn't a criminal case, an attempt to put the defrauder in jail. Those could be tough cases, because the other side had plenty of motive to fight. This also wasn't a traditional fraud case, trying to recoup the plaintiff's damages and hoping for punitive damages to punish the bad intent. Those too could be tough cases.

This case wasn't that tough. Even if I couldn't prove Shoal intentionally defrauded Dot Downing, I certainly could show negligent misrepresentation. Had he been alive to face criminal and civil charges, I wouldn't have been satisfied with a simple misrepresentation case. However, as much as I might like to punish Lionel Shoal, somebody else had already taken care of that. I needed to climb down off my trial lawyer white charger and climb on a humble little donkey. This case required gentleness and wisdom.

Realistically, all I needed to prove was negligent misrepresentation, an easier case than fraud. I likely wouldn't be convincing a jury; I'd be talking directly to a judge, asking to have the sales contract set aside.

I'd been used to defending corporations and professionals against huge, complicated cases. I needed to quit making things difficult. Most of the items on my to-do list involved simple peacemaking, just chatting with people, not battling with them. I'd been used to a more—was combative the word I was looking for? A more combative environment, where I met opponents in depositions or in front of juries. This felt, what? Mushy more cautious. Blessed are the peacemakers, I reminded myself. No need to stay girded for battle. I needed to learn that I could protect people without a fight.

I dialed Maggy Avinger's number. The answering machine picked up again. Dang, she was an early riser, and I'd let her get up and out of the house. I'd half-hoped to see her at *The Mikado* last night. Why hadn't she called me back?

I scrabbled through papers on my desk, looking for Dot Downing's phone number, and found it right where I routinely put contact information for my clients—scrawled inside a folder with interview notes for her case. A faint glimmer of organization. Which, of course, was the only folder I had for any of my so-called cases. Emma, little Miss Organizer, probably knew how to print labels on the computer. Heck, she probably had one of those little label machines.

In surveying my disaster zone, for the first time I truly appreciated all those women who'd made labels and kept my life workable. Here I was with only a handful of cases—using the term "case" loosely—and I was in a mess. I'd certainly need a heck of a lot more than a bunch of unpaid cases before I could afford to hire someone to organize me out of my mess.

I dialed Dot's number. Another answering machine. Where did these women go this early on Saturday morning?

I stared at my list, with Maggy's name at the top. All weekend, every time I'd thought about her, my focus had been how to convince her to accept both a new epitaph and the angel. Staring at my list, seeing her name with all the other names, something started forming in my mind. I tried to push it out, refusing it. But the more I looked at my list, the more shape it took.

The letter I'd seen on her hall stand, the one with the familiar handwriting. The pudgy guy at the play last night, saying the lady in charge had sent him up the hill. I'd thought he was talking about Dot Downing because it was her land, but Dot had been very low-key that day. Maggy Avinger had been in charge; she had sent him up the hill toward the mine. Toward Len Ruffin's body.

Len Ruffin's letter. Suse Knight's. Alex Shoal. Valerie Shoal.

My puzzle was missing plenty of pieces, but the edges were all in place and the central figure was quite clear. Quite sickeningly clear.

Maggy's house was a few blocks away. Maybe she was working in her yard and hadn't heard the phone. To think, I'd considered talking to her about that blasted angel, the toughest conversation on my list.

I could walk and think at the same time. Any kind of activity, to keep my heart from hurting.

Late Saturday Morning

The walk to Maggy Avinger's house took me by both the best and worst of Dacus proper. One block with stately century-old rambling houses. Turn the corner to another block crowded with small clapboard rental houses shedding chunks of paint, the yards full of weeds. Then Maggy's block, with more rambling, well-kept houses. I noted each house as I passed to distract myself from the conversation I was about to have.

Maggy's neat white bungalow stood in the middle of the block. Her yard, divided by a wide concrete walk, spilled over with azaleas and dogwoods. In just a few weeks, it would explode in color.

As soon as I set foot on the front steps, I saw the envelope taped to the wooden screen door.

FOR AVERY ANDREWS: IMPORTANT AND PERSONAL

No point in knocking. I took the envelope, the air in my chest hot and painful. I sank down on the top step and pulled out the letter, fingering the familiar thick vellum.

Dearest Avery,

Who said confession is good for the soul? Someone who believes we have souls. We confess to explain why—or fool ourselves into believing why.

Why? Because they needed it. Because I saw no other way. I was just going to write a few letters. Things I thought people should hear, things no one was willing to tell them. I hadn't intended to go any farther.

Was it my . . . disgust? displeasure? with myself for having tolerated Harden all those years. I never understood how a woman could let a man hit her. How could she have so little respect for herself? Then, lo and behold, after he's dead, after my life becomes peaceful and pleasant, I'm startled one day to realize that almost every word out of Harden's mouth had been a slap. How could I not have seen it? How could I blame myself for what he did to me? How could I not fight back? Odd how reality is altered by our own experience.

The day of my epiphany, Mack MacGregor stopped by to help me trim the azaleas. I offered to toast us some pound cake. I suppose I was a bit flustered, having him sitting in my kitchen, watching me. I had pooh-poohed the notion, but I knew he was interested in me. Whatever the reason, I got clumsy as I reached in the oven, burnt my forearm, and dumped the cake slices all over. I just stared at the mess, shaking, waiting. Waiting for Harden to yell at me. I know Mack thought I was an idiot. He kept saying, "It's okay, it's okay." He patted my shoulder, took the potholders from me, and rescued the cake slices. My entire adult life came together in that one incident. I was so surprised by his gentleness. Surprised because there was no yelling. I'd spent my whole life tensed for the next attack. I'd never stood up for myself. Never. What a waste.

We had our cake and Mack went home. He would've been shocked to know my real thoughts. In a blinding flash, I wished I had killed Harden. Then I could have visited that angel and her ugly epitaph with pride. Lucky for Harden, I was too stupid to see what he'd done, until he was safely out of it.

I couldn't say how or when I first decided how to redeem some of what I'd lost, but it was soon after that, while the thin red line I'd burned on my arm still stung. I started writing notes. I can't apologize to you, Avery. I still doubt that associating with Melvin Bertram will come to any good. In any event, the notes did little good—for me or anyone else.

One morning, drinking coffee and reading the newspaper, I saw an article about the opera workshop. *The Mikado.* I laughed out loud.

It had an artistry about it. Closure, you could say. That song your niece was singing, "I've got a little list . . . who never would be missed." I've always loved it. *The Mikado* comes to town just as I'm, so to speak, leaving town, feeling my life's been such a waste.

I pledged to help others. I just needed a list. Finding blind people who needed saving, who couldn't see their danger or pain, wasn't hard. Do people with normal eyesight see them as clearly? Or is that sight reserved only for their fellow blind travelers?

I had studied happy couples for years. I even studied your parents. Was it the way she said his name? The way he held the hymnbook for her in church? The way they teased each other? If only I could unlock the secret.

Now, with my small seared mark, I looked for others living in the worst of my old reality. As if an archangel had delivered her to me, I met Jesse Ruffin. I knew her mother from church. Jesse often checked me out at the grocery store and we chatted. She had that gangly yearling way of adolescents. One day, I saw her leaving the grocery store with her father. I knew as soon as I saw the way he looked at her, that sneer, a way no father should look at his daughter, his words, her flinch. It was as if he'd been delivered up.

Don't worry, I didn't jump to any conclusions. I did my homework. I got to know Jesse and her mom better. I studied him. I knew they needed a new reality, but I found her mother too brainwashed to help and the court system impotent unless the bruises show. I tried, but threats of court only made matters in their home worse, not better. If something didn't happen soon, Jesse would have no one to protect her.

His greed made it easy. I knew him from church, too. He and Harden both were always in church, every Sunday. Amazing, if you really knew them.

I lured him to that abandoned gold mine with a story about how Harden had left it to me and how I wasn't sure what to do, that Harden had dug out some gold nuggets and left them in a gunny sack hidden behind a rock I couldn't move. Not very creative, but he went with me.

Easy to get him there, but frightfully loud to shoot him. Nerve-racking. That did it for me and my "list." Or so I thought. Removing someone permanently gets complicated. Not what they show in movies. When someone is shot, he doesn't die right away. Sometimes he lingers, wheezing with a frightful death rattle that you hear in your sleep nights later.

I obviously wasn't well suited to life as an avenging angel because I failed to consider the problems that would arise for his family if he just disappeared. I didn't know his employer had generously insured him and that the insurance company wouldn't pay unless his body was found.

The whole endeavor was almost a fiasco, especially when Jesse showed up at the plant rescue. No matter, at least he couldn't destroy her life anymore.

I thought it would end there. I just wanted to protect Jesse, after I realized I wouldn't always be there for her. I arranged for her to have counseling. Maybe, just maybe, she has a chance now. Without dredging up ancient history (my own), protecting her was important to me.

I learned from my mistakes, though. I really am a coward. I didn't like being too close. At the same time, I wanted to do something courageous, something that needed doing, that no one else could do.

Cleaning out the shed behind the house, I found those old pharmacy bottles Daddy had collected. The bottles were beautiful. Perhaps this would be a gentler way to protect those I'd found. Did you know strychnine was once used as a digestive, to keep people regular? The chocolate-coated pills were even given to children.

Sometimes drugs used to heal aren't kind to the body. Like the treatments they offered me. I could refuse, and I did. I supposed those whose evil I set about treating could've refused, too. But of course they didn't. They assumed the beautiful box of chocolates came just for them. All good things in life came for them.

Nobody talks about evil much anymore. We used to believe in it. Maybe that kept it at bay. Or was I just more naive?

I suppose you've figured it out. I made my little list after the doctor gave me my diagnosis, while Harden was busy making his grand exit. Of course I couldn't steal his thunder, so I kept quiet. I watched what happened to him and decided not to stay around for more of the same. I had moments of regret, as I discovered what life could have been—should have been. But even with cancer treatments, no guarantee I would've enjoyed much of that life. Maybe it's all an illusion, dancing slightly out of reach of everyone.

I sent more letters. I needed to feel useful, as if it counted for something. Then Suse Knight asked her yard boy if he minded letting her take a blood sample, she needed to test some new supplies.

After hearing that, I marched out of the beauty parlor with a renewed sense of purpose. Or rather a renewed pledge not to be such a coward.

Suse destroyed at least one woman's life. I won't tell her name, but she knew who the father of her baby was. She wasn't a tramp, she was just stupid enough to fall for his promises. She took him to court, only to be publicly humiliated when the paternity test showed he wasn't the father. Again, the court was no help. The judge refused to order a second test based only on hearsay testimony. The police also refused to investigate without a direct witness. When she ran out of money, her lawyer ran out of fight. Her own family turned its back on her. She considered suicide, while the baby's father continued his comfortable, self-righteous life.

If that had been the only blood test Suse Knight had fudged, that'd be one thing. But it wasn't—and warning her wasn't the end of it. She was too greedy. How many diamond earrings or swimming pools does one woman need?

Lionel Shoal certainly won't be missed, either, except maybe by that tart posing as his wife, and she'll only miss what she thought he could give her. Come to think of it, he might have met his match in her. I didn't know about his dear wife—his real wife—until afterward. She certainly didn't deserve him, and Dot didn't deserve to lose her family legacy. He told Dot all the right things; then, one by one, he did none of them. Dot said you would look into it, but she said you didn't look too optimistic. After I saw those bulldozers on top of the wetlands and after he blew up the office—who else would have?—I knew no legal language or threat would contain him. He was Harden—at turns arrogant and hale-fellow, and at no time trustworthy.

I'm tired now and have said too much. That's what happens when you're alone with your thoughts. It all wells up inside you.

The door's unlocked, but don't feel as though you have to come inside. Just call Jackson over at Baldwin & Bates Funeral Home. He knows what to do.

A panic jolted me. I jumped up from the porch step. I knew what she'd done.

The wooden screen door swung open easily. The old iron door knob balked but finally turned. The door opened without a sound. The house was dark and cool, the curtains closed in the dining and living rooms.

I found her in a bedroom at the back of the house. Elaborate drapes covered the windows. The only light seeped around the edges.

She lay on her back under a quilt, her hands folded, her mouth slightly open. She looked asleep. I touched her, to see if I could wake her. Her mottled brown forearm felt cold. I tried but couldn't close her mouth.

I didn't want to look at her anymore. Panic had jolted me full of adrenaline; fear or reverence had slowed my pace. Now both left me shaking.

I found the phone—an old rotary dial with a heavy handset—in the hall. On the same table where I'd seen the letter with the blue writing. Who had received that one? Was the last one sent to me?

For the second time in a week, I sat waiting for the police and whoever else would come like carrion birds to take care of the dead.

I waited on the porch step. Her house smelled so much like my great-aunts' house—baked cookies, mothballs, wool rugs, furniture polish. I had tried to make myself wait with her, but I couldn't. Not that she cared, but I was embarrassed that I couldn't do that for her.

The letter's scattered pages lay on the front porch where I'd dropped them. I gathered them up, straightening the edges, rubbing the vellum with my fingertips.

Waiting, I looked down at the last page, her final words, the ones I hadn't finished.

> "—Jackson at Baldwin & Bates Funeral Home. He knows what to do."

I hadn't called Jackson first. I'd called L.J.'s office, her direct line. It would be simpler, with all that had transpired, to treat this like a crime scene until it was officially ruled otherwise.

Her sure blue pen strokes went on:

> I wish I could've known you earlier, Avery Andrews. I think we would've been friends. You remind me of myself—or, rather, who I wanted to be, who I think I was inside. You're a fighter. I hope you'll be happy back in Dacus. I just hope you'll be happy.

Tears blurred the words. What a sad plea from a woman who'd studied happiness from a distance. Somehow her hope read more like a curse than a blessing.

> Please do me one last favor. By all that's right and holy, swear you won't let them plant me beneath that angel. Carlton Barner told me about your idea, about rewording the epitaph. That's fine. Write whatever you want on the damned thing. Just keep it away from the church cemetery and away from what remains of me.

I bequeath the angel to you, Avery. I'll call Carlton and tell him. Better yet, I'll write it, sign it, and send it to him, along with a check to pay for any extra expenses in erecting it in front of your office. I reread Harden's instructions. You were right: He just said carve the epitaph; he didn't say it had to be visible. He also said "install it." he didn't say it had to be over his grave. So place it anywhere you'd like. How about right in front of your office? You could use it for a signpost. Some artistic irony, having it in front of the old Baldwin & Bates Funeral Home, don't you think?

It is a lovely work of art. I finally went out to Innis Barker's to see it, full well expecting to hate it. But I didn't. I loved it. It's quite beautiful. I just don't want it over my grave. And Harden certainly doesn't deserve it over his.

Please enjoy her, Avery. Maybe she—and you—will pray for me, if you're sure there's anybody listening.

I set out on my mission of redemption. Frankly, I found checking off my list wasn't as redemptive as I'd hoped. I am tired.

Good-bye, Avery. Please keep those of my secrets that you can.

Maggy

P.S. The contents of the house are to be auctioned, with the proceeds going to the library and to the conservation fund. I told Carlton earlier—he added this to my will—that you are to have first choice of any contents you'd like. There's quite a nice collection of historical crime accounts my father left me. I'd love for you to have them, though don't feel obligated to take them.

The sheriff's car stopped at the curb. L.J. herself had arrived. What of Maggy's secrets could I keep?

Midday Saturday

"Is this her handwriting?" L.J. asked, shoving the plastic-encased letter at me.

Maggy Avinger had thoughtfully written a suicide note and left it on her nightstand.

I've killed myself with an overdose of pills.

"Would you recognize it?" L.J. said.

I nodded. "You will, too, if you take a look at those poison-pen letters your guys sent to the state crime lab."

I had told L.J. it was suicide as soon as she got out of the car, but she wasn't inclined to take my word for it. Not because of her sharp investigative mind-set, but just because she hates for me to know something she doesn't know.

I rubbed my fingers on the vellum of the letter Maggy had written me, folded deep in my jacket pocket. L.J. wouldn't need my letter for her investigation. She could find plenty of writing samples in the house to compare with the suicide note, and I could protect a few of Maggy Avinger's secrets, at least until I had time to think.

As the number of cop cars grew, it quickly became a circus. The crime scene processing went on forever. Unlike the scene at Lionel Shoal's, the sight of the ambulance drew a crowd of concerned neighbors. At first, only a few Ghouly Boys were drawn like blowflies to the hint of violent death. They prefer car accidents— more chance for gore. But the rash of unsolved murders in Dacus provided its own irresistible allure. Maybe a serial killer on the loose, they speculated with relish.

I sat on the porch, out of sight of the street, tucked behind the shade of vines and trellises sheltering the end of the porch.

Even Carlton Barner showed up. I wasn't sure if someone had called him or if he'd been out taking his Saturday constitutional, but he was wearing a natty sweater vest that said, "Here's a man who looks like a stiff even when he's relaxing."

He joined me on the porch but didn't accept my offer of a seat on the swing, which I appreciated. That would've felt awkwardly cozy.

He stood, looking down at me. "She's asked that you be allowed to take your pick of her books and other items of personalty before the estate auction is held. I suppose she told you?"

I nodded, staring for some reason at the creases in his jeans. I doubted I'd come back here for anything.

"Whenever the police finish snapping pictures or whatever they're doing, just let me know when you'd like to enter the premises. She said the books had no special collectors' value, as far as she knew, but the firm who'll handle the estate auction will have to value anything you remove, for estate purposes."

I nodded, just barely acknowledging his words. I knew I must appear rude, but I couldn't seem to rouse even rudimentary social graces.

Carlton had enough social grace for the both of us, but he was having trouble getting around to the topic of Maggy's bequest to me. At first, I didn't think he knew about it. Then he mentioned she'd sent him a note about a gift for me.

"We can talk about—everything else later, Avery," he said. "It's all been such a shock."

I almost giggled at the thought: There was a thousand-pound stone elephant on the porch between us.

He left, and I stayed, slumped in the swing. Shock. He was right about that.

This was what happened when you died without children or family. Strangers came in and put yard-sale stickers on the things that made up your life, and other strangers picked over the bits and carried some off to absorb into their own lives. If you hadn't shared those memories before you left—where you were when you bought it, how you'd enjoyed using it—then all that was lost.

Maggy Avinger probably didn't care that the memories in this house would dissipate. She was probably glad. She'd chosen another legacy, to heal this one.

Part of me wanted to save something of hers, to save what I'd seen and liked in her. Another part of me wanted to walk away without looking back.

I sat a while longer, watching official people come and go. Occasionally a cop entering the house glanced my way. My thoughts jumped and skittered, but I was aware only of a numbness.

Finally, without asking permission, I left. If L.J. or anybody needed me, they could track me down.

Tomorrow was church. I'd spend the night with my family. I wanted to be alone, but not as alone as the cabin. I walked back to my office.

Slicing open the packing tape on a box, I began putting books on a shelf without even looking at the titles. I broke the empty box down flat and carried it to the mud room inside the back door. The darkened oak floors creaked under every step. I found myself staring down at the thick baseboards in the back hallway, then at the heavy crown molding that decorated even the back rooms in this house. The sand-cast doorknob, the heavy-hinged door, the sweeping staircase to the second floor.

This house was so much like my grandfather's. I couldn't build a new house. The only "new" places I'd lived were boxy condos or apartments. I didn't want to be relegated to one of those, not when I grew old, and not now. Why cut up good earth and plough down trees when there were already enough places to live?

I strode back to my office and dialed the phone. Aunt Hattie answered.

"I've been reading over the papers you left—"

"Avery, I meant to call and got busy. Figured I'd see you at Sunday dinner tomorrow. Vinnia and I have changed our minds. We went to visit Ava, and we were both so depressed on the drive home. When we could finally bring ourselves to talk to each other, what a relief to find we both felt the same way. So thank you, honey, for looking over those papers. Just let us know what we owe you."

The breath I'd been holding rushed out. "You don't owe me a thing, Aunt Hattie." I'd never been so relieved to be dismissed by a client. "Would you like me to explain your ownership rights, just in—"

"No, honey. No need to waste breath on that. I reckon we'll live here as we have, and you all can worry about it when we're gone."

"Aunt Hattie, you know you don't . . . have any worries about who'll take care—"

"We know that." She cut me off, not wanting or needing to hear more.

"I'll see you tomorrow morning," I said, and we hung up.

I felt buoyant, I was so relieved. My great-aunts' decision to stay meant I wouldn't have to offer to buy their interest or deal with the family upheaval. They wouldn't be here forever, but I could keep that part of my life as I'd always known it for a while longer.

That left me with my housing dilemma unresolved. I could keep looking. Maybe I could move in here, as a temporary place, a rental. Walking downstairs to the office would certainly cut commute time, but that proximity to work could also be a bane. I would still have the cabin, though, for a respite. Why did I feel such need for a nest? Maybe if I got this office organized.

I looked down at my desk. No sooner had I straightened it than

I made another mess. On top of my latest mess lay the list I'd been working on that morning.

I picked it up. No further need to see Maggy Avinger or my great-aunts. I would need to have a long talk with Sheriff L.J. Peters after she got through playing detective at Maggy's house. First, though, I needed to think through how to tell L.J. what I knew about the murders.

After reading the anonymous notes with the distinctive hand-writing, she could begin putting the pieces together without my help, but I doubted she had enough to fill in all the blanks. Not that "why" was technically part of a police report, but this case was too complicated unless you understood the why.

The remaining item on my list was setting aside Dot Downing's land transfer. How best to tackle that? Maybe a petition in equity directly to the judge? Would other investors come out of the wood-work? Had the subcontractors been paid? Was anything Alex Shoal had left protected? What a mess. I jotted down some calls I could make, but not until next week.

I craved mindless activity. And order. Right now, I needed to practice—what did that ancient monk Brother Lawrence call it? Something about experiencing the holy in mundane chores. He peeled potatoes in the monastery scullery. My piles of potatoes were all exceedingly angular: boxes and books.

The Weekend

I didn't have to go looking for Noah Lakefield. He found me. Saturday evening, I was curled up in the leather armchair in my office, thumbing through an 1895 volume of South Carolina case law. Old cases have a beautiful language—and an intimacy of wrongdoing. I absentmindedly stroked the creamy, smooth calfskin cover and flipped the pages, ignoring the gathering gloom.

Insistent knocking rattled the front door, jolting me in my chair. "Avery? Avery, are you in there? It's Noah."

I rested the book on the corner of my desk, marched into the entry hall, and swung open the door. I was pleased when Noah froze midstep, his mouth open in an almost-word. I was glaring like a fury and glad it had an effect.

"You ever hear of knocking politely? No need to shatter the stained glass. Maybe you could call ahead?"

"O-kay? May I come in?"

I stood aside, then followed him through the French doors, switching on the shadow-filled glare of the overhead light.

"You okay?" he asked. Uncharacteristic solicitousness, coming from him.

"I'm fine."

"I heard about Miz Avinger. I knew you were friends—"

"So you wanted to get the scoop."

He blinked. "No, well, in part. I just thought—I knew you'd be upset. I saw your light. Thought you might like somebody to talk to."

He seemed sincere, but then again, he was a reporter. Like lawyers, they're sometimes paid to seem sincere.

"I do want to talk," I said. "Have a seat." From my tone of voice, he knew it wasn't an invitation to tea, and certainly not the conversation he'd come to have.

"How about you explain you and Lionel Shoal getting to Dacus at the same time."

He didn't answer. He just sat slumped in his chair, his manner relaxed.

"You came here from Phoenix, same as Shoal."

"I never said I didn't."

"You didn't volunteer it, either. You followed Shoal here."

"Yes, I did."

Never acknowledge an admission when you are pushing toward the hard questions, even if it surprises you. "You blew up Shoal's model home."

"No, I did not." He seemed almost amused by my questions.

"You think you're a helluva poker player, don't you? Okay, you know who blew it up."

"No." He stretched his legs, the shaggy cuffs of his jeans puddling on top of his sneakers. "I have my suspicions, but I don't know for sure."

I tried not to let my face telegraph my surprise.

"Have you talked to L.J.?" I asked. "Told her about your suspicions?"

"Of course not. Number one, your crack law enforcement officer doesn't inspire trust. Second, I have suspicions, no proof."

"So who'd'you think did it?"

He shrugged. His elbows on the armrests kept him from sliding off the wooden chair. "Shoal's one possibility. Your new buddy, Tim McDonald, is another, though I don't think his guys had the means to carry out two operations so close together. And they wouldn't want to endanger their nuclear plant protest for something with such limited news value. Can't really get much publicity—or raise much money—protesting a local problem."

"Raise money?"

"Sure." He sat upright in the chair. "The funding that organizations like the Environmental Protest Alliance need to protect trees doesn't grow on trees. They needed donations. They had to stage an event that would give them the most buck for the bang."

"Could someone from the group have taken on Shoal as a solo operation?"

"Yeah. Maybe." He sounded skeptical.

"Your money's on Shoal?"

He wagged his head from side to side, his thick curls waving slightly. "Maybe. Heck, could've been you, for all I know. Or somebody else around here unhappy with outsiders coming in."

"Could've been you, too."

His stare didn't waver.

"Why do you care if Shoal messes up Camden County, or Phoenix, for that matter? Why chase him cross-country?"

We kept our gazes locked, stubborn.

"Wait a minute," I said. Realization dawned slowly. "You don't care, do you? Not about Dacus or Phoenix. This is about Vail, isn't it? Shoal helped mess up Vail, didn't he?"

He glanced down at the floor, then back at me. "My hometown, near Vail. He swindled my mother out of her land, plowed it up, left town ahead of the creditors. I hoped to call him to account, to make sure he didn't ruin someplace else." He paused, holding my gaze. "I didn't kill him, though."

No need to protest to me that he was innocent of murder. I knew that news of Maggy's death had spread. The rumor mill in Dacus was, as in most small towns, busy and remarkably accurate.

267

Eventually, the story that she'd been ill and that she'd committed suicide would be widely known. In this case, though, the rumors would likely bear only bits and pieces of truth. How much would people know of the full story? I certainly wouldn't be talking.

I changed the subject. "So how do you know Tim McDonald?"

"Tim's one of EPA's front men. He and a guy named Mitch Eggles usually work together. After the investigation of the Vail arson, I became interested in these fringe radical environmental demonstrators. I've followed them for years, since I was in college."

He offered a wry grin. "Incidentally, I never thanked you for the tip about Tim. If it hadn't been for you, their protest might have carried that press conference onto every newscast worldwide."

"Well, you're welcome. I didn't realize I'd turned them in."

"You didn't. But you mentioned Tim's name. Knowing he was in the neighborhood helped me put together a few other pieces, so I tipped the cops. One of the benefits of cozy small-town life, I'm finding. People know what's going on, who belongs and who doesn't."

I hoped my expression wasn't betraying my earlier thoughts about how much he didn't belong.

"Want to grab some dinner?" he asked.

"No. Thanks, though. A raincheck?"

"Sure." He ran his hands through his unruly curls. Did he ever get his hair cut? "I better be going."

Who had set those explosions? Shoal? Tim McDonald and his crew? Would the cops be able to figure it out? Unlikely. I also doubted that Noah would be around long enough to follow through on that dinner invitation. Who would he chase, now that Shoal was gone?

I locked the front door behind him, stared around my office for a few minutes, turned off the lamp, and let myself out the back door. Lydia, Frank, and Emma had invited me to join them for hot dogs and a video. That now sounded like a great idea.

––––––––

After church the next morning, I wished I'd skipped Sunday dinner at home and headed straight up the mountain. But I didn't know, until the meal was almost on the table, what Mom had planned. At first, things were going so well.

"Mr. Mack's going to join us for dinner, too," Mom said as she hefted the eye round roast out of the slow cooker onto the cutting board. Dad was warming up his electric knife. The big midday dinner meal was called lunch most places now—except on Sunday in the South.

"Avery, could you get the milk out of the refrigerator for me?" Aunt Hattie had taken charge of the mashed potatoes, while Vinnia took pan drippings with which to work her gravy magic. Aletha slid a pan of biscuits in the oven. These women had after-church Sunday dinner down to an art form, an oft-rehearsed ballet. Dad and I were just minions, nothing more than ushers.

"I was afraid he'd insist on inviting Estelle Garrett."

Estelle, the apple-cinnamon-bread lady who was so obviously interested in Mr. Mack.

"We could've made room," I said, setting the milk jug next to the stove and scuttling out of the way.

"No business making room for that Estelle Garrett," Letha pronounced. "I swear, Mack Brown has floated through life without a clue what the women around him were up to. Had business to learn, though, after he ended up married to Lucy."

"You would think he'd have learned his lesson there," Hattie said. I was surprised. They usually try to cork off Aunt Letha's sharper observations, rather than join in.

"One shrew ought to be enough for anybody," said Letha. "Lucy was a doozy. God rest her."

"Such a shame about Maggy Avinger passing," Vinnia said. "Mack and she would've made such a lovely couple. Lord knows they both deserved some happiness." Vinnia, the only one of my great-aunts to have ever married, maintains a soft, romantic view of the world, thirty years after her husband died.

"Estelle Garrett was doing her dead level best to keep Mack

away from Maggy—or anyone else," Letha said. "You know she sent Mack an anonymous letter warning him to stay away from Maggy, that Maggy had done Harden in?"

I almost dropped the gravy boat I'd gotten from the cabinet for Hattie. I caught Mom's eye. She just shrugged. She wouldn't have told them about Mack's letter, but she's not the only one in the family who mines rich veins of information.

"Well," Vinnia added, "Harden Avinger helped out there. He fed Estelle that nonsense about Maggy poisoning him. He was bound and determined to keep Maggy and Mack apart, even after he was gone. Such a pity. And so mean."

Letha made a rude sound as she lifted the plates down from the cabinet. "Harden Avinger was shriveled and consumed by hate. What misguided notion about 'til death do us part kept Maggy living with him, I'll never know."

"Scared of making it on her own, I think," said Vinnia.

Letha snorted in disgust. "The world couldn't have offered her up anything scarier than Harden Avinger."

"Pity Estelle and Harden didn't get together," Hattie said, stirring the gravy. Her grin was sly.

Letha took the bait. "Not a chance there. Those two looked for victims. They didn't look to be victims."

"Aunt Letha, we'll need an extra plate. Oh, here's Lydia. And our other guest. Avery, can you get another chair?"

Emma came in and held open the back door for her dad, who carried a baking dish full of what smelled like peach cobbler from last summer's canning. Plenty of ice cream in the freezer, I hoped.

I went into the living room to get an extra chair for the dining table. My mom is always picking up strays, so a stranger at Sunday dinner was no surprise. Lydia had met him in the driveway and was introducing him around when I came back in the kitchen.

"—and this is my older sister, Avery." Lydia likes to point out our age difference. "Avery, this is Byron Caudle. He's just moved to town to work for the sheriff's department."

Deputy Caudle and I both froze. Even out of context, we recognized each other. Officer Uptight. The one who'd stopped me for speeding. Why, oh, why had Aunt Letha left Bud at home? I could've invited Kid Deputy to play a friendly game of catch in the backyard.

He stood at attention. "We've met."

Mom looked back and forth between us, the tension not missing her notice. "Wonderful. You've met. Oh, here's Mr. Mack. What say you all grab a plate and we'll serve off the counter here. We don't stand on formality, Byron."

Deputy Caudle sat at the end of the table farthest from me, talking to Dad and Aunt Hattie. Emma, Mr. Mack, and I sat at the other end, where Mom could keep an eye on us, ensuring a peaceful meal.

I had talked to Melvin, to get his okay on the new sign outside my office. After all, it was his house, had been his family's home place. I didn't want to do anything disrespectful.

He surprised me by agreeing. His only condition was that it not mention his name. He didn't need to advertise, he said. He also picked the spot, on the left of the sidewalk as you faced the house, near the shrubs that encircled the porch.

"That way, you can enjoy it from your window," he said without a hint of sarcasm.

The morning set for the installation brought a crystal blue sky and that earth smell hinting spring won't be late. I watched two guys hunch over the base of my new sign, centering it on the mounting rods protruding from the concrete pad they'd poured days earlier. They stepped back and motioned to the crane operator. He finished lowering it into place with a satisfying crunch.

My angel was stunning. Innis Barker had carefully engraved Harden's epitaph at her feet, as instructed. He had then engraved a second thin block and artfully mounted it to cover the epitaph. AV-ERY ANDREWS, ATTORNEY AT LAW. To complete Harden's instructions to the letter, Mr. Barker arranged for the installation.

Nothing in Harden's instructions required that the angel stand at his grave. Nothing said the epitaph had to be visible.

So she rested now, in winged glory, on the front lawn of my law office, my gift from Maggy Avinger. Looking up at the angel, I wasn't sure how I felt. At first, it had seemed a quirky joke to have a grave marker for a sign, standing in front of the old mortuary. She looked sad and beautiful, luminous in the sunlight. I was surprised to find Maggy wasn't the first thought in my mind. I was simply struck by her serenity. And her watchfulness.

I couldn't wait to hear what Aunt Letha had to say about my new sign.